Scott McKenzie lives and works in Manchester, UK. In addition to writing fiction, he also writes for dvdactive.com. His first novel *Rebirth* won the spinetinglers.co.uk best unpublished manuscript award 2007.

The Rising

Also by this author

Rebirth

Scott McKenzie

The Rising

*.fiction

First edition

First published in 2008 by *.fiction
www.stardotfiction.com

ISBN 978-0-9558552-0-7

Cover art by Gabriel Powers
www.gabepowers.com

Cover title typeface
Dirty Ego by Misprinted Type
www.misprintedtype.com

Excerpt from 'Ghosts, Vampires and Zombies: Fiction vs Physics Reality' used with the permission of Costas J. Efthimiou

This novel is dedicated to my proof readers:

Lizzie
Dad
Jane
Gregg
Jonnie
Paul
Andy

Thank you. I couldn't do this without you.

Previously…

I

Escape

Private Skinner hit the button to reverse the lock-down and we made our way out of the base. We ran across the summit of the mountain to a helicopter. I could feel my skin start to boil in the blazing sunshine as we jumped on board.

'Jesus Christ,' Agent Simpson exclaimed, 'look at your skin!'

The doctor looked at my face, which felt like I had been lying in the sun all day. In reality I had been in direct sunlight for about thirty seconds.

'Lie down, Detective,' said Doctor Owen, 'I need to give you another shot.'

Private Skinner sat down in the cockpit and started the helicopter's engine. His face did not appear to have been affected by the sun as much as mine. We lifted off and the doctor plunged the needle into my arm. I wondered if the treatment would make any difference.

Have I gone too far down the path to turn back?

In a few seconds I felt the treatment start to take hold and the familiar burning started to spread all over my body. Trying to ignore the pain, I reflected on my actions.

I had new powers. I could fly through the air. I had super-strength. I had psychic abilities.

In the hangar, the human side of me had been unable to control my actions. I had become an unstoppable killer with a lust for blood. I didn't want these powers though, not if it meant I had to feed on human blood to stay alive.

I realised the human community wasn't much better. The Brotherhood had become corrupt and had an agenda of hate. The only chance I had was to stick with these three people. They were good people who wanted the best for me and the rest of the human and vampire races. I felt my new powers drain from my body and tried to be hopeful for the future as I drifted into unconsciousness.

But somewhere deep inside me, a new instinct remained. It wanted me to keep these powers. It wanted me to join my new brothers and sisters. It wanted me to complete my rebirth as a vampire and stay that way.

Forever.

II

The Survivor

Night had fallen by the time reinforcements arrived at the base. Three gunships glided in through the mountains and touched down at the entrance. The heavy figure of General Graham stepped out of the leading gunship. Six soldiers jumped out of each gunship, drew their weapons and ran down the ramp into the base.

General Graham marched down the ramp behind them. He had been playing the call he had received over and over again in his mind. Their most remote regional headquarters had been overrun with vampires. Twelve bloodsuckers had somehow got into the base and killed everyone in sight. The only survivor was Captain Stein, who had made the call to national headquarters.

At least, he was a survivor when he made the call. *'Vampires have infiltrated the base. They killed everyone. Everybody's dead. The doctor and the test subject are gone. I'm dying. Come quickly.'*

That was three hours ago.

The soldiers scattered all over the base. Each soldier reported back on their radio whenever they found a body. The updates came through thick and fast.

A body was lying face down surrounded by a large pool of blood with a sprinkling of ash on top. General Graham had to do a double take as he approached it. The body would have been lying face down if it had a face, but this body's head was missing. Turning the body over, General Graham saw the stripes on the uniform and instantly knew whose head was missing. Next to the body laid a pair of legs that had been cut off at the knee.

My God, this was a massacre, he thought. There hadn't been an attack like this for a very long time. *The vampires must be working towards something. Something bigger than this. But what?*

General Graham picked up his radio and spoke into it. 'Has anyone found the doctor or the test subject?' All he got were negative responses, which meant they had either been captured or...

'Two of the gunships are missing, sir,' a soldier announced as he approached the general, 'the inventory states they have three but only one is present outside.'

'The doctor and the test subject must have escaped,' said General Graham, 'It is possible they are in some way responsible for this. The gunship has a tracking device on board. Find it.'

'Yes sir!' The soldier turned on his heels to march towards the communications office but noticed something on the floor. There was a lot of blood everywhere but the blood he saw in front of him was leading a trail into the office.

'What is it, soldier?' asked General Graham.

'This trail of blood. I can't believe I didn't see it when we got here,' said the soldier.

'A survivor?'

'Maybe.'

'Lead the way,' said General Graham, who followed the soldier into the office. The trail of blood went round the desks and stopped at a blood-soaked telephone lying on the ground.

'This must be where the call was made from,' said the soldier.

'That's right,' said General Graham, 'but if Captain Stein had been lying here since he made the call, you would expect there to be a big pool of blood. The floor's dry apart from a few spots.'

They both scanned their eyes over the floor and around the room. Where was the body that had left this trail of blood? Then General Graham felt something lightly tap him on the shoulder. He turned around but no one was there. He wiped his shoulder with his hand and looked at it.

Blood. Where...

Very slowly, General Graham raised his eyes and looked to the ceiling. He took a step back and exclaimed 'Oh my God!' The soldier turned round and looked up.

There was Captain Stein, seemingly stuck to the ceiling, looking down at them with vacant eyes and a ghostly white face. He didn't have any legs below the knees. Captain Stein opened his mouth to show his long pointed canine teeth and opened his arms out wide then dropped from the ceiling onto the soldier's back, clawing at his neck with his long, sharp finger nails.

Before he could sink his teeth into the soldier's neck, General Graham delivered a hard boot to the body of Captain Stein, who let go of the soldier and landed in the corner of the room. General Graham and the soldier both raised their guns and the vampire stopped moving.

'Don't move, Captain!' the general shouted, 'Are you okay, soldier?'

'I'm fine. Should we shoot him?'

General Graham first instinct was to give the order, but he looked into the eyes of the vampire. Was there any sense in turning Captain Stein into just another pile of ash?

'No,' he said, 'he was useless as a Captain but he may yet be of some use to us as a vampire.'

III
Emily

Emily Owen was lying in her private cell in the police station. She had been there for two nights in a row. Captain Nash came round from time to time to bring her food and water and to apologise for the broken air conditioning system.

It's like a sauna in here, she thought to herself as she looked out of the window and wondered how it could still be so hot after the sun had set long ago. She got up and moved around, trying to generate movement in the air but it only made her feel worse. The only other option was putting her in the public cell with all of the recent arrests. She questioned whether that might be preferable, if only for a few minutes to cool down.

She was relieved when the Captain had told her that he had heard her husband was safe and well. She had feared the worst when she heard about the commotion downtown. Somehow she knew he was involved.

Andrew had told her that if she ever fell into the hands of the police then someone would try to collect her. According to him, she would be safer on her own than with the police but if there was no other option; she would have to re-join him. She had been very scared when the police arrived to pick her up but after two days of sitting around she thought her husband was probably just being his usual over-protective self and that she would be fine once he came to collect her.

She had been resistant to Nash's questioning so far. He had only spent fleeting moments with her though. It seemed to her that he didn't have a lot of time on his hands and was always rushing off to deal with something else.

There was a knock at the cell door followed by the familiar voice of Captain Nash. He opened the small flap in the metal door and peeked inside. 'Emily, how are you doing in there?'

8

'Same as before, still baking. I must be nearly done now.'

'Again, I'm very sorry about this. As soon as we have a detective available to question you or we get rid of the suspects in the holding pen, we'll be able to move you. I don't think that's going to happen for a while yet though.'

'Can you bring me some more water please?'

'Of course. I'm just going to get your dinner so I'll bring plenty of water as well.'

Emily thanked Captain Nash and heard his footsteps move away from the cell door. Then she heard something else, something she wasn't expecting.

The sound of glass shattering.

Then a woman's scream.

Then a gunshot. Followed by another, and another.

The terrifying sound of gunshots, shouting and screaming seeped into the cell. Emily banged on the door.

'Captain Nash! Captain Nash! What's going on?'

There was no answer other than more screams.

She sat down on the bed and curled into a ball in the corner.

Something terrible is happening out there. It is anything to do with Andrew? Is this anything to do with me?

As suddenly as the noise had started, it stopped. There was silence from the corridor outside. The sound of footsteps made their way down the corridor and stopped at the door. The metal flap opened for a second, then slammed shut.

'Captain Nash?' Emily asked, her voice cracking with fear.

Again, there was no answer.

A key was placed in the lock and there was a loud clunk as the door swung open and hit the wall.

Emily didn't recognise the man standing at the door with blood dripping down his face. He was dressed in black with a sword tied to his belt.

There was no one alive in the police station to hear Emily's screams as he launched himself across the room and dragged her out of the cell.

IV
The Scientist

Roxy ended the call on her mobile phone without an answer for the fourth time. There had been no contact from any of her allies at The Brotherhood's regional headquarters. She feared the worst. All the vampires she had trained to infiltrate The Brotherhood must have been killed.

Either the doctor had been killed in the battle or he had escaped, which meant they were starting from scratch again. The vampire community couldn't know for sure how much the humans knew about the biology of vampires.

Of course, the vampires were doing their own scientific experiments. They had their own agenda, something similar to the humans' plan but it would be ready to test far sooner.

Roxy lifted herself out of her chair onto a pair of crutches and hobbled down the dark hall to the laboratory door. It would be another day or so before her legs would finish healing completely after such a severe injury. She opened the door and took a step inside, telling the scientist working in the lab not to let her disturb him. She sat down on a stool on the opposite side of the workbench to the scientist and watched him work.

The scientist had two racks of bullets, a pistol, a small paintbrush and a small glass bowl of blood in front of him. One by one, he picked up the bullets, dipped the paintbrush in the bowl and coated them with a thin layer of blood. He then placed each bullet in the second rack to let them dry. When he had finished coating all of the bullets with blood, he picked one up and loaded it into the pistol.

'Let's see if it works,' he said and got to his feet. Roxy followed him out of the door and across the corridor, into the room facing the lab. The room they found themselves in was bare and well lit. The only furniture in the room was a wooden chair, to which a gagged and naked man was tied. His face was soaked with sweat and he was white with fear.

The scientist pointed the pistol at the naked man and pulled the trigger. He flew backwards and struck the wall behind him, falling into a heap on the floor, still tied to the chair. Neither the scientist nor Roxy helped him up. The scientist took a stopwatch out of his pocket and pressed the button to start the timer.

'How long until he turns, Doctor Forrest?' asked Roxy.

'Hopefully under an hour but I'm working on making it more fast-acting,' he said.

'When will we be able to execute the next phase of the plan?'

'The day after tomorrow.'

The Rising

Prologue

Two Years Ago

1
Bad Feeling

Agent Becky Clarkson had a bad feeling about her mission. She'd had a bad feeling about it ever since the manager of the emergency response team had woken her up in the middle of the night. Without giving her a chance to gather her thoughts, he gave her the details of the next crisis only she could deal with.

Here's the address. Our intel says they've got the doctor. You'll need to move fast.

Trying to put the unease to the back of her mind, she gripped the accelerator and dodged her high-powered Kawasaki motorbike around the traffic that dotted the freeway. The rain had stopped falling but the road was still wet and her back tyre sprayed water behind her like a shark's fin cutting through the ocean.

She loved riding her bike before a mission. High speed got her adrenaline pumping, which gave her the edge she needed to get the job done.

To get the job done and stay alive.

She saw her exit coming up and slowed down. As her bike drifted down the off-ramp, she heard a fizzing in her ear.

'Agent Clarkson, come in.'

Becky recognised the voice. It belonged to Will, the young guy who worked for the team that provided support for World Health Organisation agents in the field.

They had never met but Becky was pretty sure that Will had a thing for her. She found it odd that he could be attracted to someone just by the sound of their voice but that didn't matter. She made the most of it and used their relationship to get him to do things and find out information that was far outside his job description.

A bit of digging had revealed that he was twenty-five years old, only four years younger than her, and was pretty good-looking. Maybe they could have met for a drink if things had been different, but as it stood, Becky's life didn't have any room for a man.

Well, it did once but never again. I learned that lesson the hard way, she thought.

'Yes Will, I'm here,' Becky said into the tiny microphone in her helmet.

'Are you there yet?'

'Nearly. I've just gone off the freeway and I'm heading out of the city.'

'What's your ETA?'

'Five minutes.'

'Okay, I can see you on my screen now. The truck is heading towards the warehouse as well. You should be there a few minutes before it. The truck's coming from the north so make sure you get in position first.'

'Understood. Any hostiles on site?'

'I've checked the satellite feed and I can only find two. They're real movers though, so watch your back.'

'Thanks, Will. I'll let you know when I'm ready to intercept.'

The road leading Becky from the freeway into the countryside was endlessly winding and dark but when she was within a mile of her destination she turned off the headlights.

I can't alert them to my presence.

The horizon opened up and half way up a hill ahead of her, hidden among the thick trees that filled the landscape, she spotted an old abandoned warehouse. At the bottom of the hill, Becky stopped her bike and hid the heavy machine in the bushes that lined the road. She was always amazed how easily it moved at a hundred miles an hour but when she needed to quickly stash it out of sight, it became an albatross round her neck.

By the light of the moon she caught a glimpse of herself in the rear-view mirror as she removed her helmet. Clad in a black Kevlar combat suit with cropped hair, she realised it was a far cry from the floral dress and long flowing blonde locks in her graduation picture. Every morning her parents looked at that picture and wept. They wept for the passing of their only child.

For eight months they had lived under the impression she was dead. Every Black Ops agent had to disappear when they took the job. The safety of the agents and their families depended on them cutting all ties to the outside world. Agent Clarkson knew she would have to live outside real life as long as the vampire threat remained and not a day went by that she didn't question her decision to take this direction.

There's no turning back. Get the job done and stay alive.

She hopped over the bushes into an empty field and started to run towards the warehouse as fast as she could while keeping her head down.

'Will, come in,' she said.

'Go ahead, Agent Clarkson,' he replied.

'I'm almost there, what's the latest?'

'Still just two of them on site as far as I can see. The truck is almost there. You should be able to see it.'

Becky looked up the hill and saw a pair of bright headlights rise over the summit.

'Affirmative. How many on board?'

'Two. Driver and passenger seat.'

'No one in the back of the truck?'

'Negative.'

'So either they haven't got the doctor with them or the driver is holding him at gunpoint. I thought you said he was taken by them in this truck an hour ago?'

'That's the information we got from The Brotherhood.'

The Brotherhood. I can't remember the last time they provided us with any useful information, she thought to herself as she jumped over the last hedge and hid behind a tree.

All she cared about was tracking down Doctor Forrest. He had gone missing again. He had a habit of disappearing without notice and strolling back into his lab as if nothing had happened a few days later, but now no one had seen him for over a week. If they couldn't find him then all of their work would be in jeopardy. He held all the knowledge, all the secrets that gave the human race a fighting chance against the vampires.

Investigations had led them to believe he was in the vampires' custody and he might be at this location. Becky had never met the doctor but she had a nagging suspicion that there was something odd about the way he conducted himself.

She peeked round her hiding place and saw the truck stop outside the warehouse. The doors opened and two men in black stepped out onto the tarmac. The blanket of soggy leaves squelched beneath their feet. They walked round to the back of the truck and opened the doors. Two more figures dressed in black appeared from the large open doorway in the warehouse and joined them.

'The doctor's not here,' Becky said.

'What's the call, Agent Clarkson?' Will asked.

Becky was about to tell him she was aborting the mission when the four figures on the other side of the trees started to unload wooden boxes from the truck. Wooden boxes that looked familiar to her but felt terribly out of place in this setting.

'Agent Clarkson, are you going to abort?' Will asked again.

'Negative. There's something else going on here.'

'Becky,' he said, trying a personal approach to get through to her, 'the primary objective is to recover Doctor Forrest. He is not on site. I strongly urge you to abort the mission.'

'No, Will. I can't tell you what's going on here yet but I have to investigate it. I'm going in.'

2
Going In

'Okay,' said Will, resigned to the fact that he wasn't going to talk Agent Clarkson into aborting her mission, 'If you're going in, I'll do all I can. I'm looking at the satellite feed now. The marks are all positioned close together so you shouldn't have to get up close to take them out.'

'But that's part of the fun,' Becky smirked.

'Have you got your equipment ready?' Will asked, ignoring her attempt to wind him up.

Becky drew her pistol from the holster on her right hip and checked it was loaded with silver bullets. She drew the silencer from a pocket on her left thigh and screwed it into the barrel then clicked the safety catch off. To round off her arsenal she put her left hand in her pocket and gripped a set of silver-plated spiked brass knuckles.

'Ready to go,' she announced.

She glanced around the tree and saw two figures walking towards the truck from the warehouse. The other two were heading towards the warehouse, carrying wooden boxes from the truck. When they disappeared into the darkness of the warehouse doorway, Becky knew that was her best chance.

'I'm going in.'

She saw the two figures walk round the opposite side of the van and knew that was the moment to make her move. She covered the ground quickly but knew they would eventually hear her feet squelching on the soft muddy ground.

As Becky reached the tarmac, the two figures became alerted to her presence and turned to face her in shock. One started to run towards her and the other jumped in the air, far higher than humanly possible and dropped to the floor just behind her.

Without thinking twice, Becky fired off a single shot from the pistol in her right hand that hit the target in front of her directly between the eyes, then elbowed the figure behind her in the stomach with her left arm. As he doubled over, she swung her left arm up and caught him square on the nose with her spiked knuckles, which drew blood instantly. She left her hand there for a few seconds, just long enough for the reaction to silver to take hold, and watched the two bodies around her dissolve. The ash pouring from their wounds soaked into the soggy ground. Were it not for two piles of clothes left on the floor, there would be no evidence they were ever there.

Two down, two to go.

'Good work, Agent Clarkson. Get ready; the other two are on their way out,' said Will.

Becky ran to the side of the truck and crouched down. As soon as the two men emerged from the doorway, she popped up and fired two shots, just like she was doing target practice at the firing range at headquarters. The bullets both hit their targets in the chest. The impact sent them reeling backwards, their bodies dissolving as they hit the ground.

'Nice shooting,' she heard in her ear, 'now do you mind telling me why you did that?'

'Give me a second,' she said, not wanting to give anything away. If her suspicions were correct, she didn't want this going over the airwaves back to headquarters.

She walked round to the back of the truck and saw that apart from the small number that had been removed just moments before, it was stacked high with wooden boxes. Her suspicions were correct. They were all labelled with the brand name 'Virex'.

After removing the silencer, she holstered her pistol. Taking the spiked knuckles in her right hand, she punched a hole in the wooden box in front of her. Inside she saw what she feared she would find. Small plastic packages containing syringes pre-filled with yellow liquid fell out of the hole in the box onto the floor.

This is wrong. This is so wrong.

'Will, did you say that you got the information about Doctor Forrest from The Brotherhood?'

'That's correct, Agent Clarkson. It came through verified channels.'

'Are you still watching the satellite feed?'

'Yes, there's no movement. Wait a minute…'

'What?'

'I've just lost the feed.'

'Shit!' she exclaimed, 'This channel isn't secure. Someone's listening to us. Maintain radio silence for now.'

The world Becky thought she knew had shifted around her in a matter of seconds. She was quickly piecing the parts of the puzzle together. It made sense but she didn't want to believe it.

How could they do this? Everything we've been told is lies. Nothing but lies.

Somewhere in the distance, Becky could hear a low whirring noise and it was getting louder. It was getting louder very quickly.

Fight or flight.

They're coming for me.

Get the hell out of here.

She grabbed a handful of the syringes and ran back the way she came as fast as she could, over the hedge, through the field, then back onto the road. All the while she heard the whirring get louder and louder and started to feel the breeze around her turn into a gale.

Don't turn round, she told herself, *Don't slow down to look at what you know is there.*

The moment of relief at reaching her motorbike and putting her helmet on was interrupted by a voice from a loudspeaker above her.

'Stay where you are, Agent Clarkson. We are here to take you for debriefing.'

She turned her head round to look through her black visor at the gunship above her. She could make out four men in military uniforms on board. One was sitting behind a machine gun that was pointing directly at her.

She turned the key in the ignition and a patch of tarmac ahead of her exploded into dust.

'That was just a warning shot, Agent Clarkson. I repeat: stay where you are.'

There's no way I'm getting out of this alive if I stay, she thought.

'Will, are you there?'

'Will has been removed from his post, Agent Clarkson,' a female voice said in her ear.

'Who is this? Where is Will?'

'My name is Jane, Agent Clarkson. Will has been taken away by security but they didn't say why. I have been told to tell you that you must go with The Brotherhood. They need your help.'

'Have you worked there long, Jane?'

'A little while. Why?'

'I have a piece of advice for you.'

'What's that?'

'Trust no one. This is the last any of you will hear from me.'

23

With that, Becky gunned the accelerator as hard as she could and sped down the road ahead, narrowly avoiding the flurry of bullets raining down from the gunship. The helicopter above her gave chase but the winding roads made targeting difficult and she made it to the freeway before they could take her out.

Looking in her rear view mirror, she breathed a sigh of relief as the helicopter disappeared into the distance. She knew they wouldn't risk a public attack.

But they'll be coming for me.
I have to disappear again.
I'm nobody.

Part One

Early Hours

3

Excerpt from
'Ghosts, Vampires and Zombies: Fiction vs Physics Reality'
aka 'The Costas Report'

Anyone who has seen any of the host of vampire films is already quite familiar with how the legend goes. The vampires need to feed on human blood. After one has stuck his fangs into your neck and sucked you dry, you turn into a vampire yourself and carry on the blood-sucking legacy. The fact of the matter is, if vampires truly feed with even a tiny fraction of the frequency that they are depicted to in the movies and folklore, then the human race would have been wiped out quite quickly after the first vampire appeared.

Let us assume that a vampire need feed only once a month. This is certainly a highly conservative assumption given any Hollywood vampire film. Now two things happen when a vampire feeds. The human population decreases by one and the vampire population increases by one. Let us suppose that the first vampire appeared in 1600 AD. It doesn't really matter what date we choose for the first vampire to appear; it has little bearing on our argument. We list a government website in the references [US Census] which provides an estimate of the world population for any given date. For January 1, 1600 we will accept that the global population was 536,870,911.3 In our argument, we had at the same time 1 vampire.

We will ignore the human mortality and birth rate for the time being and only concentrate on the effects of vampire feeding. On February 1st, 1600 1 human will have died and a new vampire born. This gives 2 vampires and $(536, 870, 911-1)$ humans. The next month there are two vampires feeding and thus two humans die and two new vampires are born. This gives 4 vampires and $(536, 870, 911-3)$ humans.

Month	Vampire Population	Human Population	Month	Vampire Population	Human Population
1	1	536870911	16	32768	536838144
2	2	536870910	17	65536	536805376
3	4	536870908	18	131072	536739840
4	8	536870904	19	262144	536608768
5	16	536870896	20	524288	536346624
6	32	536870880	21	1048576	535822336
7	64	536870848	22	2097152	534773760
8	128	536870784	23	4194304	532676608
9	256	536870656	24	8388608	528482304
10	512	536870400	25	16777216	520093696
11	1024	536869888	26	33554432	503316480
12	2048	536868864	27	67108864	469762048
13	4096	536866816	28	134217728	402653184
14	8192	536862720	29	268435456	268435456
15	16384	536854528	30	536870912	0

Table 1: Vampire and human population at the beginning of each month during a 30-month period.

Now on April 1st, 1600 there are 4 vampires feeding and thus we have 4 human deaths and 4 new vampires being born. This gives us 8 vampires and $(536, 870, 911 - 7)$ humans. By now the reader has probably caught on to the progression. Each month the number of vampires doubles so that after n months have passed there are

$$2 \times 2 \times \ldots \times 2 \mid \{z\} \text{ n times} = 2^n$$

vampires. This sort of progression is known in mathematics as a geometric progression — more specifically it is a geometric progression with ratio 2, since we multiply by 2 at each step. A geometric progression increases at a tremendous rate, a fact that will become clear shortly. Now all but one of these vampires were once human so that the human population is its original population minus the number of vampires excluding the original one. So after n months have passed there are humans. The vampire population increases geometrically and the human population decreases geometrically.

Table 1 lists the vampire and human population at the beginning of each month over a 30-month period. Note that by month number 30, the table lists a human population of zero. We conclude that if the first vampire appeared on January 1st of 1600 AD, humanity would have been wiped out by June of 1602, two and half years later.

All this may seem artificial since we ignored other effects on the human population. Mortality due to factors other than vampires would only make the decline in humans more rapid and therefore strengthen our conclusion. The only thing that can weaken our conclusion is the human birth rate. Note that our vampires have gone from 1 to 536,870,912 in two and a half years. To keep up, the human population would have had to increase by the same amount. The website [US Census] mentioned earlier also provides estimated birth rates for any given time. If you go to it, you will notice that the human birth rate never approaches anything near such a tremendous value. In fact in the long run, for humans to survive, our population must at least essentially double each month! This is clearly way beyond the human capacity for reproduction.

If we factor in the human birthrate into our discussion, we would find that after a few months, the human birthrate becomes a very small fraction of the number of deaths due to vampires. This means that ignoring this factor has a negligibly small impact on our conclusion. In our example, the death of humanity would be prolonged by only one month.

We conclude that vampires cannot exist, since their existence contradicts the existence of human beings. Incidentally, the logical proof that we just presented is of a type known as reductio ad absurdum, that is, reduction to the absurd. Another philosophical principle related to our argument is the truism given the elaborate title, the anthropic principle. This states that if something is necessary for human existence, then it must be true since we do exist. In the present case, the nonexistence of vampires is necessary for human existence.

Costas J. Efthimiou and Sohang Gandhi
arXiv:physics/0608059v1 [physics.soc-ph] 5 Aug 2006
http://www.arxiv.org/abs/physics/0608059v1

4
Funeral Pyre

Present Day

The full moon shone through a gap in the clouds, touching the edges of the landscape with white light. The snow-covered tips of the mountains shone like beacons in the distance. It was a beautiful scene that didn't last long.

General Graham looked up into the sky and saw the clouds gathering together. Darkness descended on the regional headquarters. He stood in a clearing at the end of the tarmac, looking over the edge of the cliff at the deep chasm below.

The small gang that had caused this unholy mess were on the run. His men were tracking their helicopter from the control room inside the base. He knew they wouldn't go very far. After all, they had at least one vampire with them, maybe two if their suspicions were correct from what they'd seen on the surveillance tapes. Sooner or later, they'd have to find shelter before sunrise.

There was only the sound of wind in the air until an electric whine cut through the tranquillity. General Graham turned on his heels and saw one of his men driving a white buggy up the ramp out of the base. It stopped at the helicopter pad where he was standing.

The buggy was piled high with body bags, mostly uniformed soldiers, victims of the attack just hours earlier. It had been a long time since there was a vampire attack on a base belonging to The Brotherhood. Now they were cleaning up the mess of the second in less than twenty-four hours.

'This is as good a place as any,' said General Graham and the driver of the buggy hopped out, 'The wind's blowing away from the base so they shouldn't stink up the place while we finish off inside.'

'Good job.'

He helped the driver unload the body bags onto the ground. Even though the victims were sealed inside their zippered caskets, he could feel the softness of their bodies. Blood was washing around inside the body bags and there was a loud squelch with each body they threw onto the growing pile.

Pools of blood formed at the bottom of the mountain of bodies as it grew. Streams of red followed the imperfections in the surface of the ground and trickled in every direction.

One body bag felt a lot lighter than the others. The soldier knew exactly which poor soul was inside. Newly reborn vampires often struggle to control their hunger and unfortunately for the soldier who had been guarding the morgue, the whole squad had a taste for flesh as well as blood.

Within hours of the attack, some of the men who suffered at the hands of the vampires had already turned and were found lurking in the depths of the base, waiting for reinforcements to arrive. They were despatched quickly and all that was left of them was their clothes, which were being thrown in with the rest of the bodies.

The soldier reached inside the front of the buggy and lifted out a can of petrol and flare. He opened the can and threw the contents evenly over the pile of bodies, then handed the flare to the general.

'Is there anything you want to say first?' asked General Graham.

The soldier shrugged and shook his head.

The general lit the flare. Everything surrounding them was bathed in red light, like they were standing in the pits of Hell. He threw the flare onto the mountain of dead bodies. Within seconds the funeral pyre was ablaze.

He saluted the burning soldiers and the soldier next to him followed his lead.

Is this another random attack or is it something bigger?

Is this the beginning of the Rising?

General Graham lowered his arm and his thoughts turned to the one remaining witness of the massacre who was locked in a room deep inside the base.

5
Flashlight

The vampire that used to be Captain Stein was lying in the corner of a dark, empty room many floors below the entrance to the base. His body was doubled over and he was weeping in agony. His insides were on fire and the hunger that burned in his stomach was like nothing he had ever felt before.

He would have screamed out if he thought any one of the soldiers who walked past the door and peered through the window would have helped him.

They all want to kill me. Would that be a better fate than what is in front of me?

Familiar and unfamiliar thoughts pierced through his brain. One thought remained constant; the same thought that came first to anyone who had been wronged.

Revenge.

If I ever see that cop again, that devil who made me this way, I'm going to kill him. I'm going to rip that fucker limb from limb.

There was a metallic clunk and the door that kept Captain Stein from following his new instincts opened. He was faced with General Graham, who was holding a pistol in his right hand and a flashlight in his left.

Stein looked up at him and tried to get to his feet, but thanks to the detective, he no longer had any feet. All he had were bandaged, bloody stumps at the ends of his legs. The stumps were slowly growing, which provided Stein with a mixture of emotions; happiness that he would soon be able to walk again but also anger because it meant he was turning into a vampire and there was nothing he could do about it.

'Stay where you are,' General Graham said, his voice booming around the stone walls.

'Help me,' Stein pleaded, 'You have to help me. Get me the treatment.'

'The primary treatment?' General Graham smirked, knowing it would kill him.

'No, the cure the doctors were working on. It can make me human again.'

Stein's voice was almost unrecognisable from the way he had spoken when he was human. He had always been assertive and authoritative, but now he was desperate.

Every fibre in his being wanted to be relieved of the curse that had been cast upon him the second Detective Ryder sank his teeth into his neck. Stein no longer cared about the priorities of The Brotherhood. He paid no mind to the work he had done to sabotage the research into a cure for the virus that was now coursing through his veins. He wanted it.

He needed it.

'I can help you,' said the general without any emotion in his voice, 'but first you have to tell me what happened.'

'No, you have to give me the treatment!'

General Graham holstered his pistol and took the flashlight in his right hand. He turned it on and a violet circle appeared on the wall next to him. He shone the light directly in Stein's face.

After a second, Stein screamed and tried to crawl away from the corner of the room. The general turned off the flashlight and looked at Stein's face. It was bright red.

'Tell me what I want to know. It's only going to get worse.'

Stein groaned in pain again and conceded that he was in no position to negotiate.

'Agent Simpson brought him to us.'

'Detective Ryder?'

'Yes. He had been bitten after we picked up Doctor Owen. Jane disobeyed her orders and brought him to the doctor to use as a test subject.'

'That was before the attack on Hartley House?'

'They were evacuated and came here. One of the men on the recovery team was one of *them* and brought infected bodies into the base. They broke out of the morgue and killed everyone.'

'So where are they now?'

'Ryder, Jane and the doctor escaped with one of my men, Skinner is his name. On the way out Ryder killed the commander and did this to me.'

'Shit. I'm sure you know what happened the last time one of the doc's guinea pigs escaped. Do you know where they were going?'

'No.'

'What about the other doctor?'

'We couldn't find him. I was going to send a search party out for him tomorrow.'

'Why couldn't you find him?'

'There were no leads. We couldn't find any family or friends.'

'Thank you, Captain Stein.'

General Graham turned to walk out of the room.

'Wait!' Stein shouted, 'What about the treatment?'

'What about it?' the general asked, 'there's nothing here. If you help us get the doctor back, you'll get your treatment.'

He slammed the door behind him as he left. Stein's muffled screams were only just audible from outside the cell.

6
Waking Up

I opened my eyes.

I was expecting to be in pain, just like the terrible feeling of a hangover I had when I woke up after being bitten by a vampire twenty-four hours earlier. However, on first impressions I wasn't feeling too bad.

I sat up and found myself on the seat in the back of a helicopter. The air was cold. My shirt was soaked through with sweat. I shivered and rubbed my arms, which were covered in goose bumps below my torn and bloody shirt sleeves. Then it all came flooding back to me.

The autopsy.

The attack.

Oh my God, I killed three soldiers and the commander.

I chopped his head off.

My eyes caught a metal box sitting on the floor on the opposite side of the cabin. I lowered myself onto my knees and edged over to the box. In an attempt to prepare myself for the worst, I took a moment to try and picture the horror that was held inside.

Maybe it was all a dream. Maybe I didn't really do that.

I unlocked the catches on the front of the box that held the airtight lid in place. Very slowly I lifted the lid but I heard a shout and jumped, dropping the lid before I had a chance to look inside.

'Tom!'

I looked up, outside the helicopter. I hadn't even thought to look outside. We were sitting in a grassy clearing. Ahead of us was a thick forest and behind was a small lake. It was still dark outside, with only the moonlight illuminating our surroundings.

Doctor Owen had seen me and was running back to the helicopter.

'Tom, you're awake! How are you feeling?'

After having moved around for a minute or two, I reassessed my state of well-being.

'Okay I think,' I said, 'A bit of a headache but definitely a lot better than I felt when we left the base. How long have I been out?'

'Just a couple of hours. The treatment must have worked a lot quicker than it did last time.'

'Is that a good or a bad thing?' I asked.

I didn't get an answer and the look on his face didn't fill me with confidence. The doctor took my head in his hands and looked at my face in great detail.

'Incredible,' he said, 'you've completely healed.'

'Healed?'

'Yes. When we left the base, the short run from the entrance to the main door resulted in you absorbing a small dose of the sun's ultraviolet light. Your face in particular was heavily sunburnt. Now, just hours later, you're back to normal.'

It wasn't the first time my body had miraculously healed since I had been bitten by a vampire. He looked concerned.

'I would have expected the treatment to slow down the effects of your infection, but...' He stopped talking abruptly and his face, that had been happy to see me just moments before, turned into a look of fear and shame.

'But what?'

'You fed on Captain Stein's blood. That would have provided you with a significant amount of energy. The treatment must have reduced the ability of your body to control its movement, hence your unconsciousness, but your blood, which is starting to be self-aware, followed its natural instinct to heal your body.'

You fed on Captain Stein's blood.

My hand immediately went to my mouth. My fingers probed my canine teeth. They were back to normal.

'Your teeth only extend when you're ready to feed,' the doctor said.

I couldn't believe what I'd done. I had mutilated Captain Stein's body and drank his blood. That was surely a fate worse than death. I'd cursed him with the same destiny that I was struggling to deal with. I was still struggling to decide whether I'd be better off dead.

At least I've got the doctor to help me.

'I never thanked you for last night,' I said.

'What do you mean?'

'When they strapped me down, you talked to me. You told me I could break free.'

'Really? I had no idea that worked. I tried to project those thoughts, but I never thought you would hear them. Very interesting.'

'Where are we?' I asked.

'We're in the hills, near Lake Arcadia.'

'What are we doing here?'

'Just after I gave you the treatment, you were drifting in and out of consciousness but you said something to us. You told us to come here. You said you would know what to do.'

I was very confused.

'Where are Jane and the other guy?'

'Private Skinner? They got tired of waiting for you to wake up and went off to check the area out to see if they could work out why the hell you dragged us here.'

I started to feel very guilty.

'Their words, not mine,' he laughed.

Why have I brought everyone here? What are we going to do if I can't remember? Wait a minute…

'If I didn't say why we should come here, why did we?'

'Where else could we have gone?' the doctor asked, 'The Brotherhood are almost certainly going to go to our homes and we need somewhere unfamiliar to base ourselves.'

Then it hit me.

'Where did you say we were?' I asked.

'Lake Arcadia.'

'That's it. My old partner Dave has a cabin by the lake. He's up here right now teaching his kids to fish. He'll take us in for as long as it takes to get our heads together.'

7
Seeking Shelter

Doctor Owen called Jane to tell her and Skinner to return to the helicopter. They hadn't ventured far so it didn't take them long to get back. The air was cold but I was certain the temperature dropped by a few degrees as they arrived. They didn't look pleased to see me.

'How do you feel, Tom?' Jane asked when she saw me.

'Okay. Not as bad as I did after the treatment yesterday.'

'Good for you. Now, do you want to tell us why we're here?'

I was taken aback by how cold Jane was with me. Just the day before she had been very warm toward me and we had worked well together. However, that was yesterday and this was now. The faint metallic taste in my mouth reminded me that things had changed.

Even though I'd been out for a few hours, I realised that we were still in crisis mode. The Brotherhood were almost certainly already looking for us. No one else had taken a break from worrying about our position. I had been out cold without a worry in the world.

'My partner has a cabin at the lake. I'm sure he'll let us stay there as long as we want. There are hundreds of holiday homes up there so it should give us some time to work out what we're going to do before The Brotherhood find us.'

Jane weighed up my proposal. The look on her face told me she thought it might be a good idea but she tried her best to hide it from me.

'Well, it's the best idea we've had yet,' was her less-than-enthusiastic appraisal.

I picked my mobile phone out of my pocket and called Dave's number. He answered almost immediately.

'Hey partner,' he said in his perpetually upbeat tone, 'you're on the news.'

'I know,' I said, brushing his comment aside but wondering just how bad the report about me was. 'I need your help.'

'What do you need from me? I'll do what I can but I'm still on holiday, Tom.'

'Good. I was hoping you'd say that. I need to ask you a huge favour.'

'Sounds ominous. What can I do?'

'I'm at the lake with some people who have been helping me with this case. I need you to put us up for a few hours while we work out what we're going to do next.'

'What, you're here now?'

'We're only a mile or two away from the cabins. We can be with you in about half an hour.'

'I don't know what to say, Tom. You're not giving me much of a choice, are you?'

I didn't know what to say either.

'Anyway,' he sighed, 'thanks for calling me first.'

'Thanks, Dave. I owe you one. You should send your family home.'

'Are you in danger?'

'Yes. We'll be as quick as we can.'

'See you in half an hour. We're in cabin sixty-six, but give me a chance to break the news to she-who-must-be-obeyed.'

I hung up and Jane snatched the phone out of my hand.

'Hey, what are you doing?' I asked.

'The Brotherhood will use our phones to track us down. We have to keep the doctor's phone with us in case Doctor Forrest calls again but we have to throw the rest of them away. Get everything out of the helicopter; we have to get rid of it as well. We can be certain it's being tracked.'

'How are we going to get rid of this helicopter? It's huge,' said Doctor Owen, 'We can't blow it up. Everyone will see the smoke from miles away.'

After keeping quiet, Skinner decided to pipe up. 'I know what to do,' he said, 'Let's empty it first and I'll get rid of it.'

We pulled all of the metal boxes out of the helicopter and piled them up on the grass. Skinner then got into the cockpit and fired up the engine.

'Stand back,' he shouted to us before the whirring rotors became too loud to hear his voice.

The gunship rose into the air. Skinner floated it over our heads and hovered high above the water level of the lake. The door opened and I witnessed a sight I never thought I'd dream of seeing in my entire life.

Skinner jumped out of the open door and flew towards us, narrowly avoiding being sliced to death by the spinning rotor blades as the helicopter dropped out of the sky and plunged into the lake. An almighty splash was accompanied by the creak of metal as the huge helicopter sunk into the water. Waves were sent flowing from the centre of the lake and washed up on the shore just behind Skinner's feet as they hit the ground. The water bubbled as the gunship disappeared from view.

'Right,' he said as we stood wide-eyed and open-mouthed, 'We can't stand around looking at the view. We'd better get moving.'

8
Final Test

Doctor Forrest stepped out of his lab and walked across the stone floor of the corridor to the metal door that held his test subject in solitary confinement. He stood at the door for a long time, admiring his handiwork.

The doctor had expected his guinea pig to turn within an hour. His predictions were accurate. Now the naked man was lying in the corner of the brightly lit room among the splinters of the chair he had been sitting on, crying out in agony for help from the emotionless face that was looking down on him.

A bite from even the most powerful vampire takes a matter of hours to take hold on the weakest human, but I have developed something much more powerful. More potent than anything God himself could ever have created.

The rising vampire army had been in dire need of the missing link in their plan. Something that would allow them to increase their numbers at such a rate the human community could never comprehend. Something the humans couldn't hope to resist, even if they were to find out about it before it's too late.

The human race had expanded rapidly since great leaps forward had been made in the field of medical research, but the terms of the treaty that was signed five hundred years ago refused to allow the vampire numbers to grow at the same rate. The size of the vampire community was secretly growing but their numbers were still small. The Brotherhood and the World Health Organisation always found a way to curb the growth.

But now that we can multiply quicker than ever before, there will be no stopping us, Doctor Forrest thought to himself. *It is written that we will rise to take our rightful place as the dominant force in the world. The Rising is inevitable. This treatment is the catalyst.*

The sound of footsteps echoed around the stone walls. Doctor Forrest looked down the corridor and saw the imposing figure of

Roxy limping towards him. As ever, she was dressed in black combat gear and her awkward movement coupled with the flaming torches on the walls lighting her way made her look meaner than ever.

'How is he doing?' she asked.

The doctor pulled his stopwatch out of his pocket and showed it to her. 'Fifty-three minutes.'

'Excellent,' she said, 'Any side effects?'

'None that I can see. I'm about to prepare the treatment for your operation. How many syringes do you need?'

'At least two hundred, but make up as many as you can.'

'When are you going ahead with the plan?'

'We're moving ahead earlier than we originally planned. Tonight, just after midnight.'

The doctor turned to his guinea pig.

'Unless you've got any use for him, there's only one more test to do.'

Roxy looked through the window in the door. The pitiful figure in the corner was curled in the foetal position with his hand reaching out to her. She heard a voice in her head.

Help me, please!

She turned to Doctor Forrest. 'Do it.'

The doctor flicked a switch on the wall and the lights inside the room went out. He then flicked another switch and they both stepped back as a second set of spotlights lit up the room. He restarted the timer on his stopwatch.

Ultraviolet light filled the prisoner's cell, the purple glow illuminating the faces of his audience but the sealed doorway ensured the man in the room only felt the ill effects.

His arms and legs started to twitch. His movements became more aggressive. Within seconds, his body was convulsing violently. Blisters were beginning to form on his skin, which was quickly turning an angrier and angrier shade of red. One by one, the blisters burst and more and more began to form in their place. As they burst and pus oozed down his limbs, wisps of smoke left his skin and small flecks of dust fell to the floor.

He crouched on all fours, screaming in unimaginable pain as his skin turned to flakes of dust. The reactions in his body cut through his arms and they gave way, splitting at the elbows and throwing him face down onto the floor. He stopped moving. He lay still on the floor until every cell in his body that had been human just on hour earlier settled into a pile of ash among the splintered chair.

Doctor Forrest stopped the timer and turned the lights out.

'Just over sixty seconds,' he said.

'Thank you for your hard work, Doctor Forrest. I guess we can't expect miracles.'

'Not yet,' the doctor replied, 'but anything may be possible if I have time to complete my work.'

9
Bad News

Detective Dave Thomas hung up and turned to his wife.

'Who was that?' she asked.

'It was Tom,' Dave said, bracing himself for the usual response to a call about work when he was on vacation.

'Jesus Christ, Dave. Doesn't he know you're on holiday? What did he want?'

Dave paused for a moment to try and think of the best way of telling her what was about to happen. He realised there was no good way of telling her and just came out with it.

'He's coming here.'

'Tom? Coming here? When?'

'Right now. He'll be here in half an hour.'

'What do you mean, Dave? It's the middle of the night,' she exclaimed then lowered her voice, 'The kids are asleep. What's he coming here for?'

'He's in trouble. He hasn't got anywhere else to go.'

'Well he can't. You're on holiday. *We're* on holiday.'

Dave really wasn't looking forward to telling her the next part of the deal.

'He's in trouble so he's coming to see me.' He left that comment hanging in the air with the emphasis on *me*. After all those years of marriage, he hoped she would pick up on the hint. When her face turned from disbelief to anger, he knew he'd made the breakthrough.

That's why I love you so much, he thought.

'So you're kicking us out so your buddy can come here and take over the place?'

'I'm really sorry. It's out of my hands. He's at the lake already and didn't give me any choice. What would you do in this situation? Put yourself in his place. He's my partner.'

She let it all sink in and looked up with a glint in her eye. 'You owe me big time, big boy,' she said, patting his belly.

'Anything, sweetheart. You know I wouldn't ask you to do this if it wasn't important.' He knew she was on his side but he also knew that he would have a lot of making up to do.

'If you think you're in the doghouse with me, just wait until I wake up the gang upstairs. Leo isn't going to be happy about not going fishing with you tomorrow.'

'I know, I'll make it up to all of you. I promise. Take my car if you want.'

'It's okay, I'll take mine. I'd better get this over with.'

She got to her feet and Dave heard the floorboards creak as she walked up the stairs to the kids' bedroom. The flickering golden glow of the fireplace became contaminated as she turned the bedroom light on.

Dave's heart sank as he heard his kids' protestations at being woken up. Whispers were followed by more protestations at being told they had to go home early.

This had better be important, Tom.

10
First Strike

Marcus Verrico stood over his desk, looking down at an intricate diagram. His finger traced the locations he planned to position his men, who were significantly fewer in numbers since the loss of one hundred soldiers in the attack on Hartley House.

While they had failed in their primary objective of recapturing Doctor Owen, they had undoubtedly succeeded in telling the humans they meant business. They had shown the humans that everything they thought they knew about vampires was wrong. Their numbers would continue to grow in spite of their failure the night before.

This strike will be our first against the human race. It will be our first strike in the battle for our supremacy and they won't even know it was us until it's too late.

A knock on the door signalled Roxy's entrance and he turned round to face her.

'How's the leg?' he asked as she limped towards him.

'Nearly there,' she said, 'I'm having another treatment in a few minutes' time. After that I should be fighting fit.'

'I'm glad to hear it,' he said.

Roxy looked over his shoulder at the plans on his desk.

'Do you think we have enough men?'

'Yes. I think we can do it with fewer than twenty men but they'll have to work quickly. When we complete this attack successfully, we will have a force to be reckoned with once again.'

Their thoughts were interrupted by the ring of the telephone on Marcus' desk. Marcus reached over the plans and picked up the receiver. He answered the call and heard a strange voice utter the phrase he had been both expecting and dreading. As soon as the caller had finished what he wanted to say, he hung up, leaving Marcus no time to reply.

Roxy could tell he was shaken by the call. "Who was it?'

'That was one of the Lord Chancellor's advisors. He's coming here.'

'When?'

'He didn't say. The sun will be up soon so we should probably expect him at sunset.'

They contemplated their fates in silence. After they had killed the Lord Chancellor's deputy to save their clan, they knew it would only be a matter of time until he came calling.

To save their skins, Marcus knew he had to pull out all the stops to impress the Lord Chancellor. His attention turned to the diagrams on his desk once again.

This plan must not fail. Our lives depend on it.

11
Calling In Reinforcements

Private Hindle had been staring at the same screen for hours. The red dot he'd been watching had stopped at the digital representation of a lake an hour ago.

He had alerted the general when it stopped moving but had been told to keep an eye on it for now. After all, the sun would be rising before long and once the fugitives found shelter they would be easier to pick off. They wouldn't exactly be eager to run outside with two vampires in their gang.

It wasn't quite the exciting assignment he'd been expecting when they received the emergency call from Captain Stein. Private Hindle, like many other members of The Brotherhood, had never actually seen a vampire. Of course, he'd seen them on training videos and locked inside observation rooms but he'd never made a bloodsucker stare down the barrel of his gun. Even when they arrived at the base, he had been marched into the comms room while his squad mates got to kill all the remaining vampires several floors below.

The red dot disappeared.

'Sir,' said Private Hindle.

The general, who was looking at the screens on the other side of the operations room turned round. 'Yes, Private, what is it?'

'We've lost them.'

'How could you lose them?'

'Either the tracking device on the helicopter failed or they found it and destroyed it.'

The general thought to himself for a moment. 'They must have abandoned the helicopter,' he announced, 'Where are they?'

'The last fix on their position was just over a mile south of Lake Arcadia.'

General Graham picked up the telephone sitting next to Private Hindle and dialled the number for the regional headquarters closest to the lake.

'This is General Graham. Give me Captain Sayers,' he barked as soon as his call was answered.

Private Hindle tried to listen in to the conversation but all he could hear was the general's booming voice.

'Captain Sayers, I need your help. I am at the regional headquarters nearest Hartley House. Yes, terrible losses. We need more men.'

General Graham then read the longitude and latitude of the last position of the missing helicopter out to Captain Sayers from the screen.

'Load up a helicopter and meet me at Lake Arcadia in one hour.'

12
'Where Are You Taking Me?'

Emily Owen had kept perfectly silent during the long journey from the city out into the country. Without any interruptions, she had managed to calm herself down and accept her situation.

Thoughts of her husband were always on her mind. She hadn't seen him since he had left, promising to come back for her and telling her everything would be okay. He could be in exactly the same position as her for all she knew but it was the not knowing that was hurting her the most.

Worrying about Andrew meant she wasn't thinking about where her captor was taking her. She tried not to think about what her captor had done at the police station but she couldn't escape the images that had flashed before her eyes after he had pulled her from her cell.

The floor had been strewn with bodies, some police officers, others civilian, but all dead. Pools of blood had gathered on the floor and red splatters streaked up the walls. The commotion she heard outside her cell had lasted for only a matter of seconds, but it was all the time her burly captor needed.

Did he really kill all those people single-handedly?

She knew there was only one explanation for his strength. This was the first time she had met a vampire. Well, it was the first time she was sure she had met a vampire. Andrew had told her they were everywhere in the real world, not just hiding in dark corners waiting to suck the blood of innocent people. Ever since he told her the secret he had kept hidden from the rest of the world, she always kept her eyes open for vampires in her everyday life.

The woman who always served her at the bank. Their dentist. The postman. Members of her own family. Her friends. Politicians.

Are any of them creatures of the night? Are they all creatures of the night?

She could never tell for sure but always had her suspicions. Many times in the past she had questioned her husband's sanity and her own.

Come on, Andrew. Monsters don't exist. How can they? They're the stuff of fantasy, creatures that only show up in movies.

But she trusted Andrew. He was the last person in the world she thought would let his imagination run away with him. He was the most strait-laced and sensible person she'd ever met. That's why she loved him so much. She had no reason not to believe him so she put her faith in him with no promise of any pay-off for her devotion.

Andrew had been straight with her from the start. He knew that he might not live to see the fruits of his labour, but he was certain he was part of something big, something important that the survival of mankind depended on. Many scientists before him had tried and failed to create a cure for the vampire virus. Part of him wanted to be the man to succeed where others had failed, but he was a realist.

All he thought he could do was make one breakthrough that would allow his successors to continue to develop further. But that had all changed when he and Doctor Forrest made the breakthrough just a matter of weeks earlier.

Emily stared out of the window at the dark, empty countryside. They were driving higher and higher into the mountains, working their way round winding roads edged with metal barriers that were supposed to stop careless drivers plunging into the rocky depths below. Artificial orange light illuminated the car for a few seconds as they passed through a small village. The car was then plunged back into darkness.

After a few minutes, Emily finally plucked up the courage to ask her captor a question.

'Where are you taking me?'

As soon as the words had left her lips, he hit the brakes and turned the car off the road. A shiver shot down her spine and adrenaline coursed through her veins.

Oh my God, she thought, *is he going to kill me for asking where we're going?*

Relief hit her as she realised the coincidental timing of her question. The reason the driver had turned off the road was not to kill her and dump her body. A large metal gate ahead of them swung open and they continued down a dirt track that led into the mountains.

The relief Emily had felt left her as soon as it had arrived. She realised that wherever they were going, they were almost there and her fears turned to thoughts of what might happen to her when they reached their destination.

He didn't bring me all this way just to kill me.
Did he?

13
Plunging Into The Darkness

The car drew to a halt and Emily jumped as she heard the clunk of the doors unlocking. For the first time since she had been dragged out of the police station, Emily's captor turned round and looked her in the eye. His face was deathly white and his piercing eyes a shade of unnaturally light blue. The darkness cast deep shadows across his face and Emily looked away in fear. In a deep, gruff voice he barked 'Get out!'

She complied immediately.

Emily opened the door and stepped outside. She regretted removing her shoes in her cell that afternoon, wincing as her bare feet met dirt and sharp rocks. Looking around, all she could see was grass and patches of dirt stretching into the never-ending darkness.

'What are we doing here?' she asked as the pale man got out of the car and slammed the door. The rocks underfoot crunched as he took huge steps towards her. He reached out and gripped her tightly. Emily stifled a scream as he pulled her close to him.

'Hey, what the hell are you doing? Why have you brought me here?'

He leaned forward and whispered in her ear. 'Hold on.'

'What?'

Before she could protest any further, the pale man leapt into the air. But instead of dropping back down to the ground, they kept rising and rising, soaring high above the dirt road. No matter how much she didn't want to be within a hundred miles of this man, let alone holding on to his belt as he dragged her screaming into the sky above them, she clung on to him for dear life.

With the harsh chill of the night air rushing past her face, they arced high in the air and started heading back towards the ground. Emily screamed at the top of her lungs as they passed over the car and over a ridge that had been obscured from view by the darkness.

They plunged into pitch black for what seemed like an eternity. Emily's body tingled all over, awaiting the inevitable impact at any moment.

Then without warning, they started to slow down. They slowed down until they were hanging in mid-air. Emily felt her body shaking all over. The pale man whispered in her ear again.

'What's wrong? Never flown before?'

She didn't reply and the pale man laughed.

'Do you want to try it again?' he asked and let go of her.

Emily felt gravity take hold of her body and screamed once more, louder than she had ever screamed before. Her fingers clawed for grip on the pale man's body as it rose above her and she caught hold of his boot. His blue eyes looked down on her. Before she could plead for him to spare her life, he shook her loose from his leg like she was just something stuck to his boot.

She screamed once more, with what she thought would be her final breath.

After falling not even a metre, her bare feet hit a wooden floor. Her legs buckled and she crumpled to the floor. Emily's whimpers of fear and humiliation were drowned out by the hearty laughs of the pale man, who lowered himself onto the wooden floor. He stepped over Emily's shivering body and banged on a huge wooden door.

The sound of a metal bolt echoed around the narrow cavern and the wooden doors were flung open. Emily looked up and saw Roxy limp out from the doorway and onto the wooden platform where she lay quivering. Roxy addressed the pale man.

'Is this the wife?'

The pale man nodded.

'Good work, Jackson,' she said, 'Get her inside.'

The pale man grabbed Emily's arm and dragged her to her feet. He marched her through the entrance hall and down a long corridor. She cried out for help but no one came to her aid. The pale man slammed the heavy wooden door shut and locked it, ignoring Emily's screams from inside as he pocketed the key.

Job done, Jackson thought, *That was too easy.*

14
The Cabin

I breathed a sigh of relief as we reached the top of the second hill and took in the view ahead. A massive lake lay in the valley below, its surface shimmering in the cool night breeze. The full moon reflected in the lake, painting a scene of serenity before us, completely at odds with the crisis we were struggling to deal with.

We were under no delusions. We were in mortal danger. We knew The Brotherhood must have been tracking the helicopter and now that it had stopped moving, they almost certainly had a fix on our location.

But how did I know to bring us here?

I had no recollection of telling the others to bring us here. I knew that Dave would help us but the way I told them was very disconcerting. Sarah always said I talked to her when I was asleep. Sometimes it was complete nonsense but other times she said she could hold a conversation with me. According to Sarah I would tell her things in my sleep that I would never have thought to say in my waking life. This made me wonder if the reason for us being here was due to my nocturnal foibles or another new talent I had inherited from the vampire that had bitten me.

The vampire that sucked my blood just last night.

It felt so long ago. We had been through so much since my old friend Greg Myers had turned into a vampire and bitten me, but our journey was far from over.

We stopped for a second and looked across the lake at the cabins in the distance. Tiny dots of light indicated that most of the cabins were inhabited.

'Not far to go,' Skinner said optimistically.

'Are you sure we can trust him?' Agent Simpson asked.

'Of course,' I replied immediately, 'he's my partner. I'd trust him with my life.'

'I'm still not sure,' she said, 'He's a cop. We can't trust anyone any more.' She was still being cold with me. I was worried that we'd end up taking our frustrations out on each other, when we'd worked so well together so far.

'Well, look at it this way, Jane,' I said, 'We don't have much choice, do we?'

'No Tom, we don't. But that's because you brought us here.'

Doctor Owen walked ahead of us. 'Come on,' he said, 'we won't get anywhere standing around bitching.'

The doctor led the way down the hill to the edge of the lake and we followed it round to the path that led us through a small, tidy collection of young trees to the cabin complex.

'Which cabin is he in?' Skinner asked.

'Sixty-six.'

We walked along the road that followed the side of the lake and counted down the numbers of the cabins we passed.

'It's that one up ahead,' Skinner said.

I saw the cabin Skinner was talking about. The lights were on and there were two cars outside, one on the drive and one on the road in front. As we approached, a group emerged from the front door and walked down the drive.

I turned round to face the rest of the group. 'Wait,' I said.

'What's wrong?' Jane asked.

'He's with his wife and kids.'

'So what?'

'So they don't need us wading in, that's so what. He's getting rid of his family to help us out. Let him say goodbye to them first.'

We were so focused on finding shelter that we were in danger of doing it at the expense of everything else, including social graces. With torn clothes and dirty and bloody faces, we would have been fooling ourselves if we had expected to be welcomed with open arms.

'Remember,' I announced to everyone, 'Dave doesn't know why we're here. He doesn't know who any of you are and look at the state of us. No sense in giving his kids nightmares.'

Everyone kept silent but I knew they agreed with me.

Dave was in the same position I was in yesterday. He had no concept of vampires in the real world. I had a lot to tell him but I needed him to take it all in quickly if he was going to help us.

We watched Dave's wife load their kids into the car. She kissed him goodbye then got into the car and drove away from their cabin. I hadn't seen a through road behind us so I had assumed she would drive away in the opposite direction but she was heading right for us.

As the car passed our motley crew of strays, her stare cut through the darkness and hit me right in the eye.

She knows we're the ones who've ruined her holiday.

'Wait here,' I said.

'Why?' asked Jane.

'Like I said, he doesn't know any of you. It'll be best if I go ahead and talk to him one on one.'

Once again, silent agreement washed over our team and I realised we'd have to work on our communication skills. *Maybe it's just because we're all tired*, I thought and pushed that concern to the back of my mind.

Dave had gone back inside the cabin. I walked along the road, up the drive and knocked on his front door. He opened it and paused for a second when he saw me.

'Holy shit, Tom. What the hell happened to you?'

'Make me a strong cup of coffee and I'll tell you all about it.'

'Will do. Didn't you say there were others with you?'

'They're waiting round the corner. I thought I'd better check you're okay with this first.'

'Don't worry about it, partner. I couldn't leave you wandering the hills all night, especially looking like that. Bring them in and I'll put the kettle on.'

15
Low On Supplies

Roxy stood in Marcus' office, debating with him their tactics regarding the imminent arrival of the Lord Chancellor. The way they saw it, the Lord Chancellor was coming to kill them. They had murdered his deputy and he was going to have his revenge. The thought of running away never even entered their minds. They knew he would do everything in his power to track them down and make sure they had a fate worse than death.

In the meantime, they had to do all they could to impress him with their tactical capabilities when he arrived. They knew that if the Lord Chancellor saw that the Rising had begun and it was they who were responsible for its ongoing success, they would have a chance of being spared. This meant completing one, or preferably both, of the tasks they had set themselves.

Get the doctor back

Complete tomorrow's mission successfully and move onto the next phase of the plan.

Doctor Forrest was confident the instructions he had given Doctor Owen would lead him back into their hands. After all, Doctor Owen saw no reason not to trust him. If he hadn't figured out that he'd been working with a vampire for many years, he was unlikely to piece together the clues over the next twenty-four hours.

They turned their attention to planning the next mission. They stood over the plans once more, marking the best spots to place their men and weighing up potential losses.

'Any losses will occur on impact,' said Marcus, 'We should expect a loss of ten to twenty percent.'

'That all depends on the skills of our men on the inside,' said Roxy, 'but we shouldn't have any problems from The Brotherhood. All indications from our surveillance teams are that they are putting all their efforts into recovering the doctor.'

'The doctor's escape is a fortunate diversion, and with him running around the city looking for the samples Doctor Forrest has sent him to recover, we shouldn't have any problems executing the plan.'

There was a knock at the door and Marcus shouted for the visitor to enter. Doctor Forrest opened the door and quickly stepped inside.

'Doctor Forrest, is everything okay?' Roxy asked.

'Yes,' he replied, 'but I heard you've captured Doctor Owen's wife.'

'That's correct. Is that a problem?'

'We've met each other a few times at work functions so I don't want her to know about the work I'm doing here. I realise the holding cell is close to my lab so I'm going to remain in my lab with the door closed unless absolutely necessary.'

'Don't worry,' said Roxy, 'she will be confined to her room until we get Doctor Owen back. By that time it will be too late to keep any secrets.'

'Thank you. There's one more thing. I'm running out of the treatment. I was expecting us to have access to another supply by now but with yesterday's complications I have only two days' supply left. I have a stash at my house, the one where you were holding the doctor.'

'Jackson is here so I'll send him out to pick up the supplies for you. It shouldn't take any more than a few hours.'

'Thanks, Roxy. It'll be much easier once we are able to raid the stockpiles.'

'That time isn't far away, Doctor.'

16

Introductions

Everyone said their introductions and Dave invited us inside his cabin. It was exactly how I thought it would be. The entire structure was made from wood and a log fire was crackling in the corner. It was a small, functional place but probably as close to the dictionary definition of cosy as you could get, with the orange glow from the fire and our exhaustion making it the most inviting place I had seen in a long time.

We set the heavy boxes down and Dave told us all to sit down by the fire. We didn't need a second invitation. Even though the days had been very hot, the night air was cold, especially if you were hiking through the hills in a shirt that had been ripped open by someone who wanted to tear your guts out.

I saw Dave open a suitcase that was lying under the stairs. He walked over with a polo shirt in his hand and threw it to me.

'Here you go, partner,' he said, 'Can't have you wandering around like that.'

'Thanks Dave,' I said, a little touched that I didn't even need to ask him for a new shirt.

'Yeah, no problem. I'm putting the kettle on. Who wants coffee?'

We all accepted the offer and as Dave made the coffees at the kitchen worktop, we recounted our story so far. We told him everything, from the bomb that was planted at Mantek to stop Doctor Owen's research, to the attack on the freeway, our escape from Hartley House and the discoveries we made about vampire anatomy at The Brotherhood's base just hours earlier. Of course, this included me getting bitten by a vampire.

'What the hell?' Dave exclaimed when I told him about my condition, 'If anyone else had told me that I would have told them they were full of shit and sent them on their way. So aren't you supposed to try and drink my blood or something?'

'It doesn't quite work like that,' I said, 'I've been taking the treatment Doctor Owen has been developing. It's not a permanent cure but it keeps the hunger at bay for a few hours at a time.'

He stood in silence for a moment, taking everything in. 'Well, Tom, this is the last time I go on holiday and leave you to take a case on by yourself.'

We both laughed at the unbelievable situation. I heard Doctor Owen and Skinner laugh as well, and saw a smile break on Jane's face. Dave handed out the cups of coffee. I took a sip and realised it had been a long time since I'd eaten anything. I wondered whether my body was running purely on the blood I drank from Captain Stein's neck or if it was just our situation keeping me going. I asked Dave if he had anything to eat and he popped some bread in the toaster.

'This is a lot to take in,' Dave said, thinking aloud, 'so what do we do now? I take it this Brotherhood are going to be looking for you?'

'That's right,' said Jane, 'We have to assume they were tracking our helicopter so that doesn't give us long before they find us here. We have to keep moving.'

Doctor Owen piped up. 'Last night I received a call from Doctor Forrest, my boss and research partner. He's gone missing and wouldn't tell me where he was but he did tell me I have to recover some samples that we have stored in different facilities around the city, then we can meet up with him. He said he has a plan for moving our work forward.'

'So we need to find this guy, don't we?' Dave asked.

'Yes, but I don't think that requires all of us,' said Jane.

'I agree,' I said, trying to find common ground with her, 'we need to direct our efforts.'

'Good idea, Tom,' she said, and the tone of her voice turned darker, 'You can work out what the hell we're supposed to do with the severed head you brought with us.'

61

17
Neutralising The Base

General Graham picked up the microphone for the public address system. His voice echoed all over the base. There was nowhere his men couldn't hear him.

'This is General Graham. Prepare for evacuation. We will be leaving in ten minutes. Neutralise all infected areas and destroy all remaining samples. Upload all data from local computers to the global servers. Repeat: we will be leaving in ten minutes. If you're not top-side by then, you're walking home.'

With that announcement, everyone doubled their efforts. Deep inside the base, the soldiers who were sorting through the remnants of the regional headquarters stood aside as their squad mates fired up their flame throwers. One by one, huge bursts of fire engulfed the laboratories, the morgue and every corner where blood had been spilled.

The bodies of the victims had all been removed but there were still pieces of flesh and limbs dotted around the base, which started to crackle and fill the corridors with the stench of burning meat as they were roasted by the retreating soldiers.

The men inside the operations room were hastily removing all data from the local systems and transferring it to the global servers, where it could be accessed by anyone within The Brotherhood or the World Health Organisation. As they finished and left their stations, a soldier with a flame thrower arrived to neutralise the places that Captain Stein's bloody and disfigured body had come into contact with.

Meanwhile, Captain Stein was being carried out of the base on a stretcher and guarded by a large group of soldiers, all ready to fill him with silver bullets if he made a wrong move.

'Put him in the lead chopper. He's coming with me,' the general shouted to his men.

Stein lay still, complying with the wishes of his aggressors but that didn't stop them jabbing him in the back with their rifles as they loaded him into the helicopter, just to make sure he knew who was in charge.

All equipment that had been sitting on the tarmac above them was being moved back inside the base. One day The Brotherhood may need to use this facility again and it was necessary to keep any evidence of their tactical capability from this location out of reach of satellite surveillance. There wasn't enough time to arrange the equipment neatly so the soldiers outside the base dumped the crates inside the main doors as quickly as they could.

General Graham looked at his watch. 'Ten minutes are up, people. Let's go,' he shouted to the soldiers still inside. He hit the button to lock down the base. The siren sounded and the main doors began to close. Everyone still inside ran up the ramp and through the doors before they closed with a loud metallic clang, sealing the scene of one of The Brotherhood's greatest failures. It was their second in as many days.

The pile of bodies at the end of the tarmac was burning furiously, sending a huge cloud of black smoke into the heavens above. General Graham picked up the radio as he boarded the lead helicopter.

'Good work, everyone. All other choppers head for Hartley House. Make that your base of operations. We need to stay close to the city in the coming days.'

He put down the radio and turned to the pilot. 'We're heading for Lake Arcadia.'

'Yes sir,' the pilot said and fired the engine into life. The sound of the rotating blades grew louder and louder until the heavy gunship lifted off the ground and headed in the opposite direction to the other helicopters.

General Graham turned round and looked Captain Stein in the eye. 'Keep a close watch over him,' he said to his men.

'I'm not exactly in a fit state to run away from you,' Stein said.

'Maybe not, but you'd better help us find the doctor, and fast. The sun will be coming up in a few hours so you haven't got much time.'

18
Breaking News

The atmosphere in the room was almost tangible. Jane had it in for me, probably with good reason, and she wasn't afraid to show it. Dave broke the silence that had hung in the air since her last comment to me.

'Let's see if there's anything about all this on the news,' he said, and turned on the television. He flicked over to a news channel and I was taken aback by the image in front of us. I looked at Dave, who was staring at the television, open-mouthed in astonishment.

A news reporter was standing in front of a police station that had crime scene tape all around it. Our police station. The red banner headline across the bottom of the screen said 'BREAKING NEWS: BRUTAL ATTACK ON POLICE STATION. 6 DEAD, 1 MISSING.'

'We are getting reports that just a few hours ago, an armed man entered the police station by force and killed almost everyone inside. Apart from the prisoners in the holding cells, the only survivor, a female who cannot be named at this time, appears to have been taken from the cell where she was being held.'

I looked over at Doctor Owen, who turned to me with a look on his face that was a mixture of shock and anger.

'It's Emily, isn't it?' he said, 'They've taken my wife, haven't they?'

'But who took her?' Jane said, 'We don't know if it was the vampires or The Brotherhood. We need to get someone over there and find out.'

'I'll do it,' said Dave.

'Are you sure?' I asked, 'You've already helped us out by putting us up here. You don't have to get involved.'

'My holiday's pretty much over now anyway. I'm supposed to go back to work the day after tomorrow, but it looks like there's not much of a job to go back to. I'll do my best to get in on this investigation. You need someone on the inside with the police and with the state you're in at the moment, you're not exactly up to the job.'

'Good,' Jane said assertively, 'it sounds like we're starting to come up with a plan. While Dave is checking out the police station, Doctor Owen and I will recover the samples and documents we need. I take it you know where they're all held?'

Doctor Owen nodded.

'Don't worry,' Jane continued, 'We'll get her back. Remember, we found you, didn't we?'

'What about me and Skinner?' I asked.

Skinner spoke before Jane could jump down my throat.

'I'll take him to get registered,' he said.

'What do you mean?' I asked.

'We need to register you as a vampire. The vampires have scouts trawling the city looking for new vampires. When they pick them up, they take them to a secure location and put them on the books. They're very particular about tracking the size of their population. It means we won't run into any trouble in the future if they've got you on their records.'

'I'm not sure about that,' I said, feeling very wary of offering myself up to the vampires.

'If nothing else, it'll be somewhere to hide out until the end of the day. We need to stay out of the sun and you know we can't stay here for long.'

'Sounds like we've got a plan then, people,' Jane said, 'We'll head into the city and split up.'

As Jane spoke, I was still weighing up Skinner's plan in my head. Then it hit me. I knew why I'd removed Commander North's head and brought it with us.

'Give me the head,' I said to Jane, looking her in the eye, 'I know what to do with it.'

19
Arrival At The Lake

One helicopter was already on the ground as the second gunship glided over the hills. It set down next to a small lake just over the hills from Lake Arcadia. There were just two men on board the well-armed and well-stocked helicopter: the pilot and Captain Sayers.

Sayers had been relishing the chance to take on this mission since he received the call from General Graham. A call directly from the general meant two things. One: he had handpicked Captain Luke Sayers for this mission because he knew about his successes in the past. Two: the previous captain must have really screwed up.

Stepping out of his helicopter, Sayers marched across the grass towards the earlier arrivals. He counted five soldiers scattered around the hills, including two in diving gear who were making their way towards the edge of the water. General Graham was already walking towards him and they saluted each other as they met.

'We're in some pretty shit, Sayers. I hope your men are ready to go,' said the general.

'Yes sir. Thank you for this opportunity. Where are we at the moment?'

'This is the approximate position where we lost the signal from the tracking device on the helicopter the targets stole. We've checked the surrounding area and there's no sign so I've sent divers into the lake.'

'How could they dump a helicopter into a lake without anyone getting hurt?'

'Think about it. What if one of them were a vampire?'

Captain Sayers raised his eyebrows involuntarily, immediately realising how serious this mission was. 'How many of them are there?'

'Four. Doctor Owen, who I'm sure you've heard of, Jane Simpson, an agent of the World Health Organisation, Tom Ryder, a cop from the city and Private Skinner, a member of our force. At least one of them, the cop, is a vampire. They also took Commander North's head.'

'What? He's dead? He was my commanding officer when I was a private. Why would they take his head?'

'Who the hell knows. We discovered his decapitated body at the base and couldn't find his head so I assume they have it with them. Anyway you cut it, this situation is a real fuck-up.'

'What about the captain who was in charge?'

'Captain Stein? Just wait till you see what happened to him.'

General Graham led Captain Sayers over to the second helicopter, but put a hand on his shoulder to stop him getting inside. They were faced with Captain Stein's white figure and cold, dead eyes staring out at them. What was left of his legs was wrapped in bandages that had long since soaked through with his own blood.

'Jesus Christ,' Captain Sayers exclaimed as his hand went to his pistol, 'He's one of them. Why haven't you killed him?'

'We still need him. *You* still need him.'

'What? Why?'

'They can smell their own. You're looking for a vampire. The best way to find the cop is to use Stein to sniff him out.'

Captain Sayers took the general to one side, out of Stein's direct line of sight, and whispered to him.

'This is very irregular, sir. We can't keep him like this forever. We have to dispose of him. He's a threat to every man here and everyone out there in the real world.'

'Look, we've got to get the doctor back. I don't care if you have to use every vampire out there to do it. The doctor must finish his work.'

'But surely if we let them go, they'll let their guard down in a few days' time and we'll scoop them up.'

'No. Time is critical. I suspect we may only have a few hours until I'm given the order to cease all operations. Don't ask me why. Just find the doctor. Once you have, you can do whatever you want with the captain.'

Out of sight of the conspiring pair outside the helicopter, Captain Stein sat quietly inside wondering how he could hear everything they were saying, and if there were any other new talents he hadn't yet discovered.

20
Head In A Box

The five of us crammed into Dave's car and we headed away from the lake, towards the city. It was a long, uncomfortable journey, both physically and emotionally. We had all been thrown together by circumstance and while we had managed to come up with a plan, it didn't feel like we really knew what we were doing.

Dave was going to check out the police station to see if we could get any leads on the disappearance of Doctor Owen's wife. We listened to the radio for the whole journey but the newsreaders didn't offer up any new information. The uncertainty wasn't doing anything for Doctor Owen's nerves and he kept asking Jane to change the radio over to different stations in case one news team had more information than another. Jane told him to calm down and focus on the job at hand. After all, how could we believe anything they reported on the news?

Jane and the doctor were going to scour the streets of the city looking for the samples and documents that Doctor Forrest had told us to pick up. This also made me feel uneasy. We'd agreed to this after one phone call and we had no idea how we were supposed to get the samples to him or what we would do with them once we had them.

And then there was the work Skinner and I had to do. To register me as a vampire so we don't run into any identity problems should we be faced with a team of vampires in the future.

That's where the Commander's severed head will come in handy.

I had finally remembered why I had brutally decapitated the Commander at The Brotherhood's base in the mountains. In the time when I lost my mind, I was being driven by uncontrollable primal urges that were foreign to me. Just as I had seen glimpses of the future when Doctor Owens' treatment took hold of my body the first time, an image had flashed before my eyes when I was holding Commander North by the collar.

I saw a picture of me presenting his head to a pale-looking woman dressed in black.

I knew this meant I would come face-to-face with a vampire of influence. It seemed to me that the only way I could find out what was happening to me would be to infiltrate the vampire community. I had to get on the inside.

I looked at my watch and noted that it had been a few hours since I had woken up after Doctor Owen gave me the treatment again. The effects hadn't been as severe as the first time. I hoped this meant the virus was working its way out of my system. Thinking realistically, I suspected the exact opposite was true; that the virus was taking over my system and fighting the treatment more vigorously.

I tried to remember how long it had been between waking up and getting the hunger. I knew it wouldn't be long until I started getting that horrendous feeling in my stomach again. I hoped I would be able to control myself this time.

The car drew to a halt. 'We'll let you out here,' Dave said.

Skinner opened the door and we both got out. We found ourselves standing on a street on the edge of the city. I knew this place. The towering apartment blocks and convenience stores were familiar to me. I had been called to more than a few homicides in this area. I wondered how many of them had been committed by vampires, and how many vampires I had put in prison, unaware of who they really were.

I went round to the back of the car and opened the boot. Inside was the metal case containing the commander's head that I hoped would give us the leverage we needed to get on the inside. Dave and Doctor Owen got out of the car, but Jane remained in the front passenger seat.

'Good luck, partner,' said Dave, 'The sun will be rising in a couple of hours so if you're still here in an hour, give me a call and I'll come back and pick you up.'

'Thanks,' I said and lowered my voice, turning to Doctor Owen, 'Any chance you can keep an eye on Jane? She's on my case, Doc.'

The doctor smiled. 'I'll do what I can, Tom, but to be fair, she's had a lot to take in with what's happened to you.'

We said our goodbyes and Dave's car disappeared into the city, leaving us standing on a street corner with a severed head in a box. I immediately questioned whether this was the best possible use of our time.

21
No Bodies

Captain Sayers stood on the edge of the lake, looking across the rippling silvery surface. *Have they really dumped a huge gunship in here?*

The water was disturbed by a froth of bubbles and two masked heads emerged. General Graham walked over and joined Captain Sayers at the edge of the water to meet the divers as they made their way out of the lake. The divers removed their masks and the one in front spoke before the officers could ask the obvious questions.

'The helicopter's down there, sir.'

'Any sign of the doctor and the others?' asked Captain Sayers.

'No, sir. No bodies.'

'Good work, men,' said the captain, checking his watch, 'They can't have gone far. Go and get out of your suits. They'll need shelter and transport so we'll start our search at the cabins by the lake.'

'But there's dozens, maybe hundreds of cabins, sir. We can't search every one.'

'Leave that to me,' Captain Sayers said. The soldiers ran back to their helicopter, preparing to dry off and change into their combat gear as quickly as possible. Sayers was already asserting his authority, doing whatever he could to show that he was in change. He was the one who would succeed where others had failed.

Thoughts of failure made his attention turn to Captain Stein. General Graham instinctively knew what Sayers was thinking.

'You'd better keep your sniffer dog on a short leash.'

'Are you leaving us, sir?' Captain Sayers asked.

'Yes I am. I'm going to leave you in charge here, Captain Sayers. I will join the others at Hartley House and await your call. If you need any intel, contact Private Hindle. He should be at Hartley House already.'

'Thank you, sir. I will not disappoint you.'

'Good. It is absolutely imperative that you recover the doctor. As long as he remains in the outside world, our work will be in jeopardy. Everything we have worked for over the last five hundred years depends on finding him.'

'You can depend on me, sir,' Captain Sayers said as he looked at Captain Stein, 'We'll find him.'

General Graham left Captain Sayers to round up his men and marched to his helicopter. He was confident that this was the best man to lead the search for the doctor and his small band of fugitives but wasn't as confident that they would be found.

Sayers shouted to his men. 'Get Stein in a set of boots. He's coming with us.'

As his helicopter lifted off, General Graham's thoughts turned to the day ahead. Before long, his hands would be tied and he would be forced to call off the search. The chances of finding the doctor and getting him to a facility where he could complete the work on the primary treatment by the end of the day were so remote as to be unworthy of consideration.

He almost had to laugh at the situation. They were on the run because they believed in developing a treatment to relieve the symptoms of the vampire virus, which in turn would allow the species to co-exist. But if they knew what he knew, they would almost certainly be compelled to work together.

22
Chaos At The Police Station

Dave stepped out of the car and looked across the street at the police station. The building was bathed in blue and red flashing lights but the vehicles from news networks surrounding the compound seemed to outnumber the police cars two to one.

Reporters were buzzing around, trying to talk to anyone and everyone they saw. Dave knew he'd have to run the gauntlet to get through the rabble ahead of him but unlike most of these situations, he wouldn't have to lie.

I really don't know anything this time, he thought.

Jane got out of the passenger side and walked round the car to take the driver's seat.

'I'll try and take care of the car,' she said.

Dave smiled. 'Well, if it's life or death situation, I'll understand if you save yourself first.'

'You've got our number, haven't you?' she asked.

'Yeah, I've got it. I'll give you a call if I find anything out. If you call me, don't take offence if I don't answer it. I might not be in a position to talk to you if I'm with other cops.'

'We just need any relevant information, no matter how small,' Doctor Owen said as he leaned over from the passenger seat, 'Please find my wife.'

The doctor's face painted the picture of someone who was concerned, even scared for his wife's well-being but also one hundred percent aware of his responsibilities. He knew the job he and Jane had to do in the same way Dave knew what he had to do.

'I'll do whatever I can,' said Dave, 'If it was a smash-and-grab then whoever has your wife couldn't have covered their tracks completely. If they've left a clue behind, I'll find it.'

Doctor Owen nodded in appreciation and Jane wished Dave good luck as she closed the door. The car headed down the street and disappeared round the corner, leaving the detective to contemplate the chaos he was faced with.

Taking a deep breath, he crossed the street. As soon as one reporter saw him walking towards them, they all turned round and ran into the road, oblivious to the approaching drivers who screeched to a halt and honked their horns in disapproval.

As he expected, they talked with machine-gun speed, loaded with the usual questions asking him what happened, who it happened to and who the police were looking for. His only response was 'No comment'. Dave battled his way through the crowd and under the crime scene tape that surrounded the station. He cast his eyes around the scene and saw the familiar face of Sergeant Crawford, who was doing a bad job of looking like he was in charge.

Ambulances were trying to get out of the car park but Crawford was being sidetracked by talking to the press who were standing on the exit ramp. Dave ran over to Sergeant Crawford.

'I need to talk to you,' he said in a forceful tone.

'Detective Thomas…'

Dave didn't let him finish and marched him out of the way, waving the ambulances past. The driver in front gave him a thumbs up.

'I think you're done talking to the press, sergeant,' Dave said, 'Where's the relief captain? Where's the chief?'

'The chief's on his way down here. We were on a skeleton staff this week so there's no one to stand in.'

'Right, I'm taking charge until the chief gets down here. All I know is what I saw on the news but I don't want to talk with all these reporters out here. Take me inside.'

23
Hanging Around

Thirty minutes had passed since we were dropped off and we had barely seen anyone go past us at all, never mind the vampire taxi Skinner was expecting. I sat down on the metal box containing Commander North's head.

'Are you sure this is going to work?' I asked.

'It worked for me,' said Skinner, 'I was told to wait on a quiet corner in the early hours and someone would pick me up. There's always someone out there looking for new vampires so they're bound to come round this way eventually.'

'Well, they'd better hurry up or we're both going to need a shit load of sunscreen.'

'You especially,' said Skinner, 'I was amazed how quickly you burned when we left the base. We've got to be careful with you. How do you feel now?'

'I'm expecting the hunger to kick in at any minute. It's been a few hours since I woke up from the treatment. I don't feel too bad but after seeing that vampire's guts yesterday, I'm worried about what the virus is doing to my insides.'

'I know what you mean. For what it's worth, my body still works like it should when I need it to.'

'But you can still do all the vampire magic tricks?'

'When you flew last night, did you feel the blood flowing round your body?'

'Yes. Whenever I did anything physical, I could feel something happening in my body. It was like a warmth spreading to the part of my body I was using.'

'That's your blood moving around your body. Blood moves to your muscles quicker, which means you can punch and kick harder than you ever could before.'

I thought of the organs we ripped out of the vampire's body. Doctor Owen had been surprised to find that they were filled with blood, almost soaking it up like a sponge.

'It comes at a price, though,' Skinner said, 'You saw that guy's body yesterday. The virus breaks down the tissue in your organs.'

'I know. I'm trying not to think about it. If that's what happens to all of us, how can we ever be cured? Surely our organs can't recover from that, even if the virus is removed from our bodies?'

A silence hung in the air as I contemplated what might happen to our bodies if non-infected blood tried to work its way through my sieve-like circulatory system. What Skinner was saying made perfect sense. Doctor Owen had struggled for many years to come up with a treatment and when he did, it only worked for a matter of hours. Even if the virus was destroyed, our bodies would almost certainly collapse from the damage done to our organs.

We were distracted by the sound of a car turning the corner at the end of the road. As the car approached us, it began to look familiar. It was a blue Toyota and there was a dog's head hanging out of the passenger window, barking at us. I spotted a bullet hole in the door, but the rear windscreen had been repaired.

This is the car that picked up Officer Myers last night. If I hadn't chased after this car, I wouldn't be turning into a vampire now.

The car drew to a halt next to us. A tall, pale man got out of the driver's door and looked at us.

'Good morning, my brothers. My name is Matthew Duffy. I'm here to help you.'

24
Replay Of The Attack

Dave didn't know what to expect as Sergeant Crawford led him into the police station. Murder was a regular occurrence in his life and he had been witness to countless scenes of carnage down the years but he had never seen anything like this at a police station.

The off-white walls were sprayed with blood and pools of the dark red liquid had gathered on the uneven floor. Empty bullet casings lay on the floor, scattered around the taped outlines of where the victims of the attack had fallen. Police photographers were tiptoeing around the evidence, getting snapshots that their superiors would analyse when they finally got their act together and responded to this crisis.

'I take it all the bodies have been removed?' Dave asked.

'That's right, detective,' said Sergeant Crawford, 'They're being taken to the hospital for further investigation. Captain Nash and Officer Slater did not sustain any gunshot wounds.'

'What happened to them?' Dave asked as they reached the empty cell where Emily Owen had been held.

'Broken necks.'

'Broken necks? Is this where Captain Nash was killed?' Dave asked, pointing at an outline on the floor.

'Yes sir.'

'Did they still have their guns at their side?'

'Yes sir, I believe they did.'

'But they didn't have time to draw them?'

'No sir.'

'Did you have any other prisoners?'

'Yes, but only the woman was touched. Whoever did this wasn't interested in the other prisoners. They've all been moved to another station outside the city.'

They both looked up and down the corridor that led to the holding cells. It was long and narrow. Nash would have been able to see and hear the beginning of an attack. If he didn't have time to draw his gun, the attacker must have worked very quickly.

Dave cast his eyes around the cell but there was nothing of interest. Just a small sweaty room where Emily had been held all day.

'Have you reviewed the security tapes yet?' Dave asked.

'Not yet.'

That's one of the first things I'd think to check, Dave thought.

'Okay, I'm going to look at them now.'

Sergeant Crawford led Dave to the front desk, where they had to wait until the photographers and forensic team had finished. The police station wasn't exactly a high-tech operation but Dave wanted to thank whoever installed the security system. The feeds from the cameras were saved to a hard drive in a server that was locked away in the basement so unless the attacker had known where it was held or destroyed the whole building, the record of what had happened would be safe.

Dave sat down and loaded up the security system software, which would let him view footage from the past seven days from up to four different cameras at once.

'What time did we get the call?' Dave asked.

'About ten o'clock,' Sergeant Crawford replied.

Dave entered 21:55:00 into the time selection field in the security system and the video feeds flicked to a more ordinary situation than the one he had been thrown into. One image showed a completely still car park, with headlights on the main road in front jerking past at half-second intervals. The other images showed the main entrance area from two different angles and the corridor that led to the holding cells.

He watched as the calm scene before him changed. A pair of headlights moved into the car park and stopped right outside the front door. A tall man got out of the car and entered the police station, where a handful of police officers were going about their business. He was wearing a long black coat and Dave just made out a long sheathed sword strapped to his side.

By the time the man had moved to within the field of vision of the cameras in the entrance area, he had already drawn his pistol and shot one man, who dropped to the floor. Dave watched the silent images as the invader wiped out everyone before him. He holstered his weapon and moved towards the holding cells. As he did, another policeman approached him and was immediately grabbed with one hand and thrown head first into the wall. Captain Nash started to run down the corridor from Emily Owen's cell and met with the same fate.

The man bent down and picked a set of keys off the floor where Nash had fallen. He walked up to Emily's cell and unlocked the door. In a flash, he grabbed her and pulled her out by her collar. Dave followed the images as Emily was dragged out of the police station by her captor and thrown into the back seat of his car. He removed the sword he hadn't had call to use from his belt and got into the driver's seat then drove away.

As the car turned around in the car park, Dave paused the video. With the mouse pointer, he clicked on the image before him and dragged a rectangle around the car's licence plate. The cropped image stretched out to fill the screen and the quality slowly improved, block by block, to reveal a licence plate number.

'Sergeant Crawford,' Dave said and turned round to look at the man behind him who was dumbstruck.

'Sergeant?' Dave repeated and he snapped out of it, 'I need you to do a search on this plate: Whisky Seven Four Seven Bravo X-ray Charlie.'

'I'm on it,' the sergeant replied and sat down at another computer in the entrance area.

Dave stood up and went over to a small metal case that was mounted on the wall. He opened the case to reveal a selection of keys to the police vehicles that were parked outside the station. He picked out a set of keys for an unmarked car and put them in his pocket.

Sergeant Crawford had finished searching for the car. He stood up and shouted over to Dave. 'The car's registered address is one-two-four Castle Crescent. The owner is a Doctor Forrest.'

Doctor Forrest? Tom mentioned that name before. I must be on the right track.

'Thanks, Sergeant,' Dave said, 'I'm taking a car. I'll call if I need backup. Tell the chief to call me if he needs me.'

25
'Where Are You Taking Us?'

I had no idea what I was getting into. As a detective, I had never really done any undercover work, certainly not for any significant amount of time. Now I found myself stepping into a world I never thought existed just forty-eight hours earlier, when I was sitting in my car with Dave staking out a suspect.

Skinner took the lead and opened the back door of the car for me. We got in and were immediately hit with the pungent smell of the dog that was sitting in the passenger seat. The car was grimy and the interior was in a serious state of disrepair, like it had been permanently on the road ever since it rolled off the production line. The seams of the upholstery were tattered and fraying and all exposed surfaces held a thick layer of dust.

I put my hand down on the leather seat and immediately pulled it away when I felt it stick. A shiver shot down my spine as I imagined the blood that had probably been spilled on the back seat of this car. I thought this man who had picked us up was not a lot different from Travis Bickle; transporting the questionable types of people who only come out at night from one side of the city to the other.

'This here's Goldie,' said Matthew, patting his companion, 'Without him I might not have found you. That's why he gets to ride up front. What are your names?'

'I'm Skinner and this is Tom.'

'I take it he's a rebirth?' Matthew said, looking me up and down and trying to look into my mind to find out my story without asking.

'Yes. I had to feed. Couldn't help myself. I've been looking after him ever since.'

Matthew turned to me.

'How do you feel about that, son?'

I ignored him and looked out of the window. It was a rude gesture but I figured this guy must have come up against a lot of attitude from people who had just found out about their new vampire life and I was happy to let Skinner be the talker. This guy must have dealt with reborn vampires all the time so I was probably well behaved, especially if the state of the car's interior was anything to go by.

'Fair enough,' Matthew said in response to my silence and started the engine.

'Where are you taking us?' Skinner asked.

'I would normally take you back to the clan but the sun will be rising in a little while and I'd rather stay out of view. There's an outpost not too far from here that can put you up until the sun goes down.'

Great. We've got to spend all day with this guy and his four-legged friend.

'We'll get your friend here registered and they'll have something for you to eat.'

I didn't like the sound of that. My first thought was that they'd lay on some breakfast but then it hit me that whoever was at the outpost was probably expecting a certain numbers of new vampires every day and they would have fresh meat available for their new brothers and sisters to feed on.

Very occasionally I have a habit of immediately making situations worse in my head before I've begun to deal with them, especially when I don't have any facts available. As a detective I'm compelled to remain impartial, analysing only the facts but at that moment I was imagining an initiation ceremony where I'd have to feast upon human flesh and blood from a living body while other vampires cheered me on. I began to hope the outpost was a small place where everyone was sleeping and they would leave us alone all day, kind of like a bed and breakfast for bloodsuckers.

'What's in the case?' Matthew asked.

Skinner paused for a second. 'I'd better not show you here. It's best to wait until we get to the outpost.'

'Very cryptic,' Matthew said and hit the accelerator, taking us deeper into the derelict outskirts of the city.

26
The Box Under The Bed

For the second time in under an hour, Detective Dave Thomas found himself standing in front of a building surrounded by crime scene tape. This time he was alone.

At one-two-four Castle Crescent there were no photographers or dumbstruck police officers getting in his way. Tom had told him about the attack on this house. He had even heard about the ensuing helicopter attack on the tactical aid unit on the radio as he drove his then-happy family up to the lake. All they had said on the radio was that the traffic was grid locked due to a 'possible terrorist incident'. He had half-expected to receive a call telling him to get back to work but the more time that passed without his phone ringing, the more those thoughts faded and turned to his wife and kids.

But that happiness had been all too brief. Dave cast his eyes over the surroundings. The pleasant leafy drive was lit only by street lights and he couldn't see anyone around. All the excitement in the suburbs had happened more than twenty-four hours earlier and with all the commotion at the police station, the city's hacks had a much juicier story to get their teeth into.

He knew the early risers would soon start to make their way out of bed and into their cars to beat the rush hour traffic.

If something was going to happen here, it's best to get it out of the way when there's no audience to see me screw up.

He walked up the path to the front door and pushed it open. It had been broken from its latch and now that the evidence had been gathered from the scene, securing the building wasn't a priority for the city's over-worked police department. Dave ducked under the crime scene tape and made his way inside, shutting the door behind him.

So this is where it all started.

Dave thought about the details of the story Tom had told him. This is where he first came up against a vampire and The Brotherhood at the same time. The smashed window in the door was testament to that, as were the rank aromas of burnt flesh and tear gas residue that hung in the air.

Dave started to look round the rooms, searching for anything that might lead him to the mysterious man who grabbed Doctor Owen's wife. He passed through the living room, kitchen and dining room. Nothing looked out of place to him. Other than the front door hanging from its hinges, the downstairs could have belonged to any upper-middle class home.

Dave returned to the entrance and slowly made his way up the stairs. The contrast between the scene in front of him and the one downstairs couldn't have been starker. At the top of the stairs he stopped and stared at the remnants of the demise of the vampire and Officer Myers. There was a wide red patch of blood dried into the carpet where the policeman had fallen, right next to a pile of ash and long burns streaking up the wall.

Trying not to imagine the sticky end that both victims had met, Dave moved into the main bedroom. He scanned the room and was about to move on when he noticed a small plastic box under the end of the bed. He bent down and picked up the box. It was filled with syringes, each packaged in plastic branded with the word 'Virex'. The syringes were all filled with equal measures of yellow liquid.

The silence was broken by the sound of the front door creaking open. Footsteps made their way inside the house.

Panic washed over Dave and he quickly placed the box back under the bed, then made his way into the en suite bathroom. He moved with footsteps as light as he could manage, trying to keep out of view while leaving a crack in the door to check out the intruder. He knelt down and popped the clip off his holster and drew his gun, knowing that if he was spotted, there would be no escape from the dead-end he was hiding in.

The footsteps made their way up the stairs. Dave clicked the safety catch on his pistol just before the sound of footsteps moved into the bedroom. A tall man with a pale face and dressed in black combat gear cast his piercing eyes around the room. He was tall, at least six foot four and he was stacked. If it came to a one-on-one, Dave knew he wouldn't have a hope in hell of overpowering this man mountain.

The man's eyes focused on the box under the bed. He bent down and picked it up, then made his way out of the bedroom and down the stairs. When Dave heard the front door close behind the stranger, he left the bathroom and ran down the stairs. Through the smashed window in the front door, he saw the man get into his car that was parked in front of the house and quietly drive away. With no other sounds outside on the road, it was as if he had never been there.

Dave got his keys out of his pocket, threw open the front door and made a run for his car.

27
Deserted

With no answer to his second stronger knock, Captain Sayers kicked the door in. The wooden frame splintered as the door swung open to reveal a deserted cabin.

'Are you sure this is the one?' Captain Sayers asked, turning round to look Stein in the eye. Stein nodded but didn't say a word. His mind was filled with anger and pain. His feet had barely started to grow back but he was being forced to hobble across hills and fields to look for the man who mutilated him.

Two soldiers had their arms round his shoulders, helping him walk, but they were more bothered about their own safety than minding if he stumbled and went over on his new ankles. Stein didn't have a grip on his new powers but he did what he could to be useful to Captain Sayers. The unnatural way he sniffed out the trail of the vampires they were chasing scared everyone in the squad and they all hoped they would be given the order to kill him soon.

Sayers led his men inside. The cabin was still warm, retaining heat from the log fire that had only just burned out. The embers of the fire were still glowing so Sayers knew that they weren't far behind their targets. From the outside, the cabin was identical to the rest of the holiday homes that lined the lake. Small and functional, it was designed for sleeping and eating between hikes, fishing trips and water sports. It wasn't designed to conceal four fugitives from The Brotherhood.

Sayers surveyed his surroundings. There was no sign of a struggle. Everything looked like it was in its right place.

They must have come here for a reason. No one would let a bunch of strangers in at this time of the morning. Why this cabin above all the others?

One of Sayers' men approached him. 'Nothing, sir. No personal items were left behind. The beds have been slept in, though.'

Sayers thought for a moment. 'One of them must have known whoever owns this cabin. They must have known they would be here this week.'

'Should we start knocking on doors?'

'No. That's clutching at straws. We'd only cause distress and word of our investigation would get to them before we do.'

Sayers lifted his radio. 'Private Hindle, are you there?'

There was a moment's silence before the reply. 'Yes sir, we've just arrived at Hartley House.'

'Good. We're at the lake, in a private cabin in the Waterside development. When you get the systems back online, I need you to find out who owns cabin sixty-six.'

'Yes sir. Have you found something?'

'Maybe. Stein led us to an empty cabin, but it looks like someone left not very long ago. We're going to head back to join you at Hartley House. The sun will be rising soon and it will be better to continue the search by ground.'

'Yes sir.'

As Captain Sayers clipped his radio back onto his belt, he heard Stein's voice behind him. He sounded angry and desperate. Sayers almost felt sorry for him.

'Do you still need me, or are you going to tie me to a post outside and leave me to burn? If you want to kill me, just get it over with.'

'We still need you,' Sayers replied, 'Anyway, we don't want you to burn here. You'll stink up the place and put the tourists off their breakfast. Get back to the chopper. We're leaving.'

28
Withheld Number

With Dave, Tom and Skinner all despatched on their own missions, Jane sat in silence as Doctor Owen listened attentively to the radio, resisting the urge to change stations every few seconds.

Of course, Jane sympathised with him but she hoped his current nervous state wouldn't jeopardise the tasks they had to carry out. The attack on the police station was a distraction from the job they had to focus on. Dave knew what he was doing. He was the best person to investigate the attack on the police station, which was supposed to leave them free to recover the samples Doctor Forrest had told them to find.

The first stop on their route was Mantek Pharmaceuticals. Doctor Owen looked out of the window and recognised the surroundings. They were getting close to the research laboratory.

'Are you sure you're going to be able to get past the security at Mantek?' Doctor Owen asked.

'I was there forty-eight hours ago. I've still got my security pass on me and a lot of the work at the site was done when I was there. Hopefully the security presence will be minimal and they'll just wave us through.'

'That's a lot to hope for,' the doctor said.

'Well, be sure to let me know if you come up with an alternative plan in the next few minutes because we're nearly there,' she snapped.

Doctor Owen looked at her but didn't say a word. Jane returned his stare but her expression thawed.

'I'm sorry,' she said, 'It's all getting on top of me. I need a good night's sleep.'

'What about Tom?'

'What about him?'

'Back there, he seemed to be the one on the wrong end of your tiredness.'

Jane thought that was the most polite way she'd ever been called a bitch.

'I just can't believe the change in him,' she said, 'He was a great cop, one of the best I've worked with. But seeing him do those things last night, seeing him kill those men in cold blood, it was horrible.'

'It's not his fault, you know. He doesn't want to kill anyone. It's the virus inside him making him do those things.'

'I know,' she said and struggled to find any more words.

'Mind you, if he hadn't killed those men, we'd probably all be dead.'

Doctor Owen was right and Jane knew it. Tom was a good detective and she had enjoyed working with him for that short time. They had only worked together for a few hours but they had quickly become a good team. Many obstacles had been in their way, including her hidden alliance to The Brotherhood, but that couldn't stop him finding out the terrible secret that humanity had hidden for centuries.

'It's just so difficult,' she said, 'Seeing him like that is terrible. He's not the same person he was.'

'He can't help it, Jane. Try and go easy on him. We have all the samples from the base in the boot and once we've collected all our work and meet with Doctor Forrest, I'll do everything I can to find a treatment that will cure him once and for all.'

The vibration of Doctor Owen's mobile phone in his pocket made him jump. He took it out of his pocket and looked at the screen to see who was calling.

Withheld number.

He answered the call. 'Hello?'

'Hello Andrew,' Doctor Forrest said in a hushed voice, 'Pay attention to what I have to say, I don't have much time.'

'Are you okay? Where are you?'

'I'm at the vampires' lair. I'm calling you on a phone I've managed to get working in the room they've locked me in. They've captured me but I have a plan to escape. I will call you later to tell you where to meet me. There's something you should know.'

'What's that?'

'They have your wife.'

'Emily is with you?'

'Yes. Well, not exactly. They're holding her here as well but in a different room.'

'Can you help get her out?'

'I'm not sure. I'll do what I can. Have you recovered the samples?'

'We're on our way to pick up the first sample now.'

'You have to get them all. We don't have much time. The Brotherhood are almost ready to mass-produce the primary treatment. We have to finish our work and stop them. I have to go.'

With that, Doctor Forrest was gone.

29
Arrival At The Outpost

Heavy clouds hung above us and the sky was turning a lighter shade of grey. During our relatively short journey the cool night breeze that had felt so refreshing at the lake had turned into full-on wind. We stepped out of the back of Matthew Duffy's car. In any other circumstance I would be happy to be free of the rank stench of sweaty dog but my mind was on other things.

Skinner and I faced our destination. In a deserted industrial estate we found ourselves outside a seemingly abandoned two-storey office building. With blacked-out windows and surrounded by a ten foot high metal fence, it was a very unassuming location. The ideal place for creatures of the night to hide out.

How many more of these locations are dotted around the city, the country, the world?

Our driver's dog stuck its head out of the car window and started to bark in our direction. I then heard barking behind us and turned round to see two Alsatians just like Goldie run round from the back of the building towards us. They stopped when they reached the fence but continued barking.

I've never been a fan of dogs. It probably all started when I was chased by a big black Doberman when I was just eight years old. It was only for a few seconds and no harm came to me but ever since then I've had a bad relationship with canines. It struck me that I should try to get used to having them around if I was going to be spending a lot of time surrounded by vampires.

Matthew opened a gap in the rusty fence and waved us through. As we crouched to get through the gap, the dogs kept barking but kept their distance from us. He escorted us across the yard and knocked on the front door. I heard a faint whining sound and looked up to see a small security camera focusing on us.

After a few seconds that seemed like a lifetime, I heard buttons being pressed on the other side of the door and a low buzz to indicate the security code had been entered correctly. The door opened to reveal a short, stocky man with the friendliest look I'd seen on a vampire's pale face.

'Just the two, is it?' the man asked.

'Yes,' replied Matthew, 'I've just picked them up. I would have taken them back to the lair but it'll be daylight soon and I didn't want to risk the journey.'

The short man nodded in agreement. 'Either of you a rebirth?'

'Me,' I said.

'Hungry yet?'

I shook my head, pretending not to know what he was talking about.

He smiled. 'Well, you will be soon. Don't worry, we've got takeaway on the way. Are you coming in, Matthew?'

'No, I've got time to get back. I'll leave these guys in your hands if that's okay.'

'Fine with me. Come in.'

As Matthew turned and headed back towards his car, we followed the short man into the building. He shut the door behind us.

30
Back To Mantek

Jane fished around in her pockets and pulled out her World Health Organisation security pass. She stopped their car at the security booth at the front of the Mantek pharmaceuticals complex and hoped that she still had clearance. She showed her pass to the security guard and he snatched it out of her hand. His attention turned to a sheet of paper on his desk.

Jane looked in her mirror to check there were no vehicles behind her, in case she had to shift into reverse and make a quick exit. She rested her hand on the gear stick as her foot hovered over the accelerator.

'Your details check out okay,' the security guard said, 'Follow the road up to the main building and check in with security there.'

Jane thanked him as he raised the barrier and they made their way into the compound. Ahead of them she saw almost the exact same sight she had seen two days earlier. The corner of the research building had been destroyed, blown up by a bomb planted by The Brotherhood to stop Doctor Owen's work on the cure for the vampire virus.

Their only priority was to produce a treatment that would kill all vampires but only Doctor Owen knew how and he didn't believe in their cause. Both he and Jane believed in producing the treatment that would cure all vampires. The treatment would be the first step towards co-existence, but they would need Doctor Forrest's help and the clock was ticking.

Jane stopped the car in front of the building. They got out and walked up the steps into the reception area. Without getting out of his chair, the security guard gestured for them to come over to his desk. He asked Jane and Doctor Owen for their security passes. Doctor Owen showed his Mantek pass and Jane flashed her WHO badge. The security guard was sluggish in his actions after a long night and cast his dark eyes across their credentials.

'I'll need you to sign in,' the security guard said.

'Why?' Jane asked, trying not to get aggressive but knowing that she didn't want to leave any evidence of them being here.

'Orders from you lot,' he said, pointing at Jane's WHO badge, 'Until they've sorted out the mess upstairs I have to make sure everyone signs in and out.' He passed Jane a clipboard and pen.

Damn it. He's already seen my name on my badge.

Reluctantly, Jane signed and printed her name. She fought the urge to sign a false name, knowing that it would probably cause more problems at this moment in time. She passed the clipboard and pen to Doctor Owen, whose face told her that they'd just made life more difficult for themselves.

When the security guard was satisfied that he'd done his job, he went back to reading his day-old newspaper and Jane and Doctor Owen disappeared round the corner.

'We've got to be as fast as we can,' Doctor Owen said as they walked up the stairs, 'Anyone who turns up will know what time we were here.'

'How long will this take?' Jane asked.

'We've got plenty of blood samples in the car so we won't need to pick any up from here. All I've got to do is load samples of the primary treatment into a case and download our research data onto a memory stick from the central server.'

'And you know exactly where everything is?'

'Yes. A long time ago, Doctor Forrest and I agreed that if we were ever in any danger or our work was compromised, we would have a plan to cover our tracks and carry on with our work.'

On their way to the storage room they had to go past what was left of Doctor Owen's lab, the sight of which stopped him in his tracks.

'Oh my God,' he exclaimed and edged his way through the splintered door frame into the dry, dusty shell of the lab where he used to work. Dumbstruck, he stood open-mouthed for a moment, overcome by the wreckage.

The cold night wind blew in through the massive hole in the corner of the room that had been ripped open by the bomb. Two days on, the smell of charred wood still hung in the air. Doctor Owen saw a spot on the floor that hadn't been burned by the explosion, behind the heavy metal refrigerator that had been twisted into an unnatural shape. A patch of blood had dried into the floor.

'Is that where Danny was killed?' he asked, thinking of his assistant, who he had left on his own in the lab that night.

Jane didn't answer his question. She touched him on the shoulder. 'Come on, Andrew. We've got to get this done. We've got four more sites to visit after this.'

Doctor Owen snapped out of it and turned to look her in the eye with a renewed focus in his mind. He wasn't going to let anything like this happen to them.

Get what you came here for and get out. Don't stop to smell the roses.

'You're right. Let's go.'

31
'Welcome To Our World'

The man who had greeted us at the front door entered a code into the keypad on the wall and I heard a clunk as the door was secured. The building we found ourselves in was as plain on the inside as it was on the outside.

Fluorescent tubes hung from the ceiling but none of them were turned on, leaving us in a dark corridor, only lit by the light coming from the adjoining rooms to our left and right. Paint was peeling off the walls and the carpet was so dirty that I couldn't tell what colour it used to be. The dusty, sweaty smell in the air told me people had been cooped up in the building for a long time and no one ever opened the windows.

Just like The Brotherhood had to be able to evacuate their locations at a moment's notice, I suspected the same was true for the vampires, yet another way in which their operations were similar.

'My name's Carl,' he said, 'I run the outpost here with Craig, but he's out getting something to eat. We weren't expecting anyone else to join us at this late hour so I hope there's enough to go round.'

'What are we doing here?' I asked.

'We have to hold you here during daylight hours. It's too dangerous to move around during the day unless there's an emergency. Since you're a rebirth, I'll get your details on the system. I'll need to check you against the database as well.'

'Of course,' said Skinner, who seemed to know what he was talking about.

'Come through,' he said and led us up a set of stairs, along a short corridor and into a small office. The room was bare except for two chairs and a laptop computer that sat on a standard-issue office desk.

Carl sat down at the laptop and asked Skinner to sit next to him. He tapped away at the keyboard, then asked Skinner to swipe his finger over the fingerprint reader that was built into the computer. His action was followed by a reassuring beep.

'Cool, you check out… Private Skinner,' Carl said as he examined the details that had popped up on his screen. He then turned to me. 'Now you.'

As I sat down, he opened the desk drawer and took out a pre-packaged syringe and a petri dish with a small piece of what looked like silver sitting in it.

'Roll up your sleeve.'

'What?'

'I need to take a blood sample, just to prove that you're one of us.'

I reluctantly rolled up my sleeve. Carl took my arm in his hand and tapped it to raise a vein. I thought he must have done this countless times because I barely felt it as he stuck the needle in my arm and drew blood.

'Moment of truth,' he said as he held the syringe over the petri dish and pushed the plunger. Just as Doctor Owen had tested for vampire infiltrators within The Brotherhood, the blood that came out of the syringe hit the silver in the bottom of the petri dish and turned to ash, sending a small wisp of smoke into the air.

'Well, you're definitely a vampire. That's step one complete. Half way there.'

I'm definitely a vampire. His words rang in my ears, reminding me of what I was telling myself not to believe.

He tapped away at the computer again for a minute, then without looking up, asked 'What's your name?'

'Thomas Ryder.'

'Middle name?'

'No.'

'Okay, I've got three Thomas Ryders: a plumber, a student and a cop. Which one are you?'

I thought about pretending to be a plumber for a moment but realised that as soon as they asked me to fix a leaking tap, my cover would be blown.

Honesty is the best policy.

'I'm the cop.' That made him look up.

'Really?'

'Well, not any more. Right?'

He chuckled and read something on the screen before answering. 'That's right… Detective.'

He tapped at the keyboard again then asked me to swipe my index finger over the fingerprint reader. He then hit the Enter key with a little more flair than was necessary and announced, 'Detective Thomas Ryder, you are now dead. Welcome to our world.'

32
Purge

A cloud of bitterly cold vapour hit Jane and Doctor Owen in the face as he opened the door to his cold storage chamber at Mantek pharmaceuticals. They both squinted and took a step back as the temperature of the room started to drop. Doctor Owen disappeared into the cold darkness and emerged with an ice-covered plastic bottle filled with frozen blue liquid.

'Can you bring that box over here?' he asked. Jane slid a metal box along the workbench and opened the lid. Doctor Owen placed the bottle in the box and sealed it.

'How long are we going to keep it in there?' Jane asked, 'Isn't it going to thaw out?'

'Yes it will, but that's not important. This is the primary treatment so we're going to be disposing of it, not developing it. Once we gather together all the samples and destroy them, we'll be safe to finish the development of the secondary treatment without any distractions.'

'Are we done here?'

'No, not yet. There's still something I need to do.'

Doctor Owen closed the door to the storage chamber and they left the store room. They walked across the corridor and into an office, where the doctor sat down at a computer and logged in.

'What are you doing?' Jane asked.

'I'm going to remove all data about the primary treatment from the central servers,' he said as he reached into his pocket, took out a pen drive and connected it to the computer.

'But don't they keep backups of the data on their systems?'

'Yes they do,' the doctor replied, 'The data from the shared drive is backed up every night to a storage server. Once a week, this data is then archived to tape and sent to another facility a few miles away. That means we can restore the data and continue work from a recent backup should anything happen to this building.'

'So what's the point in deleting data off the server if they're only going to restore it?'

'I always keep my pen drive with me. It contains a batch file that will copy the data and remove all data from the storage server. Then all we have to do is recover the backup tapes and destroy them, and all of Mantek's data about the primary treatment will disappear.'

He made it sound so easy. Jane thought it must be more complicated than that. If all they had to do was waltz into Mantek, pick up a bottle, destroy a few tapes and pick up a few more things, why hadn't anyone else tried to sabotage this operation before? Why hadn't the vampires done exactly what he was doing right now?

Doctor Owen opened up the contents of his pen drive, found the location of the batch file he was looking for and launched it.

'Right,' he said, 'this will take a few minutes.'

'Won't anyone be able to tell that it was you that deleted all the data?'

'It's possible, but it's a chance we have to take.'

33
Moved Downstairs

The World Health Organisation contact centre looked just like any helpdesk or call centre. The sprawling open plan office housed a team of one hundred and fifty staff, whose job it was to answer the phones to agents in the field, coordinate resources between the World Health Organisation and their suppliers and monitor essential systems for faults and abnormalities.

For two years systems monitoring had been the sole assignment for just one man. He used to work in the Operations team on the floor above, coordinating members of the Black Ops team who were infiltrating hostile territories. Two years ago, he was found to be aiding an operative who was working outside of her jurisdiction and was moved downstairs quicker than he could say 'disciplinary action'.

His name was Will Harris.

Will had been coerced by the senior agent Becky Clarkson, and the transcripts of their conversations proved it. For this reason, he hadn't been fired. No matter how much he didn't want to continue working there, he knew he couldn't leave. He had known a few members of staff who got fired but after they were escorted from the building, no one had never heard from them again.

Not a day went by that he didn't think about Becky. Once he had been removed from his desk, she had apparently only maintained radio contact for a matter of minutes before going dark. No one had heard from her since. Her name was still on the top of the white board at the end of the office, along with a printed photograph of her and a message written in board marker that had faded in the last two years.

Wanted: Becky Clarkson. If you see her, call this number immediately…

That was such a long time ago. He doubted she would ever be found.

Now he was happy to sit at his desk and watch his systems monitoring screens. All day long, he was faced with screens of scrolling green messages, confirming that servers were up and running and file system sizes were within expected thresholds. If a check failed, the green message would change to red and he would log onto that system to sort the problem out, but that hardly ever happened and he knew exactly what to do in every situation whenever there was a fault to fix.

Everyone kept out of Will's way and while he felt lonely in his job from time to time, that was pretty much how he liked it. The usual career path was to serve your time at the contact centre then move upstairs if you showed your superiors you were trustworthy. No one ever moved back downstairs.

Except Will, and they were all too worried about being associated with him to get too close.

Will walked over from the kitchen at the end of the office with a mug of coffee and threw his bag under his desk. He had long since stopped asking his so-called team mates if they wanted to join him. For some reason they all needed a break from the almost permanent flow of caffeine as soon as he announced he was thirsty so he went directly to the kitchen as soon as his shift started and ignored his colleagues the same way they ignored him.

Will sat down and logged onto his computer to see a red alert scrolling through the monitoring system. He turned round and asked no one in particular 'Hey, is anyone dealing with this alert?'

No one in particular answered.

'I take it that's a no,' he said and clicked his mouse on the alert message to get the details. The file system sizes on the storage manager were analysed at midnight every night and alert thresholds were set for the next day. The idea was that nothing should be deleted without prior approval and if the size of the file system dropped below the threshold, Will found out about it.

```
Server whostorage01, File system /mantek 43.2% full
Server whostorage01, File system /mantek 42.9% full
Server whostorage01, File system /mantek 42.6% full
```

Will stood up and shouted down the office. 'Hey, listen up! Someone's deleting a shit load of data from the storage manager! Anyone know anything about it?'

His question was followed by the silent shaking of heads.

```
Server whostorage01, File system /mantek 40.8% full
Server whostorage01, File system /mantek 40.5% full
```

Without sitting down, Will picked up the phone and hit speed dial number one.

Upstairs.

'Hi, it's Will.'

'Will, what do you want?' It was Jodi, the manager of the team upstairs and Will's old boss.

'I've got a problem I need you to look at.'

'Look Will, this better not be another…'

'Look, trust me, this is a real problem. Someone's deleting a load of data from the Mantek file system on the storage manager. It's just gone under forty percent.'

'It's not someone down there compressing the file system is it?'

'No, of course not.'

'Okay, leave it with me.'

'Okay, but this alert will be going off all day so let me know what happens.'

There was no reply to his last comment and Jodi hung up, leaving Will thinking that would be the last he would hear about it.

34
'What's In The Box?'

'So are you gonna show me what's in the box?' Carl asked me once he had finished deleting me from existence.

'Are you sure you want to see it?'

'Of course. Who does it belong to, you?'

'No, it's his,' I said, pointing at Skinner and remembering my cover story.

I picked up the metal box and set it down on the desk. I unclipped the lid and lifted it up, leaving Carl to peer inside himself. He nearly fell back in his seat.

'Oh my God, that can't be real!'

Skinner stepped forward. 'You know who this is, don't you?'

'Of course I do. It's my job to know who all the big players are. This is Commander North. He's a senior figure in The Brotherhood. This is incredible. How did it happen?'

Realising that we had already told Carl I had only just turned into a vampire, Skinner spun him a half-true story about being a soldier of The Brotherhood, killing Commander North and escaping, then finding me and turning me. He almost had me convinced and as long as Carl wasn't trying to read his mind, I knew it would stand up to scrutiny.

'Why did you do it?' Carl asked, 'This is going to bring a major shit-storm down on us, you know.'

'I know. Roxy had me placed in the regional headquarters. I was ordered to extract someone from the base but I failed. I needed to reset the balance as much as I could to seek forgiveness for my failure so I've brought her the head of Commander North.'

Carl laughed to himself. 'Holy shit, man. That's a badass way of saying sorry! I'll need to call her', he said, 'I need to call her now. She'll want to know about this immediately.'

Skinner nodded in agreement and I did my best to look like I didn't know what was going on. Carl took his phone out of his pocket and hit a speed dial number. The person on the other end answered very quickly.

'Hello Roxy,' he said, 'Two men have just arrived at my outpost. One is a rebirth but I think you'll be very interested in the other. He says he knows you and he has a package for you. His name's Skinner.'

Carl held the phone out to Skinner. 'She wants to talk to you.'

I sensed Skinner's apprehension as he took the phone from Carl.

'Hello Roxy. Yes, I did exactly what you told me to do. The bodies turned and attacked the base. Yes, almost everyone was killed. Only the doctor and a female agent escaped. I don't know where they were going. The package? To apologise for my failure, I have brought you the head of Commander North of The Brotherhood.'

Skinner handed the phone back to Carl. 'She wants to talk to you again.'

Carl took the phone. 'He's right, Roxy. It's the commander's head alright. Okay, thanks.'

He hung up and put the phone back in his pocket. 'She said she wants to see you and it can't wait until nightfall. She needs both of you for some kind of operation and she wants to speak to you about what you did. Looks like this was just a flying visit, guys. She's sending someone over now to pick you up and take you to her.'

35
Signing Out

'Where do we need to go next?' Jane asked as they sat staring at the screen, waiting on the computer to finish deleting all of the data.

'The First National bank,' Doctor Owen said, 'We've got a safety deposit box that contains papers and notes on our work. Only Doctor Forrest and I can access the box. We then need to go to the Mantek offsite storage facility and collect the storage tapes to ensure all the data has been removed. After that, there are two more sets of samples we need to collect from different labs around the city. It should take us most of the day but with a bit of luck on our side we won't run into any trouble.'

The progress bar indicating how much longer it would take to delete the data from the Mantek file system reached one hundred percent. Doctor Owen took his pen drive out of the computer and logged off.

'Let's go,' said Doctor Owen.

They left the room, walked back along the corridor and down the stairs to the reception area. They didn't give the security guard on reception a thought until they reached the front door and heard a voice behind them.

'Hey, you two!'

Jane and Doctor Owen froze to the spot and slowly turned round. They were faced with the security guard, holding the clipboard they had signed in with.

'Just need you to sign out,' he said.

They tried not to make their sighs of relief obvious but they both knew that in the current situation, they could have done without that short rush of adrenaline.

The security guard returned to his desk as they left the building and reached the car. Doctor Owen put the frozen bottle of primary treatment into the trunk and Jane started the engine. They both breathed an even bigger sigh of relief once they had got past the security booth and were out on the open road.

Jane and Doctor Owen both cast knowing looks at each other.

'We have to be careful,' she said, but before she could finish her sentence, she had to swerve the car out of the way of the approaching traffic, which was taking up most of the carriageway. They kept their heads down when they realised what the traffic was.

A line of military vehicles thundered past them. Jane counted four transports and they were in such a rush that she was certain they would have driven over their car without thinking twice had they been in the way. They both kept their heads down and tried not to look too conspicuous.

'Oh my God,' Jane said, 'That must have been The Brotherhood.'

'Looking for us?'

'Why else would they be here? Like you said, someone must have been alerted to the fact that we were deleting data from the system.'

'Damn it. As soon as they check the sign-in log, they'll know we've only just left. We've got to stay ahead of them and gather everything together before they call in reinforcements.'

'Do you think we can do it?'

'We have to. It's the only way we're going to get Emily back and complete work on the treatment.'

'Shouldn't we pick up the storage tapes now? Won't they try and restore all the data when they realise it's all been deleted?'

'In an ideal world we probably should, but the storage facility was built on another power grid so it's on the other side of the city. The bank isn't far and it's on the way. It won't take us long in there so we may as well stop off on the way.'

Jane jammed her foot on the accelerator and headed for the First National bank, unaware of the motorbike in the distance in her rear view mirror.

36
Visitors

The rumble of trucks outside made the security guard look up from his newspaper. He rubbed his eyes and had to do a double-take. He couldn't believe what he saw.

A line of military vehicles had stopped outside the reception. He watched in awe as countless men in urban combat gear jumped out of the vehicles and made their way up the steps. One man led the way and ran up to the front door. He barged his way through the door before the security guard could hit the button to lock the doors. The security guard's hand reached for the panic button that would alert the police to an emergency.

'Stop!' the man in the lead shouted and aimed his machine gun at the security guard. 'Don't touch the panic button!'

'What do you want?' the security guard asked, complying with the soldier's wishes as he looked down at the red spot of light that marked his heart as a target.

'My name is Captain Luke Sayers. I represent the World Health Organisation.'

Still aiming his weapon, Captain Sayers reached into his pocket, pulled out his WHO pass and showed it to the security guard.

'We're investigating the potential threat of the release of an infectious disease,' he continued, 'Have you had any visitors in the last few hours?'

The security guard examined the captain's pass. 'That's funny,' he said, 'One of your colleagues was just here. You only just missed her.'

'Was she alone?'

'No, there was someone else with her. An old man with glasses.'

He pulled the clipboard out from under the desk and handed it to Captain Sayers. 'Look, they just left five minutes ago. Jane Simpson: she was the one with a pass like yours.'

Captain Sayers turned on his heels and barked orders at the men behind him. 'They were here. You and you, take a truck each and find them.'

He turned to the security guard again. 'Do you know which way they went?'

'No, I didn't see them leave, but we might have it on the security cameras.'

'We can't waste any time, they're on the move,' he said, pointing at his men, 'At the exit, you do a left and you do a right. Keep in touch.'

'Yes sir,' the men said and made their hasty exits from the building.

Captain Sayers took his radio off his belt. 'Come in, General Graham. This is Captain Sayers.'

Almost immediately, he received a reply. 'This is General Graham. Go ahead.'

'The intelligence supplied by the World Health Organisation was correct. They were here. It must have been Doctor Owen that deleted the data from the storage system.'

'They must be going for the tapes as well.'

'I agree. I'll tell the men at the storage location to be on guard.'

'Okay. Don't begin restoring the data yet. We can't risk transporting the tapes. Once you've neutralised them, we can start bringing the systems back.'

'I've sent some men out to search for them but I need to check the security tapes here.'

'Why?'

'They could easily have logged on and deleted the data remotely. There must be something else here that they were looking for.'

Out of the car park and a few miles down the road, someone on a motorbike overheard that conversation and decided to keep an eye on the rear view mirror for approaching trucks.

37
'Fight It'

Carl opened the door and we were faced with what he had called 'our room'.

All four solid brick walls were coloured with grime and brown streaks indicated where blood had splattered and long since dried. Two single metal bed frames that held yellow and brown-stained mattresses sat in the middle of the room. A toilet sat in the corner, which used to be white but was now an unhealthy shade of brown. With no windows, the only light in the room came from a bare bulb hanging from a wire in the ceiling.

'Believe it or not, this is the best one,' Carl said.

I looked at him and my face must have told him I didn't believe him.

'It's not exactly the Hilton, I know, but with the crazy shit that happens to rebirths in here, I'm fucked if I'm going to clean it.'

'What kind of crazy shit happens to rebirths?' I asked, almost wishing I hadn't.

Carl looked me up and down. 'You seem to be dealing with it pretty well so there's no point telling you any of the horror stories. Don't worry, you're not going to be here for long, just until Roxy's guy picks you up.'

We reluctantly stepped inside. The door slammed shut behind us and we heard a metal bolt slide shut.

'Hey, what are you doing?' I shouted.

'It's okay, it's standard procedure. Just taking precautions.'

'Precautions against what?' Skinner asked.

'Breakfast will be here soon,' was Carl's cryptic reply, 'You'll see.'

Left alone in the unholy cesspit, neither of us dared to sit on the dirty beds. I couldn't bring myself to go over to the corner of the room where the toilet stood and I hoped that Mother Nature wouldn't call on me any time soon.

'Have you been here before?' I asked Skinner.

'Not here but somewhere like it. There are places like this all over the city. Some of the buildings you see that look derelict or abandoned are actually used by the vampires to hold their recently-turned brothers and sisters or to provide shelter for those who are in trouble.'

The size and scale of the vampires' operation shocked me. 'This is unbelievable. How do they manage to keep such a low profile?'

'I'm not exactly an expert but in my opinion it doesn't seem very difficult at all. The humans, especially The Brotherhood, always thought the vampire community was small but from what I hear, the treaty never stated exact population levels that had to be maintained.'

'Have you read the treaty?'

'No. Very few have. You just hear second and third-hand bits of information.'

I guess it made sense in a twisted kind of way. Who would ever think that there were outposts all over the city? Who would ever think to examine the contents of all the abandoned buildings? There were so many, how would they ever know where to start?

'I was taken to a place like this and spent a few weeks being acclimatised to the way of life.'

'A few weeks?'

'That guy was right. This room is the Hilton compared to where I stayed. Trust me. At least they bother to clear the bodies out of here.'

'What bodies?'

'The vampires that drive around like the one who picked us up also search for food. They pick up people who don't look like they'll be missed. Thankfully, they were all dead by the time I got to feed on them. I don't know if I could bring myself to kill someone for food, no matter how bad the hunger was.'

'So you've never killed anyone?'

'No. I worked in the morgue at The Brotherhood. Until yesterday I only had to deal with bodies very occasionally but I managed to train myself to go days, sometimes weeks without feeding.'

As soon as Skinner finished his sentence, my hands went to my stomach. The fire in my belly had returned and I dropped to my knees. I reached a hand out and grabbed the bed frame, trying to steady myself as I fought against the excruciating pain.

'Fight it, Tom,' Skinner said, 'Remember what I told you yesterday. It hurts like hell. You'd suck anyone's blood right now to make the pain go away but remember, it does go away.'

I remembered alright. I remembered that the pain had gone away but my animal desire to feed on human blood had only been kept at bay while we made our escape from the clutches of The Brotherhood. Now that we were in the clear, the hunger had returned. My thoughts turned to Captain Stein.

What happened to him? Did they kill him? Did he turn? What would he do to me if he found me?

Another sharp stab to the guts brought me back to reality. My hand left the bed frame and my body hit the floor. I grabbed my stomach and writhed in agony.

My canine teeth shifted in their sockets. My jaw clicked, as if my whole mouth was re-aligning itself.

Skinner's hand gripped my shoulder and he started to say something that was undoubtedly reasonable and comforting but I beat his arm away with my fist and screamed at him.

'Get off me! Don't fucking touch me!'

Skinner took a step back. 'You're turning.'

I moved my tongue round my mouth. My canine teeth had grown. My mouth was filling with saliva. I tried to swallow it but the hunger had arrived and it wasn't going to go away any time soon.

I'm ready to feed.

There was a commotion outside our room. In addition to Carl's voice, I heard another man and what sounded like two other people.

Two young people. A boy and a girl.

'What are you doing?'

'Why are we here?'

'Who are you?'

'You're here because you're special. We need you.'

There were two muffled screams and then the voices stopped.

I heard the bolt sliding across and the door creaked as it slowly opened a fraction. It opened just far enough for Carl to throw something inside and say 'Enjoy your breakfast' before slamming the door shut and locking it again. Skinner edged over to the door to see what Carl had dropped in our room.

From my position on the floor by the bed, I could already see what he had delivered. My mind became ravaged by an awful tangle of hunger and repulsion, pulling my conscience in opposite directions.

Our breakfast was a little girl, no more than ten years old.

Part Two

Dark Day

38
Almost Home

Jackson Korvath was happy. After a long couple of days, he was heading home and like any other person, human or vampire, he was looking forward to getting his head down and enjoying some well-deserved rest.

He'd achieved more in the past two days than he had in a long time. He was always the first person Marcus and Roxy turned to for their dirty work and it was a job that he loved, even after nearly two hundred years of loyal service.

The first job Roxy had given him was to track down Doctor Owen and bring him back the lair. Finding him wasn't hard. Predictably, he'd driven far out of the city and checked into a dingy motel, but Jackson had been on his tail the whole time. The doctor could have kept driving all night but he still would have been found, drugged and taken back towards the lair.

Unfortunately the timing of his capture had coincided with the destruction of the Mantek lab by The Brotherhood. Jackson made the decision to keep the doctor at the nearest secure location until he thought it was safe to move him.

He had made a mistake in choosing Doctor Forrest's house as that secure location. By driving around in Doctor Forrest's car when he was scoping out the ensuing investigation, it didn't exactly make it difficult for the police to find them. Roxy had reprimanded him for that, which was why he wouldn't be able to say no to her for a long time. But he was sure even she knew that he had earned a breather for one night.

Capturing Doctor Owen's wife Emily had been fun. Jackson enjoyed the chance to draw his pistol and cut down those in his way, especially police officers who think they can stop him with their little pop guns.

It had been a long journey back to the lair. It always was. But thankfully Emily hadn't spoken much. She had been the most well-behaved prisoner he had ever taken back to the lair. There hadn't been any screaming or shouting once they left the police station.

A road sign whizzed past him that told him the town of Blackchapel was five miles ahead.

Almost home.

Jackson felt that familiar sinking feeling in his stomach as soon as his phone started to ring. He almost considered not answering the call until he picked up the phone and saw who the caller was.

Roxy.

'Hello Roxy.'

'Jackson, where are you?'

'Just approaching Blackchapel.'

'So you managed to pick up what the doctor needs?'

'Yes.'

'Good. I need you to turn round and go back to the city, I've got another job for you.'

Jackson paused before answering. There was no sense in protesting. There was nothing he could say to convince her he shouldn't follow her orders. 'Sure. What is it?'

'Two of our brothers are being held at the outpost on the Southmoor industrial estate. I need you to pick them up and bring them back here.'

'But the sun's just come up.'

'I know, but we can't afford to leave them there all day. I need them back here. Also, they have a box with them. Make sure they don't leave it there. I want to see it.'

'Who are they?'

'One of them was stationed at the base that was attacked last night. I need him to debrief me on the attack. They've only just been picked up and the other one is a rebirth.'

'Okay, Roxy. I'll pick them up. I just hope the outpost is still there. I've seen some jumpy rebirths in my time.'

There was no answer. No reply to the attempt at making small talk. Roxy had already hung up. Jackson sighed and hit the brakes. Just a few yards from a sign that read 'Blackchapel Welcomes Careful Drivers', he did a U-turn in the middle of the road and headed back the way he had come.

39

'Blackchapel Welcomes Careful Drivers'

Blackchapel? Where the hell is that?

Dave thought he knew the city and the surrounding areas like the back of his hand but he'd never heard of the town on the sign that had just passed him by. He had been tailing the car in front ever since the driver had left Doctor Forrest's house with the box of syringes that was hidden under the bed.

As far as he could tell, the man in front hadn't noticed Dave behind him. After all, Dave was a cop with too many years' experience not to know how to keep his distance.

He had followed his target all the way down Castle Crescent, onto the Expressway, up the ramp onto the Freeway then out of the city for miles and miles. After the Freeway turned into a country road, they had turned down a road that was obscured by trees and driven up a road into the mountains. The road seemed to go on forever without any signs lining the road until he was informed of a town called Blackchapel that lay five miles ahead.

With no junctions for miles, Dave allowed the car in front to get ahead, even out of sight as they wound their way round the twisting dips and inclines. As he dropped a gear to slow down for a sharp blind corner, Dave almost lost control as the car he thought he was following skidded round the corner towards him and whizzed past in the opposite direction.

What the hell? Where is he going now in such a rush?

Dave knew he had to make a decision. Whoever this guy was, he didn't drive all this way into the mountains just to shake Dave off his tail.

He'll be back.

He took his phone out of his pocket, carrying on straight ahead into the mountains. He found Doctor Owen's number and called him. Jane answered.

'Hi Jane, it's Dave.'

'Hi Dave, have you got any news?'

'Yes. The man who attacked the police station was driving a car registered to Doctor Forrest. I found the car and I was following it but I just lost him. He turned round and he's heading back towards the city.'

'Where are you?'

'I'm up in the mountains. Heading towards a town called Blackchapel.'

'Never heard of it.'

'Neither have I. I'm going to push on and check it out though. I think whoever I was following was called back to the city but they'll come back here. No one would come all the way up here to turn round again. It's the middle of nowhere.'

'You can't get back on his tail?'

'No. He'd know I was following him. I'm sure he'll be back. Until then, I'll see what I can do in Blackchapel. Where are you?'

'We've just picked up the first samples. We're going to the second point now.'

'Did you run into any trouble with The Brotherhood?'

'No, but it was a close call. They're not far behind us.'

'Okay. Be careful. I'll call you when I have an update.'

'Thanks Dave.'

They said their goodbyes and Dave hung up. Street lights illuminated the road ahead. A grimy sign approached that read 'Blackchapel Welcomes Careful Drivers'.

40
The Hunger

'They've got to be kidding!' I shouted and banged on the door. 'You've got to be kidding!'

Skinner knelt down next to the young girl who had been dumped on the floor of our room like a sack of garbage. I felt sick. Not just because of the fire in my stomach or the thought of feeding on this little girl, but the nonchalance of our hosts. How could they drop this little girl at our feet like she was nothing more than a room service dinner?

'Tom…' Skinner said.

I ignored him and banged my fist on the door again. 'Come back here! You can't do this to a little girl!'

I beat my fist on the door again and again until it felt like my fingers were going to break, but I kept on shouting and screaming.

'Tom…'

'You sick fuckers! What if this was your little girl?'

'Tom…'

'What!?'

I looked down and saw Skinner holding the little girl in his arms. Her limbs were limp and her head was hanging back over Skinner's arm.

'Tom. She's dead.'

I winced and dropped to my knees as an explosion ripped through my guts. My new instincts were telling me the only thing that could satisfy my hunger but I tried with every excruciating breath to hold onto my humanity.

'She's dead?' I asked, struggling to get my words out.

'Her neck's broken,' said Skinner as he cradled her head, looking into her lifeless eyes.

There was a knock on the door. 'Hey,' Carl shouted, 'let me know when you're done.'

I struggled to my feet, clinging onto the rusty bed frame to steady myself. 'Why are you doing this? Why this little girl?'

'The streets were quiet this morning. That's all he could find. Chow down, Detective. From the screaming in there I guess breakfast arrived just in the nick of time, eh?'

'What are we going to do?' I asked.

'If you wait long enough, the pain will pass,' Skinner said.

'And then what? What happens when the pain comes back?'

'I'm not going to lie to you, Tom. It'll be worse. A lot worse. But you learn to live with it. You have to learn to live with it if you don't want to turn into one of them completely.'

'Shit!' I exclaimed as the pain stabbed me in the chest again, 'I can't take it now. I don't want it to get worse.'

I looked at the dead girl in Skinner's arms and remembered what had happened when I sank my teeth into Captain Stein's neck. I had felt amazing. Reborn. With his blood in my system I had felt like I could take on the world. Memory of the taste flooded back and as repulsive as I found it, saliva started to gather in the sides of my mouth.

What am I contemplating here? Don't do it, Tom.

I remembered that turning into a vampire had given me incredible power. My physical form had been stronger and quicker. My mind had been more alert, hearing words that people only thought but never spoke.

I was super-human.

'Don't you get the hunger?' I asked Skinner, with the agony of my burning stomach breaking my voice.

'Yes, but not every day. I've trained myself to be able to do without feeding for days at a time. That's what you can do if you fight the hunger.'

But can I fight the hunger now?

My eyes were transfixed on the little girl. She had the ability to take away my pain. Like an oasis in the desert, she could quench my thirst and give me the energy I needed.

But at what cost? I knew what Skinner meant when he said that I didn't have to turn completely. *With every drop of human blood I drink, I become less human.* I knew that somewhere in the city right now, this girl's parents were frantic. They were searching everywhere they could think of in a blind panic, hoping to find their princess alive and well.

But she wasn't alive and well. She was dead, her neck broken so she could be food for these vile creatures of the night. Vile creatures of the night like me.

Is this where all missing children go? Do all missing children end up like this?

I stared into her empty blue eyes.

They won't hurt any more children here. You were the last, little girl. But I need your help to stop them.

41
Pouring Rain

Jane stopped the car at the side of the street opposite the First National Bank. She looked at her watch. It was 8:45am. The bank wouldn't be open for another fifteen minutes. She sat in silence with Doctor Owen for a moment and looked ahead through the windscreen.

The city was bustling. It was rush hour and the people of the city were going about their daily routines, blissfully unaware of what was really going on in the world around them, unaware of how close they were to death every single day of their lives.

The weather had turned. After the longest September hot spell in many years, dark clouds were gathering above them. A spot of rain hit the windscreen. Then another. Jane and the doctor watched as the people walking to work suddenly started to run, holding newspapers and jackets over their heads to protect them from the rain that was now beginning to fall in torrents. The falling rain became so heavy that they could no longer clearly see out of the car. A clap of thunder and a flash of lightning confirmed the heat wave was officially over.

Jane sighed. Last time she'd stopped to think, she had been on vacation. She'd taken two weeks off to recharge her batteries before the doctors presented the results of their research into the primary treatment, after which she knew her life would be turned upside down. But that was all a distant memory.

She turned to the doctor. 'I was going to ask you if you wanted a coffee two minutes ago before the rain started. There's a coffee shop just over there.'

'That'd be great,' Doctor Owen said, 'but let me go.'

'No, it's okay. I won't be long. I'll pick up a paper as well. We'll see if there's anything in there about Emily.'

Jane braced herself, then opened the door and ran for cover. The coffee shop was only two doors down so she managed to reach shelter before being soaked to the skin. There were a few people huddled together in the small coffee shop, desperately hoping the rain would stop as suddenly as it had started.

The girl behind the counter took Jane's order. As she took her coffees and paid for them, the girl said something that Jane thought was odd.

'Hey, do I know you? You look familiar.'

Jane looked at her and thought for a moment. 'No, I don't think so. Sorry.'

They both shrugged it off and smiled cordially at each other. Jane headed towards the exit but clocked the cover of a newspaper that had been abandoned on an empty table. She quickly scooped it up and put it under her arm. She was desperate to read the cover story but didn't want to risk it in front of anyone in the coffee shop.

The rain hadn't stopped outside. If anything, it was heavier, coming down in sheets and bouncing off the road. Jane ran for the car. With a coffee in each hand and a newspaper under her arm, she opened the driver's door with a spare finger and landed in the seat. Doctor Owen took the coffees from her and she shut the door behind her.

'Thanks,' Doctor Owen said, 'Is there anything in the paper?'

'What do you reckon?' Jane said with anger in her voice as she unfolded the copy of the tabloid City Star in front of him. On the cover was a massive picture of her with the headline 'FUGITIVE SOUGHT FOR LAB BOMB'.

42
The Cliffside Hotel

The small town of Blackchapel sat high in the mountains, far from the interference of the big city. Its main function was as a stop-off point for hikers, mountain climbers and those making their way up to the ski slopes in the winter.

It's definitely not skiing weather today, Dave thought as the first heavy drops of rain rattled off his car. The wipers were going at full speed as he turned his car into the car park of the Cliffside Hotel, an impressive structure with a large wooden entrance that gave it the look of an over-sized ski lodge. Overlooking the foggy depths on the opposite side of the road, it was an unexpected, imposing sight on a road that had been empty for miles.

Blackchapel was a town based solely on one side of the road. Just down from the hotel were a bar and a convenience store with apartments above and a filling station at the end of the row of buildings. Driving fast enough along the mountain road you could blink and almost miss the whole town.

At nine o'clock in the morning, Dave assumed correctly that the bar would be closed and instead decided to head for the hotel entrance. The wind outside made the rain pour into the car as soon as he opened the door. Dave jumped out, ran across the car park and up the steps to the revolving doors that led him into the hotel reception. He did his best to shake the rain off his jacket and what hair hadn't receded from the top of his shiny head.

A young man in a red jacket approached him. 'Hello, sir. Welcome to the Cliffside Hotel. I am the concierge. Can I take your bags?'

'Erm... no thanks. I haven't got any. Just passing through.'

'Passing through, sir? Are you visiting friends?'

'Something like that, yes. Do you have a room free?'

'Of course, sir. We're out of season now until the winter. The weather's turning so I don't think the few visitors we've had here over the last few nights will be staying long. Please come over to the desk.'

The young man escorted Dave to the reception desk and walked round to the other side. Dave cast his eyes round the amber-lit reception hall and noticed that he and the concierge were alone.

'You're right. It's quiet here today. Is there no one else working here?'

'Not at the front desk, sir. Just me today.'

'Must be slow out of season.'

'No, sir. Actually, the Morningside Mall rents out a lot of the rooms during the quiet season for the staff that work the night shifts.'

'The Morningside Mall? That's pretty far away, isn't it?'

'It is, but there's a bus that picks the staff up and brings them home. They'll be back here very soon, actually.'

'I suppose I'd better get my head down if I want some rest, then.'

'No, don't worry. They usually just sleep through the day.'

'Are the workers from round here?' Dave asked, expecting a shifty look to confirm his suspicions that the mall workers were illegal immigrants.

'Yes sir. They've lived round here for a long time.'

Dave thought it was odd that a mall would rent out a hotel for its workers but not being an expert in the leisure industry, he shrugged it off.

'Can you give me a room with a view of the road and the mountains?'

The concierge looked at Dave a little funny. He picked a set of keys off a numbered hook behind him and handed them to him. 'Here you go, sir. Room two-thirteen. Perfect view of the road. And the mountains of course. Take the elevator to the second floor then take a left and follow the signs.'

'Thanks,' said Dave and made his way to the elevator.

The silence of the hotel was eerie. There wasn't even any muzak playing in the elevator to put his mind at ease. He got out of the elevator and made his way towards room two-thirteen. The floor creaked under his feet. He reached the door to his room and looked up and down the long corridor to his left and right.

No one. No movement. Not a sound.

The whole place made him feel uneasy and he felt a sense of relief as he entered the room and shut the door. The bed, desk and chair in the corner made the room look just like any other hotel room he had ever stayed in but it didn't feel them same. Dave locked the door behind him.

He walked over to the window and threw the curtains open. Just as the concierge had said, he had a perfect view of the road. The wind was blowing the rain away from the hotel so there would be no problem spotting the black car belonging to Doctor Forrest, should it return to Blackchapel.

Dave pulled the chair away from the desk and sat himself down by the window. He grabbed the remote and turned the TV to a news channel, just to have some background noise and cast his gaze towards the road.

The car had better return soon. This place is freaking me out.

43

Monster

I felt hands gripping my shoulders tightly. A hard slap across the face brought me back into reality. I realised I was in the corridor outside our cell. I had lost time.

Did I black out?

Skinner shouted in my face. 'Snap out of it, Tom. Jesus Christ, what have you done?'

'What do you mean?' I had no idea what he was talking about.

'You don't know?'

'No,' I said and shrugged his hands from my shoulders, 'Get your hands off me.'

'Okay Tom,' Skinner said, 'Look what you've done.'

Skinner moved aside to reveal a scene that filled me with horror. The door to our cell was wide open. On the floor of the corridor were two twitching bodies: Carl and another man I didn't recognise. Very slowly, I took small steps towards them. Their heads were both twisted at unnatural angles. I looked closer. Their limbs twitched like they were being electrocuted and their eyes were darting around in their sockets.

'Oh my God,' I exclaimed, 'They're not dead.'

'No. They're vampires. You can't kill them by battering them and breaking their necks like you did, but it will incapacitate them for a while until their bodies heal.'

'I did this?'

'Yes. Just a few seconds ago. Don't you remember?'

'Not a thing.' I looked at my hands. They were dripping with blood. The vampires lying on the floor were injured but they weren't bleeding heavily.

Where did the blood come from? As soon as the thought entered my mind, I knew the answer.

I stepped over Carl's twitching legs and held my breath as I slowly peered round the door to our cell. Lying on the floor just inside the cell was the young girl, her delicate clothes soaked in her own blood. Her neck had been ravaged. The skin was hanging like it had been ripped apart by a savage beast.

I swallowed. A horrible metallic taste slid down my throat. My heart was pumping so fast, I thought I was going to pass out.

I didn't do this. I couldn't do this, I thought as I looked down at my shirt. It was soaked through with the little girl's blood.

All the blood in my body raced to my head. The warmth spread up my legs and arms and neck. My body crumpled and I slumped to the floor, weeping into my bloody hands.

I screamed as loud as I could. I felt Skinner's hands on my shoulders again but I didn't shake them off. I took the little girl in my arms and hugged her tightly. Blood poured from her wound as I squeezed her body. The wound where I had bitten her neck and fed on her blood. I couldn't remember a thing.

What's happening to me?
I'm turning into a monster.

44
FUGITIVE SOUGHT FOR LAB BOMB

2am Exclusive!

A woman who worked for the World Health Organisation is being sought for the bombing of the Mantek research facility that left three late night workers dead.

Jane Simpson, who performed an unnamed role for the international body, is said to be missing from her home and workplace and is the prime suspect in the race to find the bomber.

Police have also linked the Mantek bombing with the police station attack last night that left six dead and one prisoner missing but declined to comment on the link.

Chief of Police Chris Cameron said, 'We need to talk to Miss Simpson to eliminate her from our enquiries.'

Miss Simpson was believed to be investigating the bombing at the Mantek research facility but suspicion has fallen on her since her disappearance without warning yesterday from her WHO office.

Also sought in the investigation is Doctor Andrew Owen, who worked for Mantek and the World Health Organisation, and is also missing. Doctor Owen has not been seen since the day of the bombing. When asked if the two disappearances were linked and if Dr Owen and Ms Simpson could be working together, Cameron said only 'No comment'.

While there is currently no link between the bombing and the helicopter attack on the Freeway two days ago, a source close to the investigation tells us that 'It's only a matter of time until the two are linked. There's a lot of circumstantial evidence there and this is a much bigger investigation than you might think. The police believe this is just the tip of the iceberg.'

Our source continued, 'As long as Miss Simpson and Doctor Owen are still out there, we can expect more attacks.'

Miss Simpson's family declined to comment. Dr Owen's family could not be reached at the time of going to press.

45
Nothing Has Changed

Jane felt nauseous. She rolled down the window a little to get some fresh air.

My family declined to comment?

She didn't want to think about what was happening to her mother and father. Reporters were almost certainly camped outside their little house in the countryside, laying siege to the old man and woman inside who had no knowledge of the terrible accusations being directed at their daughter.

She looked again at the last comment by the unnamed source.

I may as well draw a target on my head for everyone to shoot at. I'm guilty until proven innocent.

Jane wasn't as media-savvy as Tom but she knew that when newspapers cited 'a source', what they really mean is that they made up the whole damn thing themselves. She was certain all this stemmed from their escape from The Brotherhood. They were trying everything they could to draw them out as soon as possible, but the urgency of their attempts to turn the world against her and the doctor was unexpected.

'2am Exclusive' meant that the lead headline had been changed through the night. The first edition that hit the streets would have had a completely different lead story. Jane flicked through the paper but found no other mention of her or the doctor.

'Is that all they wrote?' Doctor Owen asked.

'It looks like it. The Brotherhood had a hand in this. They must have knocked this story together overnight, knowing that we'd see it this morning.'

'They're trying to draw us out. At least we know they're struggling to find us. They're clutching at straws.'

Jane started to read through the article again but Doctor Owen grabbed the newspaper out of her hands and threw it onto the back seat.

'Hey, there's nothing you can do about it.'

'But…'

'No, Jane. It's not important. The only thing that matters is getting our hands on the samples and documents and meeting Doctor Forrest. As soon as we left The Brotherhood, we knew they'd be after us. Even with the newspaper article, nothing has changed.'

Jane spent a moment with her thoughts. 'You're right. It's just so difficult. Everything's changed since the attack on your lab. I'd give anything to go back to two days ago.'

'How do you think Tom feels?'

Jane didn't answer, choosing to look at her watch instead. 'It's nine o'clock. Do you want me to go into the bank?'

'No. They'll want me to sign for the box and they'll only let me open it.'

'Okay. Don't be long.'

'I'll be as quick as I can,' said Doctor Owen. He opened the door and ran for the shelter of the bank as the rained continued to pour down. Jane reached for the paper and started to read the article once more.

46
I Feel Nothing

I dried my eyes on a patch of my sleeve that wasn't soaked with the little girl's blood. I felt the warmth of my blood move from my head and back through my body. I got to my feet and looked down on the lifeless young body sprawled out on the floor.

I feel nothing.

Just moments before, I had been weeping for the lost life of an innocent soul but now I found myself struggling to care either way. Sorrow had passed as quickly as it had arrived.

Is this what happens to all humans who become vampires? Am I going to stop feeling anything at all?

I inched away from the dead girl and out of the cell, shutting the door behind me. Skinner was standing just behind me, observing the sudden change in my emotions.

'It passes quickly, doesn't it?' he said.

'I've just fed on the blood of a little girl. I'm an animal! Why can't I feel anything?'

'Did you feel the blood rush to your head?'

'Yes. What did it mean?'

'Like the doctor found out yesterday, it must have been moving to where it was needed most. As soon as you started to feel guilty, the blood moved to your brain to change your state of mind. I remember feeling that sensation when I first started to feed on dead bodies. It passes quicker every time you feed.'

'So my blood is programmed to make me get over the emotional impact of sucking someone's blood?'

'That's right. Eventually it will feel natural to you.'

Natural. It will feel natural to feed on the blood of children.

I felt helpless. I was a slave to the monster that was growing inside me. The only way I could stop this was to help Doctor Owen's cause any way I could. I thought of what he had told me at The Brotherhood's base.

'*You've got a very common blood type, O positive. If you start to feel hungry, you won't have to kill very many people to find a match.*'

He was right. Beneath my disgust, I felt renewed. The little girl's blood was now flowing through my body in the new unnatural way that was becoming sickeningly familiar.

'We've got to get out of here,' I said.

'We can't,' said Skinner, 'it's sunlight outside and the door is locked with a code from the inside. Unless you want to wake up your friends down there and try and get the code out of them, we're stuck here until Roxy's man comes to pick us up.'

'How are we going to explain all this when he gets here?'

'They're not dead. You're a new vampire and you flipped out when you had your first taste of blood. They were hurt while trying to restrain you. It's not the first time something like this has happened.'

'But will he buy it?'

'It's the best chance we've got. You'd better get cleaned up.'

I walked down the corridor and found a bathroom. Unlike the disgusting cell our hosts had confined us to, the bathroom was gleaming white all over. Spotless.

I looked at myself in the mirror. I couldn't believe what I saw. From my nose down, my face was caked with blood. The tears from my eyes had carved flesh-coloured tracks in my cheeks. I ran the hot water and quickly splashed handfuls on my face over and over again. The blood poured off me and turned the sink a light shade of red.

I looked up again and opened my mouth, prodding my teeth with my fingers. My canine teeth had retracted. Other than the blood that was soaking the shirt Dave had loaned me, I was back to my tired, stressed-out looking best. The white towel sitting next to the sink turned a deep shade of pink as I dried my hair, face and neck.

I threw the towel in the sink and left the bathroom. I passed a closed door as I made my way back into the corridor to join Skinner. Somehow I knew the body of the little boy we had heard from inside our cell was in there. Nothing made me want to open the door to see if he was still alive.

I stepped over the twitching bodies without a thought for their well-being. Carl has started to make a faint gargling noise and his eyes followed me as I stepped over him. I could tell that very slowly, their bodies were starting to heal, but I felt the same way about them as I did about the children they had brought here. They were nothing to me.

Skinner was about to say something to me when our attention was distracted. Through the heavy door, we heard the dogs outside the building start to bark.

47
Two New Friends

The rain was still bouncing off the road as the black motorbike stopped on the corner, watching the car that had pulled in to the side of the road. The figure on the motorbike was a little confused.

They can't be vampires and they're definitely not members of The Brotherhood, so who are they? Agent Becky Clarkson thought as she watched Jane run to and from the coffee shop. After two years on the run from The Brotherhood's attempts to find her, she was in no mood to stick her head above water, but she had to know more about the two people in the car.

As Doctor Owen opened the door and ran across the road into the bank, Becky knew she had an opening. She unzipped a small pocket on her jacket and took out a small, round piece of plastic with a magnet fixed into one end. Holding it between two gloved fingers, she unzipped another pocket and pulled out a PDA. A gloved hand tapped on the screen with the stylus and loaded up a road map. A red dot was blinking in the centre of the screen.

She put the PDA back into her jacket pocket and slowly rode the bike down the road and pulled in just behind the car. Kneeling down at the front of the bike, Becky pretended to check the tyre and when she was certain no one was looking, delicately stuck the magnetic tracer to the underside of the car.

As she stood up, Becky saw the car's rear wiper clean the back window. Jane adjusted the rear view mirror. At that moment, Becky knew it was time to leave.

Jane stepped out of the car in time to see a black motorbike with a rider clad in black leather heading down the street. She made a mental note of the registration plate and walked round to the back of the car to take a look. Everything looked okay and with the rain already soaking her, she ran back to the car and jumped in.

Stop it Jane, you're just being paranoid, she thought as she picked up the newspaper and started to read the cover article again.

Becky looked over her shoulder and saw that the car hadn't followed her. She pulled into a side street and stopped to examine the PDA. The red dot was still blinking in the middle of the screen. Confident that the tracer she'd planted was working perfectly, Becky moved her bike into an alleyway to find some shelter and decided to wait and see where her two new friends would lead her next.

48
Picked Up

Almost as soon as the racket outside had started, the dogs stopped barking.

Skinner and I moved towards the door, in a futile attempt to obscure the bodies on the floor behind us from whoever had just arrived. A strange sense of realisation struck me, knowing there was one man standing behind the door.

The keypad by the door beeped and a clunk announced that it was unlocked. Very slowly, the door creaked open to reveal a tall, wide man standing in the doorway, sheltering from the rain and sunlight.

He was holding a pistol but tucked it in his belt when he saw that we were no immediate threat. He stepped inside and looked us up and down. Skinner was about to talk but the man pointed at him and told him not to say anything.

The man moved in closer and went toe-to-toe with Skinner, looking deep within his eyes. After a few seconds, he took a step to his right and did the same with me. He then looked over my shoulder at the bodies on the floor. He didn't bat an eyelid, like he already knew they were there. He stepped round me and knelt down to take a closer look at the injured vampires on the floor.

'They're not dead,' Skinner said.

The man looked up at us and narrowed his eyes. 'I know,' he said and got to his feet. He looked at me and said, 'You're the rebirth, aren't you?'

'Yes, I am.'

He pointed at the door of the cell we had been held in. 'There's a body in there. Was that your first feed?'

'Yes.'

He cast his eyes around the room and knelt down next to the vampires again. His footsteps squelched in the wide pool of blood that had gathered around the bodies. He turned Carl's body over and found a leather holster attached to his belt. Carl's gun was still clipped into it.

'He's still got his gun,' the man said as he got to his feet, wiping his bloody hands on his jacket, 'Your story checks out.'

'Our story checks out? We never told you anything,' I said.

'I got all I needed to know from your eyes. I can tell we've all got the same blood flowing through our veins and I believe I can call you brothers. My name is Jackson.'

Skinner and I did our best to breathe a sigh of relief without looking like we were worried and introduced ourselves.

'Roxy said you had a box,' Jackson said.

'Yes,' I said and made my way into the office, 'It's through here. It's…'

'Whoa, I don't want to know what's in it,' Jackson said, 'I've only got orders to take it back with us. Just bring it with you. We're leaving.'

'Where are we going?' I asked.

'I'm taking you home. Roxy is very anxious to talk to you.'

I picked the box up from the office and followed Jackson to the door. He escorted us outside into the pouring rain and shepherded the dogs inside the building before closing the door behind us.

'I take it you're both photo-sensitive?' he asked.

'I am,' Skinner said, then pointed to me, 'Not sure about him yet though.'

'It's not far to the car and with this cloud cover you won't get a massive dose of UV before we get there.' Jackson pointed his keys at the car and pressed a button. The lights flashed to tell us the car was unlocked.

'Ready?' Jackson asked.

We nodded, then I ran for the car like my life depended on it.

49
Two Hundred And Fifty Syringes

Roxy opened the door to Doctor Forrest's lab. As ever, he was working hard and didn't allow her entrance to break his concentration.

He acknowledged her importance to the cause and knew full well that she had the ability to end his life in a heartbeat, but he was a scientist. He took his direction from the experiments in front of him, irrespective of the seniority of the people who supported him. They needed him a hell of a lot more than he needed them.

On the bench in the centre of the lab a plastic box held over two hundred capped syringes, each containing a dark red liquid. Doctor Forrest picked up the last empty syringe and dipped the needle into a basin that held a few dregs of crimson. He pulled the plunger to suck the remnants into the syringe, then wiped it down with a cloth and slid a cap onto the end.

'That's your lot. Two hundred and fifty, ready to go,' he said, finally looking up at Roxy.

'Excellent,' she said, 'It was a lot of work at short notice but once we put them to good use, we will be on our way to an army of thousands. What's the target time?'

'Obviously it depends on the physiological make-up of the subjects but it should take about two hours to take hold.'

'Perfect. We should have the subjects at the drop-off point by that time.'

'It almost makes me feel sorry for the poor bastards who are going to be on the receiving end. Any news on my treatment?'

'Yes,' said Roxy, 'I've just received a call from Jackson. He has picked up your treatment and he is also bringing two of our brothers with him.'

'Rebirths? It's too early in the day for a pickup isn't it?'

'One of them survived the attack at The Brotherhood's headquarters. He was the one who helped smuggle the bodies into the base. According to our brother at the outpost, they have the head of Commander North of The Brotherhood.'

Doctor Forrest removed his glasses. 'If that's true, it affects our plans.'

'That's why I'm bringing them in. If it is true then it will work in our favour. The Brotherhood will be running around trying to find whoever killed their Commander and won't worry about us for the rest of the day. By then, it will be too late and they'll have to do whatever we want. Don't worry, we're still going ahead with the plan.'

'Are you sure we have enough brothers and sisters to coordinate this operation?'

'I'll make sure we've got enough. The only thing we need to worry about is completing the operation successfully. If we don't, we're probably all going to die.'

'What? Why?'

'The Lord Chancellor is coming here tonight. He wants to know what happened to Luca.'

'But you had to kill him. He was going to ruin everything.'

'Let's hope he sees it that way too.'

50
SPRAY: SLOW DOWN

Doctor Owen ran across the road through the pouring rain and got into the car, rubbing the rain water out of his hair. He had only been gone for fifteen minutes but to Jane it had felt like an eternity. In his hand he had a manila folder full of papers.

'No problems?' Jane asked.

'None at all. That's two down. Let's get going. We need to head to the offsite storage facility to pick up the tapes.'

Jane hit the accelerator and took them down the road as fast as she could, dodging in and out of the traffic and paying no mind to the honking horns that greeted her manoeuvres.

She was happy just to be moving. All that time spent sitting in the car made her feel more and more like a sitting duck. The newspaper article had put the frighteners on her and the fact that the girl in the coffee shop had recognised her, even if it was only subconsciously, made her think everyone out there was looking for her. They had to get these jobs done as quickly as possible, then find somewhere to lie low. If anyone recognised her then that would be it. They wouldn't have a chance.

Doctor Owen directed them away from the city but rush hour traffic was slowing them down. Jane cursed the city's one-way system that took them on a convoluted route to get them on the right course for the Expressway.

'How long will it take us to get there?' Jane asked.

'No more than ten minutes once we get on the Expressway. As long as it's clear, of course,' Doctor Owen said, 'It's not far out of the city.'

'The bank was too easy,' Jane said, 'The Brotherhood must know we're going to pick up the tapes. It's stupid going there. We might as well call them and tell them we're coming, for God's sake. Isn't there any way we can miss this place out?'

'Not at all. The pact I made with Doctor Forrest was that whichever one of us had the ability would retrieve all samples and documents. The tapes are essential to continuing our work without allowing The Brotherhood to continue without us.'

Doctor Owen stopped talking when he saw the worried look on Jane's face.

'The story in the paper has hit you hard, hasn't it?' he asked.

Jane avoided answering his question directly. 'No point in worrying about anything else. If we don't get the samples, we're all going to die in the end, aren't we?'

They reached the Expressway and drove up the ramp to see a cloud of spray ahead of them reaching up into the grey sky above. Visibility was poor and the electronic signs that hung overhead at regular intervals advised drivers to slow down. One driver that didn't heed the warning was the rider of a black motorbike that sped past them and disappeared into the misty spray.

'Hey, that's weird,' Jane said.

'What's that?'

'I'm sure I saw that motorbike before, when you were in the bank. It pulled in behind us.'

'Are you sure?'

'I recognise the plate.'

Jane tried to shrug it off, hoping it was a coincidence but couldn't shake the nagging feeling that something was amiss.

51
Time To Come Out Of Hiding

As soon as she saw them take the ramp onto the Expressway, Agent Becky Clarkson knew where Doctor Owen and his companion were going. She'd tracked them out of the city using the PDA mounted on her motorbike, following the blinking red dot along every road and round every corner.

She had already checked out the offsite storage facility a long time ago, not long after her disappearance. She made it her mission to know as much as she could about every installation that belonged to the World Health Organisation or The Brotherhood, both official and unofficial.

What the unsuspecting souls in the car she had been following didn't know, at least not for sure, was that The Brotherhood would be waiting for them. And they were armed and ready. Becky had been listening in on Captain Sayers' chatter with his men all morning. When the patrols failed to find the fugitives, Sayers had predicted they would attempt to pick up the backup tapes.

They should have gone there first, Becky thought.

In the time it took for them to visit the bank, Sayers had already sent a team of men to assist the man on site and more were on their way. Becky thought there had to be at least five men waiting for them when they arrived, with at least another five en route.

They haven't got a chance.

Faced with the almost certain death of the subjects she was pursuing, Becky couldn't intervene if she was going to remain out of harm's way. It was the philosophy she'd lived by for two long years as she tried to get to the bottom of what she'd seen that night. Above all else, self-preservation had been her motivation, above even the lives of others.

But Becky knew she didn't have a choice. Everything that was going on right now pointed to the beginning of something. Something she heard from people she had met on her travels all over the world. Something that was going to happen here, and was going to happen soon. It would shake the world and wake every man woman and child up to the terrible secrets that had remained in the domain of the underworld for centuries.

The Rising.

She knew that if Doctor Owen was deleting data and had The Brotherhood chasing after him, he was no longer part of the plan. He was working outside the terms of the treaty, unaware that the wheels were probably already in motion and nothing could stop the plans of both sides.

But he must know something. Something I don't know. There's very little time left. I have to help him.

With no more than ten minutes until they reached the storage facility, Becky knew she would have a window of only five minutes, even if she could get there twice as fast as the doctor. There was no other option in her mind. Five minutes was all she needed to neutralise the threat at their destination.

She hit the gas and roared past the doctor's car into the mist that filled the Expressway.

Time to come out of hiding.

52
Out Of Hiding

Traffic was heavy on the Expressway and the rain continued to pour in torrents. Becky Clarkson put some distance between her and the doctor by dodging in and out of the slow-moving cars, ignoring the honking horns that were becoming all too familiar.

After taking the exit ten miles down the road, she turned the corners that led to a plain, uninspiring industrial estate. The roads were relatively quiet, with the last of the commuters arriving late to their office jobs. Becky slowed down and stopped her bike in the car park of the building that sat opposite the storage facility. She stared at the building for a moment. There were no vehicles parked in any of the spaces at the front, but she hadn't expected The Brotherhood to leave military jeeps sitting outside.

Looking around to ensure she was out of sight of any security cameras, Becky unzipped a long pocket on her right thigh. She took her pistol out of her pocket, checked it was loaded and the safety catch was on, screwed the silencer into the barrel and tucked it into the back of her leathers.

She then turned her bike round and zoomed across the road, splashing through puddles and stopping just in front of the main door. Her heart was pumping fast as she dismounted and walked up to the door. She took off her gloves and dropped them on the ground under the shelter of the awning above the door so the rain wouldn't soak them through before she returned. If she returned.

'Who is it?' was the reply almost as soon as she hit the intercom button.

'I've got a delivery,' she said, lifting her visor just enough for her voice to be audible.

'What have you got?'

'I don't know what it is. Look man, I just get paid to deliver this crap. Do you want to sign for it or not?'

There was a brief silence, followed by 'Okay. Wait there.'

For an insufferable amount of time nothing happened but as soon as the lock buzzed and the door opened slightly, Agent Clarkson was unstoppable.

In one swift move she booted the door open, smacking the man behind who answered her call right on the nose. His hands instinctively went for his bleeding nose when he should have reached for his gun, but he didn't get the chance. Becky drew her gun and shot a hole directly between his eyes. There was no immediate noise from inside so she knew he was on his own.

Stepping inside, Becky pointed her gun left and right but the only route was up the stairs ahead of her. Removing her helmet to improve her vision, she spotted a security pass around the dead man's neck and tore it free. With no time to lose, she ran up the stairs and spotted a security camera at the top. She shot it with pinpoint accuracy, shattering it and debris rained to the ground but she knew her face must have been recorded.

Got to move quickly.

The door buzzed as she swiped the security pass and she took a step inside, holding her pistol behind the open door. Two men in camouflage combat gear stood in the reception area, their pistols clipped in their holsters.

'Hey, who are you? Where's Bill?'

Without replying, Becky revealed her gun and shot the man furthest away from her in the throat. Blood sprayed over the white wall next to him and he fell to the ground, clutching his neck and gurgling blood in his throat with his final breath. Before the man closest to her could react, she grabbed his right arm with her left and twisted it behind his back. She pushed the gun hard into his neck.

'What the hell are you doing? You won't get away with this.'

'Where do you keep the tapes?'

There was no reply. Becky cocked the hammer on her pistol.

'None of that counting to five bullshit. Tell me now or you're dead.'

'Okay,' he relented, 'There's a safe in the main office.'

'Where's the key to the safe?'

'Behind the desk.'

There was a loud bang of a door being flung open around the corner followed by two sets of heavy footsteps. In a flash, Becky released her grip and pushed the man forward, then took a step back and went down on one knee, obscuring her from the view of two more men in combat gear who appeared round the corner. Before they could react, she fired a shot into the back of the man she had interrogated.

As he sunk to his knees, she used the cover of his body to fire a shot over either shoulder. Both bullets hit their targets, one hitting a soldier in the eye and the second tearing through the other soldier's ear. The man with one ear gripped his head and didn't have time to return fire at Becky before she finished him off with a bullet to the forehead.

Anticipating the appearance of more soldiers, Becky got to her feet and took deep breaths to regulate her heartbeat, but there were no more obstacles in her way. There was no one else for her to kill. She took a second to take in everything that had happened and tucked her pistol back into her leathers, pleased with the fact that none of her shots had missed their targets.

She searched behind the desk and found the long safe key hanging on a hook. She checked her watch. Almost four minutes had passed since her arrival.

They'll be here any second. Better get my calling card ready for them.

53
Out Of Your Depth

Jane did a U-turn and stopped the car on the road outside the storage facility. She checked her pistol was loaded and clipped it back into the holster under her jacket.

'Okay, Doc, you're the expert. What's the plan?'

Doctor Owen looked at Jane with a blank expression on his face. She'd known the answer to her question before she asked it but she wanted to see his reaction. Unfortunately, it was exactly what she suspected.

'You mean you haven't got a plan?' she asked, anger growing in her voice.

'Have you still got your Mantek badge?' he asked.

'Yes,' she said and fished it out of her pocket.

'That's our best option.'

'Jesus Christ, Andrew. This is a shambles. We're going to get ourselves killed.' Jane shook her head and rubbed her eyes. 'Come on, let's go.'

They got out of the car and ran through the rain to the front door. Jane was despairing at their lack of organisation. Her work was always so well planned but now she felt helpless. She always had to have a plan A, B and if possible C, but they barely had a plan A. For all she knew, they were walking right into a trap and there was nothing they could do about it, but as Doctor Owen had told her, they didn't have a choice. They had to recover everything on his list. If they didn't, they wouldn't be able to stop The Brotherhood developing and distributing the primary treatment.

'Wait,' she said as they approached the front step, 'the door's open.'

Jane drew her pistol as they reached the door. With the fingertips of her left hand, she slowly eased the door open.

Blood.

There was a pool of dark red blood on the floor. Jane stepped inside and took a deep breath as she saw a dead body lying in front of her, stopping the door opening all the way. He was clad in combat gear, with blood was still slowly pouring from the hole in his head. Jane grabbed Doctor Owen's arm and dragged him inside the building, closing the door behind them.

'Oh my God,' he exclaimed.

'It looks like someone's beaten us to it. We're too late. What the hell is going on here, Andrew?'

'But this is a Brotherhood facility. Who did this?'

They slowly followed a trail of wet footprints up the stairs. At the top they found a security pass hanging from a cord tied to the handle of the door. They shared a look that told each other they had no idea what was going on. They were out of control, out of their depth and they knew it.

Jane removed the pass and opened the door to the reception area. She had no idea what to expect when she opened the door but the sight before her left her speechless.

The bodies of four dead soldiers were lined up on the floor next to the reception desk. Just in front of Jane as she stepped through into the reception area was a heavy clear plastic bag that was filled with data tapes.

A hand-written note sat next to the bag. Jane picked it up and read it out loud. 'Doctor Owen, you and your companion are out of your depth. If you want to stay alive, go to the following address: 112 Abbey Tower. The Brotherhood are coming. Go now.'

54
Virex

'How long will it take to get there?' I asked.

Jackson looked in his rear view mirror at me. 'A little while, so make yourself comfortable.'

I checked the backs of my hands. They had turned a strong shade of pink in the short time it had taken us to run to the car, but my skin was now back to normal. I couldn't imagine how the incredible healing power of the vampire virus would ever cease to amaze me.

I looked out of the window and watched the city rush past me and turn into countryside. The events that were unfolding were not what we were expecting when Skinner had the idea of officially registering me as a vampire. We had thought it would help my safe passage should we run into any bloodsuckers, but now we were being taken to their home. As it turned out, carrying the head of Commander North around with us had worked – we were about to find out so much more about what was going on. But at what cost?

I had many concerns going round in my head. The biggest worry of all was what the vampires knew about us without asking any questions. The vampire driving the car had worked out the whole situation at the outpost just a matter of seconds after he had arrived. Without saying a word, he had known who we were and whether we posed a threat to him or not.

Can he read our minds? Can he tell what I'm thinking now?

'What's going to happen to those men we left back there?' I asked.

'Don't worry about them,' Jackson said, 'You're not the first rebirth to go crazy after your first taste of blood. You won't be the last, either. You only broke their bones. Their bodies will heal in time. If you had removed their limbs, it would have taken a lot longer to repair the damage. It's their job to look after guys like you so I'm sure they won't hold a grudge.'

'Wow, us vampires are a friendly bunch, aren't we?' I quipped, trying to figure him out.

His stony face cracked a tiny smile. 'Up to a point, new boy. Up to a point.'

He shot another glance at me in the mirror. 'How was your first taste of blood?'

I wondered if he knew how I felt. *Does he know how sick I feel after drinking the blood of a child, no matter how sweet it tasted and how much it quenched my uncontrollable thirst?*

'I can't remember,' I lied.

'Do you remember why you went crazy?'

'I would have preferred my first feed to be a little older.'

'I understand. Get used to it though, new boy. When you have to feed, you don't have a choice. Boy, girl or some old dear doddering along the street, they're all the same to you now.'

I looked out of the window again and let his words ring in my ears. *When you have to feed, you don't have a choice.*

As the hours went by, I was beginning to think there was no way back for me. Even if the doctor could finish work on the treatment, was I too far gone to turn back? I had already tasted the blood of two people and slaughtered more. As time ticked by, I was becoming less and less human.

The box containing Commander North's head sat on the back seat next to me. *Our ticket into the underworld.* I knew The Brotherhood would be looking for us and I thought of Jane and Doctor Owen, hoping they were safe. In a perverse way I was happier to be with the vampires than on our own. I knew that at least if The Brotherhood found us, we would have a better chance of surviving their attack. *Safety in numbers.*

Jackson asked Skinner about what had happened the previous day at The Brotherhood's regional headquarters. I took Jackson's advice and sat back in my seat to get comfortable. As I tried to stretch my legs out, my feet hit something under the seat in front. I looked down and saw a small plastic box. Intrigued, I gripped the box between my feet and slowly drew it out into my foot well.

I was surprised at what I saw. The box was full of individually wrapped syringes, each filled with a yellow liquid. The plastic packaging around the syringes was printed with the word 'Virex'. The yellow liquid looked exactly the same as the treatment Doctor Owen had given me. I was confused. This was too much of a coincidence.

If this is the same treatment I received, what is it doing in the back of a vampire's car? And why is it packaged with a brand name?

I knew I had to get a sample of this back to the doctor. He would certainly want to check this out for himself. With Jackson still talking to Skinner, as quietly as I could I bent over and lifted two syringes out of the box and slipped them into my sock.

My actions had been quick enough not to warrant another glance in the mirror from Jackson. I sat back and watched the countryside go by, trying to work out the significance of my discovery.

55
Moved Upstairs

Will Harris took the last gulp of his third cup of coffee of the morning. With no help from any of his so-called colleagues, he was getting nowhere and starting to despair.

The Mantek file system had been completely wiped and it was his job to restore all the files from the offsite backup. This was proving impossible because he would need someone from the offsite storage facility to bring the tapes over to him but no one was answering the phone over there.

Will had tried to escalate the problem to his manager but as usual, he had something better to do. Will knew that as soon as someone important decided this was a big problem, his manager would be interested but until then he was on his own. He had half a mind to get in his car and drive out there himself. After all, it's just outside the city and he could have been there and back in the time he'd been hanging on the phone.

To hell with it, he thought, *No one would thank me for it. Time for another cup of coffee.*

Will got out of his seat and as he turned round to leave his cubicle, he was faced with a dark-haired woman in a sharp suit and glasses. She had blanked him for the past two years on the rare occasions they saw each other but now she wanted to talk. It was Jodi Carr, his old boss from upstairs.

'Will, I need you to come with me,' she said in the unfriendliest way she could.

'Hi Jodi, how are you?' he asked in a mischievously upbeat tone.

'I need you to come with me, Will. Right now.'

'I can't. I've got to sort out this file system problem. I reported it to your guys upstairs but I haven't heard anything back so I guess it's up to me.'

'This is related to the file system problem, Will.'

'Well, there's no answer at the storage facility. I don't know how I'm going to restore the files.'

'You won't be able to,' she said, 'We have a bigger problem that we need your help with.'

A bigger problem that they need my help with? This should be fun…

'What could you possibly need my help with?'

'This,' Jodi said and handed Will a photograph. It was a picture of a female with short dark hair, dressed in black running up a flight of stairs with a gun in her hand.

'Who's this?' Will asked.

'That is Agent Becky Clarkson. She has reappeared this morning. That picture was taken at the offsite storage facility less than an hour ago. She murdered everyone there. When our people got there, the dead bodies of the men were all neatly piled up and all the tapes were gone.'

Will was stunned. She was back. After two years, he thought he'd never hear anything from her again.

'You were closer to her than anyone here.'

'Close to her? I worked with her a few times but I wouldn't say we were close.'

'You're the best shot we've got at bringing her in before anyone else gets killed. Pack up your things. You're being moved upstairs.'

'What, permanently?' he asked, with hope in his voice.

Jodi didn't answer his question. 'Follow me.'

56
No Missed Calls

'Room service!'

Dave got out of his chair for the first time since he arrived at the hotel and opened the door to his room. He found himself faced with the concierge, carrying a tray that held a silver platter, a bottle of water and the smallest bottle of tomato ketchup he had ever seen.

'Jeez, are you doing every job today?' Dave asked as he let the concierge into the room and watched him place the tray on the end of his bed.

'Pretty much,' he said, 'Have you managed to get some rest?'

'A little.'

Dave signed for his meal and saw the concierge to the door.

'If you need anything else, just give me a call,' the concierge said.

'Thanks,' Dave said and closed the door on him.

He ran back to his chair by the window and gazed outside, just as he had been doing all morning. The rain was still pouring heavily from the dull grey sky, falling diagonally as the wind got stronger and stronger.

He lifted the lid on his lunch and took the plate full of over-priced cheeseburger and fries in his hands. He hoped he hadn't missed the car going past in the few seconds that it took to get rid of the concierge. That's the reason there was always two people on a stakeout, so one could cover while the other went to get refreshments or take whatever type of relief was required.

The television news channels were still reporting on the investigation into the attack on the police station. Unsurprisingly, there appeared to be no progress until Dave heard a reporter's voice say, 'We can now go live to the police station. Chief of Police Chris Cameron is about to make a statement.'

Dave moved his chair to allow himself to keep one eye on the road outside while taking in the announcement. The chief appeared outside the police station, walking directly into an onslaught of flashing cameras.

'Thank you for your time,' he said, 'I will keep this brief and I will not take any questions following this statement.

'I wish to announce the names of the individuals we need to speak to in the course of this investigation. I would encourage these people to come forward to allow us to eliminate them from our investigations.'

Yeah, right, Dave thought, *These are the people you've got down as prime suspects.*

The chief continued. 'They are Jane Simpson of the World Health Organisation, Doctor Andrew Owen of Mantek pharmaceuticals and our own detectives Dave Thomas and Tom Ryder. All attempts to contact these people have proved fruitless so I am appealing to these people and anyone who may know where they are to call us with information.'

What the hell?

Dave took his mobile phone out of his pocket.

No missed calls. They haven't tried to contact me.

He had a terrible thought. He called his wife and was relieved when she answered.

'Dave, where are you? I was just about to call you. Have you seen the news? The police are looking for you.'

'I know. I'm safe. I'm at a hotel in Blackchapel. Something weird is going on. Where are you?'

'Blackchapel? Where the hell is that?'

'It's up in the mountains. Just tell me, where are you?'

'I'm at home. Why?'

'I need you to take the kids away. Rent a car and go up the coast.'

'What? I'm not leaving.'

'Trust me, please. We're in danger.'

'Danger?'

Dave almost dropped his burger as he got out of his chair. On the road outside, a black car was approaching. *The* black car.

'I'm sorry,' he said, 'It's very important. Believe me, you have to leave. I have to go now.'

He hung up, cutting his wife off as she continued her protests, and sprinted for the door.

57
Nowhere To Go

Jane opened the boot of the car and found a space for the bag of tapes next to the medical boxes of samples they had taken from The Brotherhood's base. She slammed the boot shut and ran round to the driver's door.

'Do you know where Abbey Tower is?' Doctor Owen asked her, shouting through the noise of the rain bouncing off the car.

'No,' Jane replied, 'but there's a road atlas in the car. You can navigate. Come on, let's go.'

They got into the car and Jane hit the accelerator. Under Doctor Owen's guidance they got back onto the Expressway. With most commuters now at their places of work, the traffic was moving along at a decent pace, even if the conditions were still wet.

'Keep on going,' the doctor said, running his finger along the map, 'The exit isn't for a while yet.'

'What the hell happened back there?' Jane asked, not for a moment expecting a coherent answer from her companion.

'Whoever killed all those people must have known we were going there.'

'Who knows about that place?'

'Doctor Forrest springs to mind, but why would he give the location away to anyone else if he wanted us to retrieve the tapes?'

'Are you sure you can trust him? Maybe he's putting us through all this to set us up.'

'No, we can trust him. I've known him for a very long time. He has my total confidence.'

'Anyone else?'

'Apart from Doctor Forrest, you can take your pick of pretty much any member of The Brotherhood. If they saw us deleting the data from Mantek, they probably would have assumed we would try to get the tapes.'

'But whoever killed those soldiers couldn't have been from The Brotherhood, and I'm sure that none of them were vampires either. Something else is going on here.'

'Look, we've still got two more stops to make. Whoever this is must be able to help us. Why else would they leave us that note?'

'I hope so. Otherwise we haven't got a chance of standing up against another building full of armed guards.'

Jane slammed her fist on the dashboard and yelled obscenities in frustration.

'What is it?' Doctor Owen asked.

'Look at us. We haven't got a clue what the hell we're doing. We left The Brotherhood last night with boxes full of samples for you to carry on your work but now we've got nowhere to go. We've been trailing round the city picking up more of your crap and now we're blindly going to another random address just because someone wrote us a note. It's amazing that we've stayed alive this long!'

'We're out of options, Jane!' Doctor Owen shouted back, 'It's a shitty situation but it's the best we've got.'

Jane cast a look in her rear view mirror. A big black object was far behind in the mist. A few seconds later she looked again. This time the black object was bigger, joined by identical companions on either side.

'Have you seen the trucks behind us?' she said.

Doctor Owen turned round. Before he could check out the trucks that were moving quickly towards them, they heard a faint rattle of gunfire. The rear windscreen shattered into a thousand pieces.

58
'Pull Over Now!'

Jane floored the accelerator and weaved in and out of the traffic. The wet road made manoeuvring difficult and she felt the wheels of the car spinning as they passed over patches of standing water.

Most of the cars on the road were either slowing down or veering wildly across the lanes to get out of the way of the massive trucks that were thundering along the Expressway. Jane had to keep her wits about her just to avoid the panicked movements of the car ahead of her, never mind the firepower that was being unleashed just behind them.

Soldiers of The Brotherhood were hanging out of the passenger windows of each truck, firing their rifles in the direction of Jane and Doctor Owen. They didn't think twice if their bullets found another target. The sound of tearing metal and screeching tyres drowned out the rain, which was interrupted by regular crunches of metal on metal and blaring horns.

Captain Sayers sat in the lead truck, watching the attack unfold. *Don't kill them,* he had told his men, *but make sure you scare them and run them off the road.*

The car Jane was driving was more nimble than their trucks but they had all three lanes of the Expressway covered and all she could do was swerve across the road from the gun sights of one truck to the other. The back of their car was being torn apart by all the gunfire it was taking but it kept on going. It wouldn't last forever but they were living by the second, just doing their best to survive with no thought of how they could escape the attack.

Sayers picked up the radio. 'Jesus Christ, can't any of you hit the tyres?'

He didn't expect a reply and didn't get one. 'Okay,' he continued into the radio, 'Cease fire and hit the lights.'

A huge set of spotlights on the top of each truck illuminated and cast a blinding beam of white light onto the road ahead. Captain Sayers hit the button on the radio to turn it into a loudspeaker.

'Agent Simpson,' his voice boomed across the Expressway, 'Pull over now and you will not be harmed.'

Jane straightened the car's movement but did not slow down. Captain Sayers nodded to the soldier who was hanging out of the side of his truck. The soldier fired off a short burst that tore through the rear of the car. Sayers picked up the radio again.

'Agent Simpson, pull over now!'

She slowed the car down and started to pull over towards the edge of the road. The road ahead was almost clear. Everyone on the road had either pulled over or hit the gas to get as far away from the gunfire as possible.

Jane was about to stop the car when there was a loud bang from the truck on the right. Sayers looked out of the window to see it swerve and spin off the road, with smoke pouring out of the back. It smashed through the barrier at the side of the road and fell onto its side as it hit the grassy verge. Jane put her foot to the floor and moved back to the middle of the road.

'What the hell is going on?' Captain Sayers shouted into the radio at the other trucks.

'Grenade, Captain. No casualties but our truck is out of commission. It was a single attacker on a motorbike. Look out behind.'

Sayers turned round to look out of the back of the truck and saw a figure in black on a motorbike speeding towards them.

59
'She's Back'

Agent Becky Clarkson had only one magnetic grenade left but there were still two trucks ahead of her. The soldiers on board were now well aware of her presence and had diverted their attention away from Jane and the doctor, who were still struggling to pull away from the thundering military vehicles on their tail.

That's exactly what she wanted but she wasn't prepared to let them use her as target practice for long. Bullets whistled past her and she dropped back, knowing it was only a matter of time until one of them found their intended target.

She took the grenade in her hand and flicked the plastic cap off the end. A red diode lit up to indicate the grenade was primed.

I've got to time this perfectly.

With her other hand Agent Clarkson yanked the accelerator and moved closer to the trucks, keeping her head down from the gunfire. When she was confident she was within range, she pressed the button on the end of the grenade. It made a small whining noise that wasn't audible to her through her helmet but she knew how much time she had.

Three seconds until it turns magnetic.

Becky threw the grenade into the air and hit the brake. The bike slid all over the road and she had to speed up again to re-gain control.

One... two...

Before the grenade hit the road, it changed direction in mid-air and flew towards the truck on the left. There was a clunk as it hit the rear bumper.

Five seconds.

Becky watched from a distance as one of the soldiers on board the doomed truck knelt over the tailgate to see where the explosive had landed. He held onto the back of the truck with one arm and tried to lean over to reach the grenade. He gripped it and tried to wrestle it free but the magnetic force was too strong for one man to break the seal.

Five seconds are up.

The back of the truck exploded in a ball of fire, and the top of the soldier's body turned into a cloud of red mist that blew away in the torrential rain. The rest of him fell off the back of the truck onto the road. Becky had to swerve to avoid the bloody pair of legs that flailed towards her.

The remains of the flaming truck skidded to the right and crashed into the back of the remaining truck, which lost its grip on the flooded road and spun through one hundred and eighty degrees, coming to a halt in the emergency lane.

Before the soldiers could compose themselves and pick up their weapons, Agent Clarkson hit the accelerator again and zoomed past the wreckage. She pulled her bike up alongside what was left of Jane and the doctor's car and looked through the driver's window.

Both the driver and the passenger had shock written across their faces. They stared at her, unsure if they were next on her hit list. Becky pointed forward to indicate they should follow her and moved ahead of their car.

Captain Sayers kicked the truck door open and stumbled onto the road. Two soldiers got out of his truck and ran over to the burning shell next to them. They dragged one of their squad mates out of the driver's seat. His uniform was on fire and he screamed as they rolled him on the road, trying to extinguish the flames in pools of rainwater.

Sayers lifted his radio. 'Come in General Graham, this is Captain Sayers.'

'This is General Graham, come in Luke.'

'We've lost two vehicles.'

'Did you capture the fugitives?'

'Negative. We were ambushed.'

'Was it a lone attacker on a motorbike?'

'Affirmative. How did you know? Do you know who it was?'

'Yes. We've just found out this second. It's Agent Clarkson. She's back.'

60
Ghosts From The Past

It was a dark day outside and the clouds were gathering in the sky. It was a day for ghosts from the past to make their reappearance.

Steve Ellis stood at the door to his office, watching the return of Will Harris, their prodigal son. As soon as they realised that Becky Clarkson had come out of hiding he had ordered Jodi, his deputy, to move Will back upstairs after two years in exile. Steve had been sorry to lose Will. He was one of the most capable operatives on the team and had clocked up more hours on Black Ops support than anyone else. Even now, no one had come close to his achievements. Steve was certain he would fit back in to the team in no time.

He needs to fit back in if we're going to track down Agent Clarkson.

The phone on Steve's desk rang and he shut the door to his office. The plaque on the door read 'World Health Organisation Regional Operations Director'.

He sat down in his Italian leather chair and answered the call.

'Mister Ellis,' a deep voice boomed down the telephone. Steve had been expecting the call but this did not stop him being gripped by fear at the mention of his name.

'Marcus,' Steve replied in a hushed voice, 'To what do I owe the honour?'

'I understand there are complications. Enlighten me.'

'Agent Clarkson went dark two years ago. She has just come out of hiding this morning. We are still investigating her reappearance but she has already caused casualties today.'

'I thought she had been taken care of.'

'A Black Ops mission was thought to have resulted in her death but there were no survivors so we could never say for sure. We thought it was safe to assume she had been neutralised.'

'We cannot afford to make any assumptions. Will this affect our plans?'

'No sir. I guarantee this will not affect our plans at all.'

'Excellent. We will be moving ahead with the plan tonight.'

'Tonight?'

'That won't be a problem, will it Mister Ellis?'

'Of course not sir, I would let you know well in advance if we had any problems.'

'That was not intended as a question, Mister Ellis. The plan will be moving ahead. Your protection will be required at sunrise tomorrow. The location remains the same.'

'Understood.'

'I would also like to remind you that for now the treaty remains in place. The Brotherhood have operated without their usual level of secrecy for the last three days. You must ensure that they maintain a low profile until tomorrow morning.'

'I will speak to General Graham immediately.'

'And inform your superiors that the next phase of the plan will be going ahead. We have all waited a long time for this moment and finally it is within reach. The Rising must proceed without interruptions.'

With that, Marcus Verrico was gone. Steve knew General Graham would not appreciate being told to scale back his efforts. That would make it very difficult to pick up Agent Clarkson, but there was nothing he could do. The plan had been written and agreed many years ago and there was nothing anyone could do to change it. He checked his watch.

Less than twenty hours until the Rising reaches the point of no return.

61
Change Of Plan

General Graham hung up the phone and only just resisted the urge to pick the portable comms unit up and throw it across the stone-floored entrance hall of Hartley House.

The general hated taking orders from anyone at the World Health Organisation, but he especially hated taking orders from that pencil-pushing bastard Ellis. All Ellis cared about was the treaty and following the conditions of the agreement between humans and vampires to the letter. He didn't care about the effects of the Rising, only what it meant for the people they were supposed to protect. All he cared about was getting paid.

General Graham didn't believe in the treaty but he followed it. He had no choice. After all, the plan had been laid down fifty years ago when it became clear that medical treatment for the virus might be possible.

Both species knew they needed to secure their future. If the vampires broke the treaty, they knew they wouldn't have the numbers to mount an effective resistance against the humans, and if the humans broke the treaty, there would be widespread panic if the vampires came out into the open. Now, fifty years since the treaty was signed and five hundred years since the first agreement between humans and vampires, the plans for the species to co-exist would come to fruition.

Fearing what would happen on the day of the Rising, General Graham had unofficially empowered Commander North with the task of developing a weapon that could be used to wipe out vampires once and for all. This had to happen before their numbers grew too large to deal with. But just as Doctor Owen and Doctor Forrest had almost completed work on the primary treatment, they had both gone missing and all the work they had done was quickly disappearing from their locations around the city.

If that wasn't bad enough, the World Health Organisation had just called and told him to scale back their operations until tomorrow morning, when they would be informed of their new mission. If he didn't recover the doctor before that operation, he suspected it would be too late.

Too late to stop the Rising.

General Graham stepped out of the main doors and looked across the grounds. Debris from the previous day's battle was still scattered across the lawns, which had been torn apart by gunfire and the falling remnants of the wooden lookout towers. The falling rain was quickly turning the once-beautiful grounds into a muddy bog.

The general's attention was taken by a battered truck chugging down the gravel drive. It stopped at the front steps and two men immediately jumped out. They took one of their men in their arms and ran up the steps into the house. General Graham winced as he saw the burns on the face of the unconscious casualty, whose camouflage gear was charred and falling apart.

He walked down the steps to meet Captain Sayers as he got out of the truck.

'We need a recovery crew to go to the Expressway,' Captain Sayers said, 'We've got two trucks sitting on the road holding up the traffic. This is going to make the news. Too many people saw everything. Private Blondheim was blown in half trying to stop the explosion. It's a fucking mess.'

'I've already sent a team to pick up the wreckage,' said General Graham.

'If we're going to stop Agent Simpson and pick up the doctor, I'll need more men.'

'There has been a change of plan. The World Health Organisation are pursuing this line of investigation. We will remain here and await their call.'

'What? With Agent Clarkson out there? We need to stop her at all costs. She's going to screw up everything. I've just lost good men today to a chick on a motorbike. We've got to get back out there and take that bitch apart!'

'Keep that attitude in check, Sayers. We all have orders. I have mine and you have yours. Shit rolls downhill.'

'Yes sir,' Captain Sayers said grudgingly, 'How is our resident vampire?'

'Stein's still alive for now. Have you got a use for him? I was thinking about leaving him out here to get a suntan.'

'The detective is still missing. He could still help us out.'

'Okay, you check on him. Unless he's causing any trouble, we'll keep hold of him until this is over.'

62
Introductions

Agent Clarkson had been listening to The Brotherhood's radio conversations all day.

They had been completely focused on the capture of Doctor Owen and his companion, Agent Jane Simpson. There was also talk of a detective called Tom Ryder and a missing soldier called Private Skinner. She had heard no talk of anything else, which is why she was shocked to hear the general's announcement go out across the airwaves.

'This is General Graham. All troops abort your missions and return to Hartley House immediately. Repeat: return to Hartley House immediately.'

A sign at the side of the road indicated that a lay-by was coming up soon so when she saw that it was clear, she slowed down and stopped her bike in the clearing. The car that was following her did the same. She knew it would take another twenty minutes to reach the address on the note she had left with the tapes so now that The Brotherhood had called off the search, it was time to say hello to her new friends.

She dismounted and took off her helmet, leaving it perched on the seat of her bike, then approached the car and made her way into the back seat. The faces of the man and woman in front of her were still trembling slightly with shock from the attack. They had only just escaped and had no idea who this person was.

'Who are you?' Jane asked, with more than a small dose of fear cracking her voice.

'Forgive me for what has happened this morning. I felt compelled to help you,' Becky began.

'Why?'

'You're Agent Simpson, aren't you?'

'That's right.'

'I was once an agent of the World Health Organisation as well. Because of the situation we're all in I guess you already know they are not to be trusted. When I realised you were not following orders of the World Health Organisation or The Brotherhood, I knew I had to find out what you know. You're Doctor Owen, aren't you?'

'That's correct.'

'And you're picking up all the materials you have on the primary treatment, is that right?'

'Yes. How did you know?'

'Why are you doing this now?'

'Wait a minute,' Jane said, 'why should we be talking to you? We don't even know your name.'

Becky looked Jane straight in the eye. 'You may have heard of me. My name is Becky Clarkson.'

Jane's eyes widened. 'Oh my God. Agent Clarkson. But you've been off the grid for...'

'Two years. I had no choice. I discovered something that put my life in jeopardy.'

'What was that?' asked Doctor Owen.

'I know of an agreement between humans and vampires. The treaty is not in place to maintain the current populations. It is there to support a concerted effort to balance the populations of the species.'

Jane shook her head vigorously.

'That's not possible. The vampire community is compelled to maintain a small population. Their numbers would grow exponentially if they came out into the open. The Costas report states that the human species would be wiped out within just a few years. That would also result in the extinction of the vampires because there would be no human blood to feed on.'

'I know the report you're talking about but it purposely doesn't take all factors into consideration. It neglects the idea of collusion between vampires and humans, where the populations are actively maintained at mutually beneficial levels. That report was leaked into the public domain on purpose in an attempt to keep the idea of vampires a fantasy.'

'I don't understand,' Jane said, 'How can the population levels be maintained?'

'I have evidence at the address on the note,' Becky said and opened the door, 'I think the doctor will be particularly interested in what I have to show you. Follow me.'

'No,' Jane said, 'how do we know we can trust you?'

'I saved your life. Don't worry, you don't have to thank me now, but if you don't follow me, you're on your own against the vampires and The Brotherhood. Your choice.'

Becky slammed the door and marched back to her motorbike.

63

Knowing Looks

I wish I knew what the hell is going on, Dave thought.

The black car that had passed the hotel was indeed the black car that Dave had followed from Doctor Forrest's house to Blackchapel. Now, on what was quickly turning into the strangest day of his life, Dave was back doing what he seemed to do best.

Following this damn car and not knowing who is driving or where they're going.

The road out of Blackchapel led them further up into the mountains. There were no turnings whatsoever so Dave could afford to back off and let a large gap build up between them. After all, if the driver in front cottoned on that he was being followed by the same car again, Dave wouldn't have room to turn round and make his getaway.

Dave tried to call his wife again but the mountains obstructed the mobile phone signal. He hoped she had taken his advice and got the kids out of the city. He didn't want the same thing to happen to his family that had happened to Doctor Owen's wife. It had only been a few hours since Tom had come knocking but he suspected he wouldn't be able to return home for a while. This investigation was sure to take a long time so he knew it would be for the best if his wife wasn't waiting at home worrying about when he might return.

He was trying to piece together the events of the morning so far. The police station had been attacked; most likely by a vampire from the description Tom had given him of their techniques. This had led him to the house where Officer Myers was attacked. Now he was following a car being driven by a man who had visited that house to pick up some syringes that had been hidden in the main bedroom. At the same time, the police had changed their line of enquiry to the very people who had asked him for help at the lake.

And they're counting me as part of that gang.

As Dave turned a corner, he saw that a large part of the road ahead was visible and just before another turning, he saw the black car hit the brakes.

It's slowing down.

It's stopped.

If Dave stopped as well, the driver would be alerted to the fact that he was definitely being followed. He decided to take the risk that the driver had stopped for a different reason and kept going. When he reached the car, he saw the door behind the driver swing open. A head popped out and threw up onto the road. The head then looked up at Dave.

Tom.

Dave kept driving and went past the black car and round the corner without incident.

As soon as he saw Tom, Dave knew that he must have stopped the car on purpose. Tom must have known Dave was following them and wanted him to know that he was with whoever that was in the car. There had been a third figure in the car, which Dave assumed was Skinner.

Dave pushed on ahead and about a mile further down the road, saw a turning. He didn't take the turning, however, due to a metal gate obstructing his path. Just further down the road was a lookout point that allowed travellers to admire the views of the mountains.

Dave stopped the car and got out, pretending to take pictures with the camera on his mobile phone as soon as the black car appeared at the top of the road. He saw the car stop at the gate, wait for it to open and drive through.

Looking around the tall mountains, Dave noticed that they were casting long shadows everywhere, even though the middle of the day had only just passed.

You could probably walk for miles without being in direct sunlight. The perfect place for vampires to make their home.

64
Unmarked Car

Just a few moments after we saw the sign telling us we were entering Blackchapel, we'd passed through the small town high in the mountains.

In a town that comprised a hotel, a filling station and a few shops that whizzed past the car window, I noticed something out of the corner of my eye that drew my attention. A lone car was parked outside the hotel. A lone car that looked suspiciously like one of the police department's unmarked cars. Unmarked cars are supposed to blend in anywhere but the sight of a slightly battered dark blue Ford out here in the middle of nowhere made me a little suspicious. I hoped this was my cop's instinct rather than another one of my new powers.

We made our way through the mountains in silence. Skinner had long since lost topics of conversation with Jackson and I had lost the will to interrogate him about being a vampire. I had learned all I wanted to learn so far today and I didn't want to think about what surprises were in store when we arrived at the place our driver called home.

The car turned a corner and we were faced with a huge chasm. As we worked our way round the sheer drop next to us, I looked round and saw a car on the road behind us.

The dark blue Ford.

I knew this was far too much of a coincidence and had to do something to find out who was in the car. If it was Dave, I needed to know. I needed to know that he was okay and I needed to know that he was nearby if I ran into trouble.

I grabbed my stomach and shouted, 'Stop the car!'

Jackson looked in his mirror, 'What's wrong back there?'

'I think I'm going to be sick.'

'What? We're nearly there.'

'Pull over. Please!'

Jackson stopped the car before the corner at the edge of the chasm. I flung the door open and stuck my fingers down my throat. As the burning flow of vomit moved up through my throat and splashed onto the floor, I wondered if I could have thought of a better way of getting him to stop the car.

The car that had been following us drove past and I made eye contact with the driver. As I suspected, it was an unmarked car and the driver was a police officer. A detective called Dave to be precise.

I spat the last piece of vomit onto the road and closed the door.

'Are you okay?' Skinner asked.

'Yeah, I'll be alright,' I said, 'Must have had too much for breakfast.'

Jackson took us barely a mile down the road until we reached a metal gate at the side of the road. I saw that Dave had pulled over just ahead and I'm sure our driver didn't fail to notice him either. He took a radio control out of his pocket and pressed the button. When the gates were open, Jackson took us into the darkness ahead.

65
Hanging In The Darkness

The car stopped in a clearing at the edge of a cliff. Shadows from the mountains kept us in relative darkness but I was still worried about getting out of the car.

I had no idea how much ultraviolet light my skin could absorb before it started to burn. One of the few things I remembered about leaving The Brotherhood's regional headquarters the night before was lying in the helicopter feeling like my skin had been removed inch by inch with a potato peeler. I had only been in direct sunlight for about thirty seconds.

Jackson got out of the car and opened my door. My hesitation spoke volumes. 'Don't worry,' he said, 'We won't be out here for long.'

'Why, are we getting picked up?' I asked.

'No, this is the end of the road. Have you flown yet?'

'Erm, no. Not really. Why?' I asked. I almost forgot that I was supposed to have been a vampire for only a few hours, not a flying, murdering, Captain-eating son of a bitch.

'You know the fight or flight theory?'

'Yes.'

'Well, for your brothers and sisters it's more literal than it was when you were human. Get out of the car and I'll show you what I mean.'

I hesitated again, but Jackson had finished being friendly. He leaned over, grabbed me by my shirt collar and dragged me out of the car.

'Hey, what the hell are you doing?' I shouted as Jackson picked me up and lifted me above his head, 'Put me down!'

'Time to learn how to fly, new boy.'

Jackson ran to the edge of the cliff and threw my struggling body into the darkness below. My whole body tingled as I felt myself tumbling down. It was like the dream where you're falling forever and only ends when you wake up in a cold sweat.

Only I didn't wake up. I was more awake and alert than I'd ever been in my life. I screamed as I fell feet first. The warmth of my blood spread up through my body and collected in my head and shoulders. The air in the dark chasm became colder the further I fell.

Then, just when I thought I was destined for a bloody end on the rocks, I stopped falling.

My descent slowed and slowed until I was hanging in mid-air. I stopped screaming and looked all around me. It was the strangest feeling I had ever had. I could see the sharp rocks below me on the base of the cavern but something was stopping me from falling, suspending me in the air just a few metres from a small ledge and a pair of large wooden doors built into the rock.

Did I do this? Am I controlling my body?

I looked up and saw two figures appear in the bright band of sky above and fly down towards me. In a swift intricate move, Jackson flew headfirst towards the ledge and performed a back flip in the air to land perfectly on his feet. Skinner stopped next to me, holding our metal case in his arms.

'That was a shitty thing for him to do,' he said, 'Are you okay?'

'I guess so,' I said, still in shock from the fall.

Skinner grabbed me by the collar and dragged me across the chasm, setting me down on the ledge as he landed. I took a couple of steps, steadying myself on my feet.

Jackson banged on the wooden door. After a few seconds the sound of unlocking bolts filled the chasm. The doors creaked open.

Two vampires dressed in black cloaks, with swords at their side held the doors open as a female figure dressed in black combat gear stood waiting for us.

'Welcome home, Jackson,' she said, 'All of you come inside. I need to speak to you. Now.'

66
Revelations

Becky Clarkson had gone on ahead so Jane and Doctor Owen were left to find their own way to Abbey Tower.

The address Becky had given them could be found in one of the less desirable areas of the city, outside the centre but not far enough away from the hustle and bustle to be considered suburbia. Jane stopped the car next to a concrete park where children that should have been in school were playing football.

'What should we do about the samples in the back?' Doctor Owen asked as he got out of the car. He looked at the bullet holes in the bodywork and wondered how much of their treasure had survived the attack.

'Just leave it locked away for now,' Jane said, 'We'll find out what she wants and come back for everything. It would look pretty suspicious walking into a place like this with armfuls of medical equipment.'

They approached Abbey Tower. It was a twenty-storey apartment block, run-down and imposing, but Jane suspected it didn't look much worse now than it did the day it was built. Smashed windows peppered the high walls and many of them that weren't smashed had nationalist flags hanging outside. Graffiti adorned every free patch of wall space at the entrance as far up the building as the artists could reach, telling any would-be invaders that they wouldn't be welcome, although why anyone would want to invade this place was anyone's guess.

The door to the entrance hall was locked, with a keypad on the wall next to it. Jane entered the apartment number Becky had given them and hit the 'call' button. A few seconds later, a mechanical buzz told them the door was open and they ventured inside.

Jane hit the button to call the elevator, trying not to inhale too much of the rank stench of urine that hung in the air. The elevator arrived and took them up to the eleventh floor. As the doors opened and the aroma of an unmaintained building that housed hundreds of people hit them in the face, Jane and the doctor looked at each other.

What the hell are we doing here?

They found apartment one-one-two but before Jane could knock on the door, Becky had opened it from the inside. 'Get in, quick,' she said and they followed her order.

'Sorry for the rather unpleasant surroundings,' Becky said, 'I've been out of work for two years. You need to make the savings last, you know?'

She took them through the barely furnished apartment, the cleanliness of which was a stark contrast to the rest of the building, and sat them down at the kitchen table. The kettle was already boiling and she offered her visitors a cup of coffee, which they both accepted.

Becky sat down at the table and took a sip. 'You must forgive me for our dramatic introduction,' she began, 'but I know the capabilities of The Brotherhood. I also know what they are protecting and the lengths they will go to stop anyone interfering with their plans.'

'You mean the primary treatment?' Jane asked knowingly.

'No. Forget what you think you know. Development of the treatment to rid the world of vampires may appear to be the main motivation of The Brotherhood but that is far from the truth. In fact, it is the exact opposite.

'The primary treatment is an unofficial project launched by the leader of The Brotherhood, General Graham. On the record he goes along with his orders from the World Health Organisation but off the record he was actively sponsoring the work Doctor Forrest and Doctor Owen were doing.'

'Why was it off the record?' Doctor Owen asked, 'Everything we've seen from The Brotherhood has indicated that the primary treatment was their only priority.'

'That's because it's the only work they've been doing off their own backs. Without overseeing your research, their only role would have been to act as the military arm of the World Health Organisation. General Graham knew he couldn't stand by and take no action. He had to do everything he could to develop a weapon to use against the vampires.'

'Why did all of this have to go on under the radar?' Jane asked.

'Simple. Because of the treaty.'

'But the treaty just lays down the rules between vampires and humans and restricts their actions. It defines the rules which the communities have to live by.'

'That's what you're meant to think and to a point, it does. But what you don't know, and only a few key people know this, is that it lays down the plans for ongoing co-existence of the communities. This includes a schedule for balancing out the population levels.'

'No no no,' Jane said, shaking her head, 'You're talking about the Rising, aren't you?'

'Exactly.'

'But that's just a myth, a conspiracy theory.'

'No, Agent Simpson. It's a fact. Everything I've seen and heard over the last two years tells me it's due to start soon, and it's going to start here.'

67
Smokescreen

Jane got out of her chair and paced backward and forward on the wooden floor, her footsteps amplified by the bare walls. 'I can't believe what you're saying, but I know who you are. I used to work in the Black Ops support team before I joined the emergency response unit. I was the one who took over from Will on the night you went dark.'

Becky raised her eyebrows. 'Really? What happened to him? I tried to track him down but found nothing. Was he killed?'

'No. I believe he was moved downstairs.'

'Figures. I bet those bastards never let him leave.'

'Why did you leave the World Health Organisation?' Doctor Owen asked.

'I discovered proof of the plan to balance the populations. My life was in danger so I went dark. Since then, I've travelled all over the world looking for evidence to back up my theory.'

'What did you discover?'

Becky got up and opened a kitchen drawer. She took something out of the drawer and placed it on the table in front of Doctor Owen. It was a pre-packaged 'Virex' syringe.

'What's this?' he asked, picking it up and examining the yellow contents of the syringe.

'I thought it might be familiar to you,' Becky said.

Doctor Owen couldn't believe what he was holding in his hand. 'There's no way this can be the same treatment I've been working on. We only just made the breakthrough a few days ago.'

'Your research was a smokescreen. As long as you were developing the primary and secondary treatments, everyone at your level would assume you were the only person who could find the cure. It was designed to divert attention from the facts.'

'That the treatment had already been developed?'

'Correct.'

'But my treatment is imperfect. It works for less than twenty-four hours.'

'No, that's exactly why it's perfect. In the minds of everyone concerned, it was never supposed to be a permanent cure. No one ever wanted to wipe out the virus. They wanted ongoing treatment. There's no money in a one-shot cure.'

'You mean this is all about money?' Jane asked, raising her voice in anger and frustration.

'Not really, but it's a logical side effect of producing a pharmaceutical treatment on this scale. It is the motivation of some people at the top of the World Health Organisation but the sole driver behind the Rising is the treaty. It is written that the destiny of the two species is to co-exist.'

'What's going to happen?' Jane asked.

'The plans for the Rising are based on the vampires quickly and deliberately increasing their numbers. They will reveal themselves to the general public as allies of the powers-that-be, who want us all to exist in harmony. This will be backed up by The Brotherhood, who will provide military support under the pretence of protecting the lives of the general public.'

'What? So The Brotherhood are complicit as well?'

'Only the general and a few other key people. They had no choice, though. The treaty was signed at a time when vampires stood on the verge of overthrowing the human race. In an attempt at self-preservation, the humans agreed to population balancing and co-existence once a treatment had been developed.'

'But that was fifty years ago,' Jane said, 'Things change in such a long period of time. Surely they can't hold us to a treaty that was signed so long ago?'

'That may be true if we were dealing with humans. Politicians tend to forget their policies, re-prioritise, retire or die. However, the same vampires that signed the treaty are still around today and their priorities haven't changed. They've been waiting for this day. In the lifetime of some vampires, fifty years is nothing.'

Doctor Owen thought to himself for a moment and rubbed his face with his hands in frustration.

'So all that crap we took from the base is useless, isn't it? There's no point working on a cure if there's already one out there and the Rising is expected to begin any day now.'

'There's always the chance that a permanent cure will be found,' Becky said in an upbeat tone.

'But don't hold your breath?' Doctor Owen said, finishing her sentence for her.

'But what about Doctor Forrest?' Jane said.

'You're right,' the doctor said, 'He's our only chance. If we meet with him, we can use the samples and documents we've got to finish the work on the primary treatment. Maybe the poison is the only answer. I never thought I'd hear myself say that.'

'What do you mean?' Becky asked.

Before Doctor Owen could answer, his phone rang.

68
Meeting Roxy

As the tall wooden doors closed behind us, a loud bang of wood hitting stone echoed off the cold bare walls of the entrance hall to the vampires' lair.

The hall was huge. The ceiling was at least twenty feet high and shrouded in darkness. The only light came from the flaming wooden torches that hung at regular intervals on the walls along the full length of the hall. A massive fireplace in the middle of the opposite wall roared and crackled and warmed the hall against the cold stone walls. I struggled to imagine how long ago this lair had been carved out of the rock and how many generations of human life had passed while vampires lived down here.

Jackson handed the box of syringes to the woman in combat gear.

'Excellent,' she said, 'He will be pleased. Thank you for your work today, Jackson. You are excused. Get some rest. I'll deal with these two.'

Jackson nodded and walked away, leaving me and Skinner faced with the baddest looking woman I had ever seen. Dressed all in black, with a pistol on one side of her belt and a knife on the other, I wondered what manner of weapons were held in the multitude of pockets on her pants and vest.

'Welcome home,' she said to Skinner, completely ignoring me.

'Thank you, Roxy,' he replied, 'I thought I might never see this place again.'

'You have been away from here for a long time but I must press on with the matters at hand. What happened at the regional headquarters?'

'It all went according to plan. The bodies from Hartley House were smuggled into the base. They turned and escaped. Almost everyone at the base was killed but they managed to kill all our brothers and sisters before I could get away with the doctor. He escaped with an agent from the World Health Organisation.'

'Where did they go?'

'I don't know.'

'But you got away. How?'

'I fought my way out.'

'How did you do that?' I could tell Roxy didn't know whether to believe him or not.

'While everyone else was preoccupied with the attack, I got a chance to get away and I took it. I couldn't get the doctor but I did leave a message for The Brotherhood.'

'What was that?'

Skinner bent down and opened the metal case at his feet. Roxy looked surprised when she saw the face staring back up at her from the case. I suspected she wasn't lost for words very often.

'That's Commander North,' she said with an air of respect for our achievement in her voice.

Skinner nodded.

'Impressive,' she said, 'I will take you to Marcus. He will want to meet the man who killed such a senior member of The Brotherhood. This will be an excellent addition to his collection.'

She turned to me but kept talking to Skinner. 'And what about him?'

'I had no choice. I turned him after my escape. My hunger was uncontrollable.'

Roxy smiled. 'So you've got a taste for live flesh now? This is certainly a day for surprises. Take him down to the training room. At midnight we will need as many of our brothers and sisters as we can pull together.'

'Why is that?' Skinner asked.

'You'll see. Follow me,' she said and led us down the hall into the darkness ahead.

69
Walking In The Dark

We left the entrance hall and made our way down a corridor lit only by burning torches mounted on the walls. The ceiling was a lot lower than in the entrance hall but a draft blowing towards us made it feel colder. We stopped at a door on our right.

'Skinner, take our new brother on ahead to the training room,' Roxy said, 'then come back and meet me. Marcus will want to speak to both of us.'

Skinner started to walk away but Roxy stopped him.

'The box, leave it here.'

He set the box down on the stone floor and led me down the corridor, further and further into the darkness. We passed many doors. I tried to listen out for goings-on inside but couldn't hear a thing apart from our loud footsteps and the occasional drip of water through the walls.

'You've been here before, haven't you?' I asked.

'Yes,' Skinner replied, 'I spent my first few months as a vampire here. I expect they want to put you through the same training they gave me.'

'What kind of training?'

'Different things really. Not just combat. I learned the best ways to remain inconspicuous in the human world, the best ways to operate in daylight, that kind of thing. I'd say you've almost got the hang of flying already.' He smiled.

'I thought that son of a bitch was trying to kill me. I bet he does that to everyone.'

'You're probably right. But I do know that if you hadn't stopped falling, you wouldn't have been the first new vampire to spend their first few weeks here in the recovery room.'

I was still finding it difficult to comprehend the fact that falling down a massive chasm and hitting the jagged stone floor wouldn't kill me. Okay, it would take a long time for my body to heal but eventually it would heal and I would be back to normal. I wondered if the vampires I attacked at the outpost had fully recovered yet. Either way, I wasn't interested in seeing them ever again.

'It doesn't sound like I'll be training for long though,' I said, 'What did she mean when she said I'll be needed at midnight?'

'They must be planning an attack. I'll do what I can to find out what's going to happen. There must be some way of getting a message out to Jane and the doctor from in here.'

'And Dave. I saw his car in the town we passed through just before we got here.'

'Is that what all the throwing up was about?'

'Yes. I had to be sure it was him.'

We continued walking down the seemingly endless corridor, further into the heart of the lair.

'Can you read their minds? That's what the guy who picked us up was doing, wasn't it?'

'No, Tom. It's very difficult to control. Some have the gift but most haven't. I've never managed to develop that ability. Have you noticed any voices or images popping into your head?'

'One or two,' I said, without offering any further detail.

'It's very difficult to harness the power and focus it all on the mind of one person. Only very old and experienced vampires have a complete grasp of it. Even then, they also have to block their mind out from being read by other people.'

I crossed reading the minds of other vampires off my personal to-do list. I wasn't planning on remaining a vampire long enough to learn how to do the difficult stuff, although something told me we'd be hanging around the lair a lot longer than we'd planned to stay at the outpost.

'You know,' I said, 'We're going to have to get out of here and get back to Jane and the doc. We can't stay here forever.'

'I know. Once they've gathered all the samples together and met with Doctor Forrest, they'll have to disappear. We might not be able to find them if we can't get out of here soon.'

We reached the door at the end of the corridor. 'You've got other things to worry about right now,' Skinner said.

'Like what?'

Skinner flung the door open to reveal a huge hall carved out of the rock. A small number of vampires, maybe ten, were dotted around. Some were sparring with wooden replica swords, some flying from one side of the hall to the other. I stood in the doorway and stared up at the vampires above me as they moved through the air in formation.

'Like meeting your new classmates. See you later, Tom.'

70
'Before Sunrise Tomorrow'

Doctor Owen answered the call from the withheld number.

'Doctor Owen, isn't it?' asked the female voice on the other end.

'Who is this?'

'My name is Roxanne Maria di Santo Ramirez. But you can call me Roxy for short.'

'What do you want?'

'If my intelligence is correct, you are currently running around the city picking up scraps that you've left behind and you're planning to run away into the night with Doctor Forrest and complete your plans of saving the world.'

Doctor Owen said nothing.

'From your silence, I take it my intelligence is correct. Unfortunately I must throw a spanner into the works. You see, Doctor Forrest had the mistaken notion that he would be able to escape from us. And if that wasn't audacious enough, he thought he could run off with your wife as well.'

'What have you done with them? If you've hurt her…'

'Calm down, Doc, they're both fine. However, I need you to do something for me to secure their safety.'

'What's that?'

'When you have all of the samples and documents, you must bring them to me and I will exchange them for your wife and the doctor. Okay?'

'Let me speak to my wife.'

'I thought you might ask to speak to her so I've got her right here.'

'Andrew, don't believe her. I haven't…' Emily said, her voice filled with fear and panic.

'That's enough,' said Roxy, 'So what do you say, Doc? The samples for both of them. Seems like a fair swap to me.'

'Okay,' he sighed, 'When and where?'

'Before sunrise tomorrow. I will call you to tell you where to meet us.'

Roxy hung up. Doctor Owen rubbed his eyes with his hands and let out a roar of frustration. Taking deep breaths, he calmed himself down and explained the situation to Jane and Becky. They all looked at each other across the table with one thing on their minds.

There's nothing we can do.

'Are you sure you can trust Doctor Forrest?' Becky asked.

'Of course,' Doctor Owen said, 'We've worked together for a very long time.'

Doctor Owen had a spark of inspiration. Roxy hadn't let him speak to the doctor. Was she bluffing? He took out his mobile phone and called Doctor Forrest's number. After a few rings, there was an answer.

'Don't waste any time, Doc,' Roxy said and hung up.

'Shit!' Doctor Owen exclaimed.

'Look,' Becky said, 'All we can do is carry on what you were doing. We finish picking up the samples and work out a way to get your wife and the doctor back without doing the swap.'

'How are we going to do that?' Jane said, 'There's only three of us and we haven't got any weapons.'

'Well, that's not strictly true,' Becky said.

Becky got up and walked into the next room, coming back with a large black case in her arms. She threw it onto the table and opened it up. Before Jane and the doctor, an arsenal of pistols and silver blades made their jaws drop. It was clear that Becky was a one-woman army. She had an array of weapons that would make Rambo jealous and from what they had seen of her in action so far; she knew exactly how to use them.

'Okay,' said Becky, 'I've got an idea.'

71
Training Begins

Skinner shut the door behind me. I knew he wouldn't slam the door on me but the stone walls of the dome-shaped hall magnified the sound ten-fold. Everyone stopped what they were doing to turn round and look at me.

One man was standing on the ground, looking up at the rest of the men and women as they moved gracefully from one wall to the other and stopped where they landed. He approached me and shouted at the others. 'Get back to work! We only have a few hours.'

We shook hands. He was just under six feet tall and clad in black combat gear, with a face as pale as any vampire's. He was one of the friendlier creatures of the night I had met in my life as a vampire, a life I hoped would be mercifully short.

'Welcome. My name is Peter. I take it you're here to join this group of misfits?'

'I guess so.' As soon as I replied, I could tell he was reading into the tone of my voice.

'You're a rebirth, right?'

'It's that obvious, is it? Yes, just this morning.'

'Well, you seem to be taking it well. Some rebirths can go a bit crazy on their first day. What's your name?'

'Tom.'

'Okay, Tom. How do you feel about being a vampire?'

'Beats being dead, right?'

Peter erupted with laughter.

'Exactly. That's the best attitude to have, Tom. I'll start you off easy with these guys but be warned: they're coiled tightly and ready to pounce. You see, there was an attack on the humans yesterday and they weren't allowed to go. Neither was I. They didn't want to send everyone out for the attack, so now we're all looking forward to tonight's operation.'

'What's happening tonight?'

'Honestly? I don't know. All I know is it's big. Bigger than last night. And if Roxy sent you down here then she wants us to get you involved.'

I looked at Peter blankly like I didn't know what he was talking about.

'Of course, you don't know what happened last night,' he said. I was grateful he hadn't mastered the art of reading my mind. 'We launched an attack on the humans at one of their military outposts. There were hundreds of them and only a handful of vampires. We almost wiped them all out but only Roxy got back here alive.'

Propaganda obviously isn't exclusively the domain of the human species, I thought.

'You're so lucky to be joining us now, at the beginning of the Rising.'

'Sounds exciting.'

My heart felt like it jumped into my throat. Our small band thought we were doing something important, like we could make a difference. Jane and the doctor were trailing round the city picking up bits and pieces and they thought that meeting with Doctor Forrest would give them a chance of coming up with a permanent cure. But I realised the truth.

We haven't got a chance.

How long would it take the doctor to finish his work on the cure? Weeks? Months? I had no idea what the hell this guy was talking about but something told me the Rising wouldn't stop and wait for our set of amateurs to catch up. I hadn't known any of them for a decent length of time. For all I knew, they had no hope of finding the first set of documents, never mind everything else we had to do.

'So what do you need me to do?' I asked.

'We haven't got long,' Peter said, 'We'll need to get you through some of the basics. I haven't been told much but what I do know is that the mission will be fairly simple. No weapons, no direct combat. If there is a problem, the only ability we will need is to fly away.'

'Okay. Sounds pretty cryptic to me.'

'I know, but missions this critical cannot be revealed until just moments before they begin. With a bit of luck we'll be able to feed tonight.'

With that comment, the feeling of belonging that had been growing inside me during our conversation left me alone with this bloodsucker. He may have been charismatic, but he still stood for everything I didn't want to become.

'Have you flown yet?' he asked.

'Well, I fell half way to the floor when Roxy's friend threw me down the big hole outside.'

He laughed again. 'That's a good start. Falling halfway is better than hitting the floor. When you're done here you'll be doing loop-the-loops.'

72
Return To Blackchapel

It was late afternoon when Dave made it back to the Cliffside Hotel. He was tired and confused, having spent the whole day chasing people around the city and the countryside, achieving what felt like absolutely nothing. Sneaking around the corridors with steps as light as he could manage, he got back to his room without running into the concierge and sat down in his chair by the window.

After seeing Tom and Skinner disappearing into the darkness of the mountains, he decided to check in with Agent Simpson. He took out his phone and saw that he still had no missed calls from his superiors who were supposedly looking for him.

'Dave, how are you doing?' she said as soon as she answered his call.

'Okay I guess. Feels like I've been chasing my tail all day.'

'Have you seen Tom and Skinner?'

'Yes. I've just seen them. They were being driven into the mountains. I lost them as they took a turning onto what looked like private land. I'm back at Blackchapel now.'

'Okay. Wait there for now.'

'Have you picked up everything you were looking for?'

'Not yet. We've got two more stops to make but we have met someone.'

'Who?'

'I'd better not give you too many details over the phone. I'm confident we'll be able to recover everything we need. Just stay there and keep an eye out for Tom and Skinner. I'll give you a call when we've got everything.'

They said their goodbyes and Dave was alone again. *To hell with this*, he thought as he got to his feet, *I'm not sitting here looking out of the window all day.*

Dave suspected that wherever Tom and Skinner were being taken, they would be there for a long time. After all, it was bad news for them to spend too long outside during daylight hours. He felt sure he wouldn't see them again until sunset. This gave him plenty of time to kill so he decided to explore his new surroundings.

More specifically the bar next to the hotel.

He managed to avoid the concierge on his way out of the hotel and found himself faced with a wall of rain that refused to stop. Careful not to slip on the wooden steps at the front of the hotel as he ran from the front door and across the car park to the bar, he flung the door open and stepped inside, shaking the rain from his clothes.

The bar was as dead as the rest of the tiny town. It was a sports bar with a large plasma TV hanging on the wall that would usually show football games but with no sports events worth watching, it was tuned to a twenty-four hour news channel. Thankfully, some B-list celebrity had been caught driving under the influence so the reporters had lost interest in Dave and his friends for now.

Dave cast his eyes around the dimly lit room. It was empty apart from the barman, who was leaning on the bar watching the news. Another man returned from the bathroom and perched on a stool, addressing Dave in his chirpy voice that was really beginning to become annoying.

'Hello sir,' the concierge said, 'Fancy seeing you in here. Did you have a good rest? How was your lunch?'

'Fine thanks,' Dave replied and approached the bar.

'I haven't seen you here before,' the barman said, 'Do you work at the mall?'

'No, but I'm starting to think everyone in this town does.'

The barman looked at the concierge. 'You're not too far from the truth. You want a beer?'

73
Crying

Skinner walked back up the long corridor from the training room towards the entrance hall. He was worried, but not just about whether Roxy believed him about Tom.

He was worried about what was happening to Tom. From the first day that Skinner had started to turn into a vampire, he had been able to resist his hunger. Even before he knew what changes were going on inside his body, he had trained himself to ignore the voices inside telling him that drinking human blood was the only way to stay alive, no matter how much pain he felt in his stomach.

But Tom seemed unable to resist, even for a few minutes. It was a well-known fact that great irresistible hunger brought with it great power. But at what price?

Skinner also thought of Jane and Doctor Owen. He had no way of contacting them and no way of knowing if they were being successful in their mission. *Have they been killed? Have they been captured and are they on their way here right now?*

His thoughts were interrupted by a sound from behind one of the wooden doors that lined the corridor. He stopped and put his ear to the door. Inside, a woman was crying. Not wailing, but sobbing like she had been crying for hours and had run out of tears.

Skinner looked up and down the corridor. Confident that no one was around, he knocked on the door.

'Hey, are you okay in there?' he asked in a hushed voice.

There was a brief silence inside, followed by the voice of a tired and emotional woman. 'Yes, I'm okay. Who are you?'

'I'd rather not say. What's your name?'

'Emily.'

'Emily Owen?'

'Yes. How did you know?'

'I've seen your husband.'

With that, Skinner heard her get up from wherever she was sitting and run to the door.

'Is he okay?' she whispered through the door.

'I believe so. I haven't seen him for a few hours but he was fine when I left him. He's in good hands.'

'Can you help me?'

'I'll see what I can do. I think almost everyone here will be leaving just after midnight. I'll do my best to get you out. Then we can go and find your husband.'

'Thank you. Thank you so much. Can't you tell me who you are?'

'I'm a friend. It's best if I don't tell you any more. Just try and stay calm for now. I'll be back.'

74
Learning To Fly

'Go on, Tom,' Peter said, 'Just try it.'

I was standing ten paces away from the jagged stone wall of the training hall. Pete had spent the last ten minutes trying to convince me I knew how to fly. He had told me it's programmed into us from the moment we become vampires. Our blood knows what to do and all it needs is a helping hand from our minds.

'Just run towards it as fast as you can, jump towards it, get a foothold and push yourself away with your feet.'

The look on my face told him that I wasn't as confident in my abilities as he was. I knew he must have been right though. I thought back to when I saw Officer Myers behind the hospital. He had only been a vampire for a matter of minutes and had instinctively scaled the hospital walls without thinking about it.

That's the key. Don't think about it.

I realised that my moments of gravity defiance thus far had also been instinctive. I had jumped high into the air to kill the vampires that were feeding on Commander North and stopped falling outside the vampire lair because somehow my body knew it had to be done, not because I stopped to think about it first.

To hell with it, Tom. Just do it.

I took a deep breath and sprinted for the wall. Two paces from the wall, I jumped with both feet forward, planted them and pushed away from the wall. The warmth in my legs flowed up through my body into my arms. I threw my arms forward. For a moment I was flying. I was suspended in the air without support. Another moment later, my face hit the floor.

My private curses failed to drown out the cackles I could hear from the other vampires in the hall. Peter walked over to me and extended a hand, helping me to my feet. As I got up, I felt for the syringes I still had stashed in my sock. I breathed a sigh of relief when I knew they were intact.

'Don't worry,' he said, 'That happens to everyone.'

'Great. Thanks for telling me first.'

'If I'd told you to expect to hit the ground on your first attempt, would you have felt more or less prepared?'

My silence was enough of an answer for him.

'Exactly. All you can do is keep trying.'

The other vampires were all drawing near, leaving their training positions to see who the new guy was.

'Hey Peter,' said one burly-looking man who must have stood a clear six inches taller than me, 'I hope you're not pairing him up with me tonight. I don't want to baby-sit another noob.'

'Don't worry,' Peter said, 'We're not doing this mission in pairs. Everyone has their own job but we're part of one big team. Right?'

Everyone apart from the big guy nodded their heads. He walked over to me, stood toe-to-toe and had to look down to eyeball me. 'You can just stay out of my way, okay?'

In any kind of normal situation this man mountain was the last guy I would be messing with but I had an idea. Without warning, I took a step back and punched him in the face. It was a good, fast jab that landed right on the end of his nose. I took a quick step to the side as blood sprayed from his nostrils.

'What the fuck?' he exclaimed, with tears in his eyes, 'Come here! I'm gonna tear you apart!'

With the giant in hot pursuit, I made a run for the wall. Just like my last attempt, I leapt, planted my feet and stretched my body out when I felt the warmth of my blood start to flow through my body. But unlike my last attempt, I didn't hit the ground after a couple of seconds. Instead, I kept rising. I kept my eyes focused on the stone wall directly ahead of me. Before I knew what had happened, I had reached the ceiling of the training hall.

I could hear whoops and cheers from the crowd far below me. I wanted to bask in the glory of my first flight but my inspiration was hot on my heels. I turned round to see him heading right for me. I instinctively moved to my right as quickly as I could, narrowly avoiding his charge. He hit the wall head-on and knocked himself out cold.

His huge, limp body fell from the wall towards the floor. The warmth of my blood quickly moved to my feet and I pushed myself away from the wall again. I fell towards him, faster than he was falling.

As I neared him, I reached out an arm and just managed to catch hold of his boot.

We stopped dead.

We hung in mid-air just inches above the stone floor of the training hall. The warmth spread around my body and we slowly dropped to the ground. I lowered him onto his back and I landed on my feet.

There were no whoops and cheers this time. As I looked around, all I could see were stunned faces. 'What's up?' I asked.

Peter walked up to me. 'Tom, that was incredible. Are you positive you only turned today?'

'Yes. Why?'

'Because some of your brothers and sisters here can't do what you just did and they were reborn many years ago.'

75
Hitting The Road

'Are you sure you don't want me to go with you?' Jane asked.

Becky checked her pistols were loaded and secured them in the pockets in her suit. Like a pilot going through pre-flight checks, she methodically checked each pocket and space on her belt to ensure all her equipment was loaded and accounted for.

'No,' she said, 'Without you I can take the bike. I'll be a lot quicker on my own. You have to stay here and protect the doc and your samples.'

'What if you run into trouble?'

'I don't think I will. The sun won't set for a few hours so I doubt I'll run into any bloodsuckers.'

'What about The Brotherhood?'

Becky lifted a radio out of her huge box of weapons and turned it on. The only sound it emitted was the low crackle of radio silence.

'Hear that? That channel is usually buzzing all day long. Even when there are no operations going on, there's always chatter over the radio. But today, ever since I picked you up: nothing. Either they've got bigger fish to fry or the general has called for radio silence. With a bit of luck, either of those options will keep them out of my way for the next hour or two.'

'You've got the addresses of the labs, haven't you?' Jane asked.

'Yes. I know where both of these places are. Shouldn't be too much trouble.'

'And you've got my number to call me in case there's any problems?'

Becky looked at Jane like she was answering to an over-protective mother. 'Yes, I have. What time's curfew? I want to make sure I don't get grounded.'

'Sorry,' Jane said, 'I just want to make sure we're all organised before you leave us.'

'Look, I'm not going to be long. One hour, maybe two. The doc's got plenty to do until I get back. Just wait here, keep an eye on him and keep watching the news.'

Becky put her helmet on and said her goodbyes, then closed the visor and headed for the door. Jane followed her out and watched her get into the elevator. She looked over the edge of the balcony. The rain was still pouring down. Jane thought that she'd love to be able to have nothing to worry about other than the changeable weather but the last forty-eight hours had given her so much more to think about.

Jane had been moving non-stop ever since she got the call that woke her up from her pleasant slumber and called her back into action from her holiday. She had taken the time off while Doctor Owen was finishing off work on the primary treatment, expecting to return to her superiors and receive instructions to move his work to a secure location.

Everyone's plans had disappeared into thin air when The Brotherhood decided to take the matter into their own hands and destroy the Mantek lab. Now they were on the run from The Brotherhood, the vampires and the police. And Tom... Poor Tom.

From eleven floors up, Jane heard the faint sound of an engine revving followed by the sight of Becky shooting away from the apartment block towards the city.

Grey clouds blanketed the skyline in the distance. Even though the sun wasn't due to set for a few hours, the city streets were becoming darker. Looking down, Jane saw a few street lights flicker into life, a sure sign that night time was coming in quicker than expected.

Jane turned round and went back into the apartment, locking the door behind her. Doctor Owen was sitting at the kitchen table, never looking up from his microscope. It was small and most unsuitable for the work he needed to do but it was all they could manage to take when they had escaped from The Brotherhood.

They had retrieved the samples and documents from their car, only to find that some of their hoard had been destroyed during their battle with The Brotherhood. One of the cases had taken a direct hit and had leaked infected blood all over the boot of the car. Some of the backup cartridges had taken direct hits as well, reducing them to nothing more than a pile of mangled plastic and tape. They both knew they would have to dispose of the car soon and find a new mode of transport.

He placed a small drop of blood that had been taken from Tom about twenty-four hours earlier into a petri dish and placed it under the lens with the highest magnification. He then unwrapped one of the syringes Becky had given them and removed the cap. Very carefully, he pressed the plunger and allowed one drop of the yellow liquid to fall onto the blood sample. He examined the reactions in silence for what seemed like an eternity.

'What's happening?' Jane asked.

Doctor Owen rubbed his eyes as he looked up. In addition to the tiredness that was written all over their faces, he also wore an expression of total disbelief.

'As far as I can tell, the syringes that she said she found two years ago are filled with the same treatment I developed last week.'

76
Blast From The Past

The pain in Becky's right leg was starting to grow. It usually didn't bother her too much but riding her motorbike aggravated it.

Beneath her cool exterior, she desperately hoped she could make it through the rest of her life without having to perform surgery on herself ever again. She had plenty of scars to show for her confrontations with creatures of the night and the countless attempts on her life over the past two years, but no cut was deeper than the one she had to make herself to remove a bullet from her thigh.

Becky shook those thoughts out of her head. She had spent most of the day on her bike, so the pain in her leg was just another reason to complete this mission as quickly as possible. End of story.

Now that she had some time by herself, she could reflect on the things she'd have preferred not to think about. Like being back in the open. As soon as she decided to intervene in Jane and Doctor Owen's mission, she knew it would mean that she would instantly come out of hiding, whether she liked it or not. She'd had run-ins with The Brotherhood and made connections in the real world since that night two years ago but had always maintained a low profile.

This is different.

The situation she now found herself in wasn't just helping one family break away from the clutches of a town full of vampires. It wasn't breaking into a warehouse protected by vampires to investigate the stockpiles of Virex that could be found all over the world.

The Rising is beginning. It must be stopped at any cost.

She was also thinking of the future. If they do recover the samples and meet with Doctor Forrest, they would need to find somewhere to hide out for a decent length of time if the doctors were to have any chance of completing their work. A number of people had sworn their lives to her and they had all said she could call on them at any time to help her out. Becky knew exactly who she would need to call on to help them out.

Her thoughts were interrupted by a break in the radio silence she had been monitoring on the radio in her helmet. It was a voice she hadn't heard for a very long time.

'Agent Clarkson, are you there? It's Will.'

The shock almost made her lose control of her bike. She gunned the accelerator to retain her balance.

'Agent Clarkson? Becky, are you there?'

Becky maintained her silence but Will continued.

'Becky, if you can hear me, you don't need to say anything. Just listen to what I have to say. We know what you did at the offsite storage facility. You won't be in any trouble if you come in now. Everyone here needs to know what you know. They need to debrief you. A lot has happened over the last two years. We need you to come back in.'

That little speech sounded so rehearsed, Becky wondered if her old friend had a gun pointed at his head and a script in front of him.

'I guess she's not on this channel,' Will mumbled, 'Let's try the next channel.'

As soon as Will had come back into Becky's life, he was gone.

77

Interrogation

Confident that no one had heard his conversation with Emily, Skinner made his way back through the long corridors of the vampire lair to the door where he had left Roxy.

The whole place felt like a tomb. It had been a long time since he had been there but he had never seen it so empty. The long corridors and large halls were usually buzzing with squads of vampires training and sparring. Now the only sound was Skinner's footsteps. The effect of the attack on Hartley House was plain to see. The vampires had increased their numbers considerably, but now they were back down to the levels that The Brotherhood had previously thought were normal.

How can they possibly be planning an attack now with such a small clan?

Skinner reached the door and noticed it was slightly ajar. He heard Roxy talking to Marcus inside. Skinner had met Marcus several times but didn't really know him. He always seemed very hands-off unless something major required his immediate attention, delegating many of his responsibilities to Roxy. Skinner couldn't hear what they were saying but the tone of their voices was very serious.

Skinner stood at the door for only a second before the talking stopped. He raised his hand to knock on the door but it swung open before he made contact. Roxy stood before him with an intense expression on her face that told him she was eager to get him inside and find out everything he knew. Marcus moved round his desk and sat in his chair.

'Come in, please. Take a seat,' she said and he complied with her orders.

'This is the survivor?' Marcus asked Roxy as soon as Skinner sat down in the creaky wooden chair.

'That's correct, sir.'

Roxy's interrogation began immediately and Skinner quickly began to feel like he was being cross-examined in court.

'Skinner, you survived the attack at The Brotherhood's regional base.'

'Yes, that's right.'

'How?'

'I smuggled the bodies from Hartley House into the base as planned. They turned into vampires when we expected them to. The Brotherhood were preoccupied with fighting our brothers and sisters, so I had the opportunity to get the doctor out.'

'Why didn't you?'

'There was an unforeseen complication. In addition to Doctor Owen, The Brotherhood also had an agent of the World Health Organisation in their custody. Between her and the doctor, they used the vampire attack as cover for their own escape.'

'But they are all part of the same team. Why would they want to escape from The Brotherhood?'

'They don't believe in the work they were forced to do. They believe in curing us, not killing us.'

'The secondary treatment?' Marcus asked incredulously and looked at Roxy. They both cracked a smile.

'If only they knew,' Marcus laughed.

'Yes sir,' Roxy said.

Skinner looked round, hoping they would let him in on their secret, but they didn't.

'So they somehow gave you the slip, did they? Then they hot wired a helicopter and made their getaway?'

'That's correct.'

'I'll be honest, Private. I don't like your story. Something about it doesn't add up, but for now I have no choice but to believe you.'

Skinner tried not to look like he was breathing a sigh of relief. There were no more questions for him.

Skinner noticed something sitting on Marcus' desk that hadn't qualified for his attention when he was being bombarded with questions. On a marble base, a skull was suspended on a wooden stake. Marcus noticed that Skinner had spotted it.

'You like it?' Marcus asked and turned the skull round to face Skinner.

'Impressive,' was all that Skinner could think to say.

'It's yours,' Marcus said, 'Roxy had him cleaned up for me. Commander North will take pride of place beside me from now on.'

Skinner raised his eyebrows in surprise. He was lost for words. How do you respond to someone who just told you he's had a human skull cleaned and mounted on his desk?

'Do you have a job for him?' Marcus asked Roxy.

'In the absence of any brothers or sisters who have seen action recently, Private Skinner is automatically my second-in-command. He will be leading the extraction team.'

'Extraction team?' Skinner asked, 'Is there going to be another attack? What can I do?'

Roxy looked at her watch. 'I'll need to tell everyone else soon anyway. I suppose I can give you the details now.'

78
Contact

Time passed to the end of the day without incident. The rain had stopped but the clouds were gathering, looking almost too heavy to remain in the sky above the city.

Bad weather sapped the few attractive qualities away from the city. The green belt was quickly being gnawed away by retail developers and an over-active manufacturing industry sixty years earlier had resulted in massive factories dotted all over the landscape, which were now abandoned and falling apart. The smashed or boarded up windows were a deterrent to everyone, with the exception of the homeless community that had grown in size year on year for a long time.

It's good to be back, Becky thought as she surveyed her surroundings before putting her helmet back on. The building behind her used to be a small office block but now it doubled as another inconspicuous storage facility that housed the kind of things The Brotherhood didn't want anyone else to know they had.

The only difference between this building and the site she had visited earlier in the day was that this one was empty. There was no one there at all. Only one thing was worthy of note in the whole building: a thick metal safe that had been left open. The building had been abandoned in a hurry. The soldiers who had been guarding the safe obviously received orders to get out but Becky wanted to know why they would go to the trouble of leaving the safe open for her. Surely they knew she was coming?

It had been the same story at a lab just a few blocks away. Doors open, no one home. Becky had taken what she had been sent for and walked out the front door as easily as she walked in.

Too easy.

Easy or not, Becky had what she needed. She just managed to squeeze the folder she had just liberated into her backpack, which she threw over her shoulders. Now they had until sunrise to get their heads together and work out what the hell was going on.

What are we going to do when we meet up with Doctor Forrest?

How do we know we can trust him?

Can we do anything to stop the Rising or are we just wasting our time?

Becky was about to start her bike when the speaker in her helmet crackled.

'Agent Clarkson, are you there?' asked the familiar voice.

She didn't say a word.

'Agent Clarkson, it's Will. There's no one listening in. Can you hear me?'

Becky wanted to respond, if only to share a conversation with someone she had thought she would never speak to again in her life. Even if someone was monitoring the channel she was on, they couldn't track her position and it was safe to assume they knew she had come out of hiding

What the hell.

'Hello Will.'

'Agent Clarkson,' Will whispered, 'It's so good to hear your voice. I thought you were dead for sure.'

'As good as, Will. It's good to hear your voice. I hope you're okay. What's going on?'

'I don't know for sure. I've only been moved back upstairs for the day. They want me to bring you in but luckily they all got bored listening in and left me to try all the channels by myself. I've got to be quick.'

'Okay, what have you got?'

'The Brotherhood have been ordered to abandon their positions all over the city.'

'They must be coordinating an operation. Can you find out what?'

'My access is severely restricted but I'll see what I can find out. I've got to go.'

'Thanks Will.'

'It's good to have you back, Agent Clarkson.'

Part Three

Glorious Night

79

The Visitor Arrives

High above the clouds that blocked the moonlight from the mountains, an Airbus A320 cut through the night sky, flanked by two Mirage 2000 fighter jets. As the pilots had expected, the journey had not been interrupted but with such precious cargo aboard the airliner, they knew they could never be too careful.

Inside, the Airbus was the height of luxury. Designed to seat over one hundred and fifty passengers, the interior had been ripped out and now comfortably housed a crew of twenty, a dark figure clad from head to toe in black robes and his team of six bodyguards. The windows running down the sides of the main compartment were blacked out and only a low emission from the strip lamps above cast a token amount of light over the passengers.

Seated in Italian leather chairs secured to the compartment floor in a semi-circle around their respected and feared leader, the six bodyguards all kept their silver-plated swords at their side. Their long hair almost obscured their faces as they sat in meditation, contemplating their important mission.

Protect the Lord Chancellor.

The intercom system made a low ping and crackled. 'We will shortly be passing over our destination. ETA two minutes.'

The bodyguards jumped to their feet in unison. They moved the swords from their sides and threw the straps over their shoulders, securing them on their backs. The Lord Chancellor rose to his feet and led the way to the rear of the compartment, where they waited by a custom-made double door that had been fitted into the side of the Airbus.

In the cockpit, the pilot spoke into his radio. 'Guardian Angels one and two, we have one minute till the drop.'

'Roger that,' was the reply from the pilots of both jets.

Outside, the two Mirage jets dropped away from the Airbus and spread out until they were almost half a mile away from the airliner. They continued to slow down and reduce their altitude until they were below the clouds. The Airbus also dropped and levelled off just above the cloud cover.

'Twenty seconds,' the pilot announced and hit the button to open the double doors in the main compartment. The Lord Chancellor and his bodyguards gripped the metal railings next to the door to steady themselves. Cold air rushed into the compartment and blew their hair and robes over their faces. As the doors opened fully, only a blanket of grey clouds were visible from inside the plane.

Even though they were his sworn protectors, the bodyguards rarely saw anything of the Lord Chancellor. He was so heavily decked in black that he could hide under his robes and barely be seen. Very few had ever seen his true face. Somehow the powerful wind didn't reveal the face beneath his robes.

One of the bodyguards registered the sight of the Lord Chancellor's hand on the metal railings. It was incredibly pale, almost white, and the fingers were unnaturally long and thin, with long, sharp fingernails. The bodyguard tried to fight the thoughts that were entering his mind.

The Lord Chancellor looks old.

He can't have long left, can he?

The bodyguard knew he had failed to contain his thoughts when he felt the deadly stare of the Lord Chancellor's eyes pierce his mind from beneath his black robes. Before he could do or say anything, the Lord Chancellor leapt through the open doors, into the darkness outside. The six bodyguards all followed.

The doors closed behind them, leaving all seven figures hurtling towards the mountains below. The bodyguards swooped round the Lord Chancellor to form a protective circle. The Mirage jets flew in sweeping arcs, forming a second circle around the falling team. One thousand feet from ground level, the jets pulled up and continued to circle around the target landing zone, a deep, dark chasm hidden from the casual view of anyone passing through the mountains.

Five hundred feet from ground level, the Lord Chancellor and his bodyguards stopped falling and started to fly. They adjusted their direction and swooped in a long line over the clearing where a small number of empty cars were parked. Falling deep into the chasm, they all stopped in mid-air just in front of the wooden platform at the front door to Marcus Verrico's lair.

Two vampires dressed in black were standing guard on the platform. When they saw the figures floating before them, they knew exactly who they were. They nodded and disappeared inside the door, closing it behind them. After a short wait, the doors were flung open. Marcus and Roxy stepped out onto the platform. They knelt on one knee and bowed their heads.

The Lord Chancellor nodded and they got to their feet.

'Welcome, Lord Chancellor,' Marcus said, 'It is an honour to have you here. Please, come inside.'

80
Stakeout For One

Dave was staring out of a window again. Just as it had been all afternoon, the bar was empty and he sat in the corner watching the small volume of traffic go by.

He had breathed a sigh of relief when the concierge decided to go back to work and leave him alone in the bar. There was something about his over-energetic brand of wanting to please the customer at any cost that wound Dave up the wrong way. It was like the chain store owners that wanted to give their customers an 'experience' when all they should do is let their valued customers buy what they want and get the hell out of there.

Thankfully the barman was at the opposite end of the talkative spectrum and only ventured over to Dave's table to bring the food he'd ordered and to refresh his glass once in a while. Dave had quickly switched from beer to soft drinks when he realised he may be waiting a long time for Tom and Skinner to go through Blackchapel.

For all he knew, they could have gone past already. For the second time in a day, Dave was doing the best he could as a stakeout force of one and he resigned himself to the fact that he didn't have much choice. Jane and the doctor seemed to be getting everything they needed so he tried to convince himself that if anything came from his investigations, it would be a bonus.

It was his job to find out who attacked the police station. He'd managed that pretty quickly but that had led him to try and keep an eye on Tom as best he could. It was starting to get dark outside though and it would be more and more difficult to see the vehicles going past on the road, never mind the people inside them.

The noise of a lower league football game on the big screen was interrupted when the bar door was flung open and thirty or so men and women swarmed inside, chatting and laughing loudly. They spread around the bar like they were invading the building, dividing and conquering the free tables. Within seconds a crowd had gathered by the bar and the barman reacted as quickly as he could be bothered to.

Dave found it odd that most of the new arrivals were looking at him. Not just glancing in his direction like you might do a double take at a stranger, but every so often one of them gave him the once-over. Then without invitation two young dudes with long hair sat down opposite him.

'Hey man, I'm Ali. This here's Bill. We haven't seen you here before.'

Dave extended his arm and they both shook hands with him.

'My name's Dave. I've just arrived here today. I'm waiting on a friend.'

'I hope you're not planning on going skiing, dude. After the heat wave and the rain, whatever snow's left up on the mountains is gonna be some seriously slushy shit.'

'No, I'm not sure what our plans are to be honest.' Dave looked around the bar at the crowd that had just arrived and quickly changed the subject. 'Do you know all these people? Where did they all come in from?'

'Our bus just got back. You know the Morningside Mall?'

'Oh right, you're the guys that work at the mall? The concierge was telling me that you guys were staying in the hotel during the off season.'

'Yeah man, pretty sweet deal, isn't it? Bus into work every day, everyone's got their own room in the hotel. Can't wait for the snow to come back, then we can do so serious boarding. Ain't that right, Bill?'

Bill had been silent up to this point but chose that moment to agree with Ali by making a noise that to Dave sounded like 'Yaw', and went back to looking at his bottle of beer.

'Sounds pretty good,' Dave said, 'I've never heard of arrangements like this.'

'Naw, I don't think they tell many people about it. I don't think they want everyone in the world to know about it.'

'So this is the deal every night? Work all day, drink all night?'

'Pretty much, man,' he nudged Bill, who was still enthralled by his beer bottle, 'Don't know about you, dude, but tonight I've got to eat.'

'Yaw.'

81
Picking Thoughts

Silence washed over the lair as the Lord Chancellor stepped inside the entrance hall. He turned to one of his protectors, the bodyguard who had let his thoughts betray him on board the plane, and muttered just two words to him in a voice that was almost too low to hear.

'Ten minutes.'

The bodyguard stepped back onto the wooden platform outside the main doors and jumped far into the air, disappearing into the sky above.

Ten minutes was longer than the Lord Chancellor usually spent with any clan. He hardly ever ventured outside his secure compound and when he did, everyone worked hard to get him back there as soon as they could. No one was sure exactly how old he was but he was widely regarded as the oldest vampire in the world and he didn't reach whatever age he was by inviting assassination attempts by staying out in the open.

High above the lair, the bodyguard rose out of the chasm and unclipped a radio from his belt. 'Ten minutes, but be ready in five,' he said into the radio.

'Understood,' was the crackly reply.

He returned the radio to his belt and flipped his body over, free falling headfirst back into the chasm. His feet hit the wooden platform with a thump, crouching to take the impact of his dramatic landing. He got to his feet and stepped inside the entrance hall. Resident vampires closed the large wooden doors behind him.

The Lord Chancellor stood in silence opposite Marcus and Roxy, who were doing their best to hide the fear that gripped them from head to toe. He raised a white, shrivelled hand. The resident vampires followed the lead of bodyguards and filed out of the hall into an adjoining chamber.

Marcus and Roxy were alone with the Lord Chancellor. The torches on the wall and the roaring fireplace did nothing to combat the deep cold they felt on their skin. The hairs on the back of their necks stood to attention as the Lord Chancellor took a step forward. Never in the centuries of their existence had they felt fear as pure as the feeling that was making them quiver involuntarily.

Marcus opened his mouth to speak but the figure approaching him stuck a finger out from beneath his robes, pointing directly at Marcus' face.

The black robes flowed all the way to the ground, obscuring the Lord Chancellor's feet, so that he appeared to slide across the floor. He stopped almost toe-to-toe with Marcus. Face to face at long last with his leader, the one man he respected almost as much as he feared, Marcus was frozen to the spot. Even though they were just inches apart, Marcus saw nothing but shadows beneath the robes.

But he felt something.

He's in my mind.

The Lord Chancellor was motionless, but Marcus could tell he was using every ounce of strength to delve into the depths of his mind. He wanted to know about what happened to Luca, his deputy who Marcus had murdered, and he was going to dig as deeply into Marcus' mind as he could to get what he wanted.

Is this it?

Is this the end?

Is he going to kill me?

But Marcus had murdered Luca with good reason. Luca was nothing more than a brown-nose who threatened to screw up the plans Marcus and Roxy had intricately planned. The plans that would bring the vampires towards their rightful place as rulers over the humans.

The Rising.

With that final thought, the Lord Chancellor took a step back. He turned to Roxy and stared deep into her eyes, picking memories from her mind with the ease of picking low-hanging apples from a tree. Within seconds, he was finished with Roxy. As he turned away from his subjects, his bodyguards left the chamber and followed him towards the main doors.

Roxy and Marcus looked at each other with confusion painted all over their faces. The trailing bodyguard stopped and turned to face them.

'The Lord Chancellor wishes to **thank** you for your hospitality. It is with regret that he must leave your **home** as quickly as he arrived.

He knows that you did what you did for good reason. You are both true believers in the cause and he wants you to know that he is very happy for you to take the lead in these early stages of the Rising. He wishes you all the best for your operation tonight. You can expect to hear from him again following its success.'

Two bodyguards opened the wooden doors. One by one, the group of visitors leapt into the air and disappeared from view. Marcus and Roxy looked at each other and didn't need to read each other's minds to know what they were thinking.

Luca deserved to die. If we hadn't killed him, this never would have been possible.

82
First Mission

The big guy I'd socked in the nose wasn't the only one of my new brothers and sisters who was giving me a wide berth. Over the past few hours his nose had healed itself but the feeling of animosity remained.

For a brief period, maybe five minutes, a strange sensation hit me, like a dark cloud had formed over my mind. I noticed that everyone around me stopped talking and continued to work as if someone was watching them. Then, just as quickly as the feeling had arrived, it was gone and everyone started talking again.

However, there was another new feeling that I enjoyed very much. The feeling of free flight was addictive. I couldn't get enough. For hours I had been swooping from one side of the training hall to the other. With practice I was learning to control my speed mid-flight.

On my first flight I had almost slammed into the stone ceiling. At first I thought of flying like swimming in the air but I quickly realised there was a significant difference. Whereas the water causes drag that slows a swimmer down, there is only gravity to slow me down in flight and the blood flowing around my body was working with forces stronger than gravity. So when I found myself hurtling towards a stone wall, I had to tell myself that I wanted to slow down. After that, my body seemed to do the rest itself.

I was confident I could pull off the loop-the-loop Peter had told me was possible but I resisted the urge. Everyone else was putting a large distance between themselves and me and I didn't want another reason for them to give me the cold shoulder. After all, if Peter was to be believed I'd have to work with all of them before the end of the night. The thought of joining the vampires on a trip to attack and kill humankind didn't fill me with warm fuzzy feelings though.

One by one, the figures around me dropped to the ground and I found myself the last one to notice that Roxy had entered the hall. I followed suit, practicing my landing which had become more graceful as the night had progressed. I was aware the syringes were still in my sock and breathed a sigh of relief every time I landed and didn't hear them break.

We all stood in a semi-circle in front of Roxy, who was joined by Skinner. My brothers and sisters around me all stood to attention and I uncomfortably attempted to do the same.

'This won't take long,' Roxy said, 'I appreciate you've been training all day and you will be allowed a short time to rest before the operation begins.'

She had the whole room gripped, eagerly awaiting the news of their first mission together. No one knew what to expect, but they couldn't have dreamed what she had planned for us.

83
Plans

Roxy cast her eyes across everyone standing before her and took a deep breath.

'Tonight will be a glorious night for our kind. Our numbers will grow at a rate that has been unprecedented in more than fifty years. You will all play your part. At midnight you will leave here. We have two buses waiting at ground level. One will take most of you, led by Peter, to the airport; the others will head for the coast, led by Skinner.

'The team heading to the airport will board flight BA159. You will have no problems getting through the check-in process. We have allies at every point along the path through to the plane, including the pilot. You will board the plane and take your seats at previously reserved strategic positions. Five minutes after take-off, gas will be released into the ventilation system that will put all the humans on board to sleep. You will then…'

'How will we stay awake?' a voice from the group piped up.

'At take-off you will mark the time on your watches. After five minutes you will put on the gas masks that will be stowed under your seats. Peter will have everything he needs to review the finer details of the mission with you on the way to the airport. Please do not interrupt me again.

'With the gas masks you will each find a supply of hypodermic needles. Between you, you will use them to inject everyone on board the plane with the blood of one of our brothers. You will have exactly five minutes to complete this section of the mission and return to your seats. Exactly ten minutes after take-off, the pilot will crash the plane into the sea. Skinner and the rest of you will be waiting on board a boat, ready to take the bodies back to land, where they will be stored until they complete their rebirth.'

Roxy looked at her watch and turned to Peter. 'Finish your preparations. I expect everyone at ground level in one hour.'

'Understood,' he said.

I was in shock as Roxy left the hall. Skinner stayed behind and approached me.

'Holy shit, Skinner,' I exclaimed under my breath when I was sure we weren't in ear shot of anyone else in the hall, 'This is mass murder. What the fuck are we going to do?'

'I don't know, Tom. They're keeping you and me apart. I'm not sure if that's because they don't trust me. I'm supposed to take two of these guys in here and pilot a fake coastguard boat to the crash site. I don't have any choice. I can't see a way out of it.'

'Can we contact the airport first?'

'I haven't got access to a phone. But if we call the airport and they stop the flight, they're bound to work out it was us that made the call. Even then, they probably won't do anything. You heard what she said: they've got people on the inside.'

We turned futile thoughts over in our heads.

'Look,' Skinner said, 'I've found the doctor's wife. She's being held here. I'm going to try and give her the chance to get out when we leave. I'll see what I can do to let you get away as well, once we pick you up.'

'You mean after the crash?'

'If you survive it, of course.'

84
Shouting And Screaming

Skinner chose to ignore Tom's reply to his suggestion that he might not make it back to dry land. They said their goodbyes and Skinner left the training hall.

He had been hoping to hang back from Roxy and Jackson so he could have another quiet moment to talk to Emily. Looking up and down the corridor once more, he knocked on the door to her cell when he was confident no one was looking.

'Emily, are you there?'

'Who is it?' she asked.

'I've got an idea of how to help you try and get out of here, but I need your help.'

'Thank you so much. What can I do?'

'I need you to scream as loud as you can and bang on the door. Shout and scream like you're going to kill yourself. If you're dead then they'll have no leverage over your husband. That'll give me a chance to get in to your cell and help you.'

She paused for a moment. 'Do you think you can do that?' Skinner asked.

'Yes,' she said with a renewed confidence in her voice, 'I'll do it.'

Skinner looked up and down the corridor again. The coast was clear. 'Okay,' he said, 'Ready when you are, Emily.'

With that, she started to scream at the top of her lungs. Even from behind the wooden door, her screams echoed off the stone walls and down the corridor. Her threats to kill herself could be heard up and down the lair.

Excellent, Skinner thought, *Here's my chance.*

He ran as fast as he could down the corridor, even breaking into partial flight as he took longer and longer strides. Roxy and

Jackson were waiting at the end of the corridor with inquisitive looks on their faces.

'What the hell is going on down there?' Roxy asked Skinner as he met them.

'It's Emily. She's threatening to kill herself!'

Roxy turned to Jackson. 'Get the key and shut her up.'

'No, wait,' Skinner protested, 'Let me go.'

'Jackson, get the key. What are you talking about?'

'We need to keep her alive, don't we? You're not going to keep her calm by tying her down. I've met her husband. I can set her mind at rest and calm her down. Let me prove it to you.'

Roxy thought about it until Jackson returned with the key.

'Give him the key,' she said, 'Let's see if he's a social worker as well as a soldier.'

Jackson held out the key and Skinner snatched it out of his hand, immediately running back down the corridor. He knew Jackson and Roxy would follow but he needed every second away from prying eyes as possible. Reaching the door, he turned the key in the lock and stepped inside, shutting the door behind him.

'Keep screaming,' he said under his breath for only Emily to hear.

Emily looked tired, really tired, like she hadn't slept for days. Skinner suspected her shoulder length hair was usually immaculately maintained but now it was matted and hanging over her face. Her eyes were red raw, the result of non-stop crying. Skinner knew Roxy and Jackson would be behind the door by now, so he'd better start proving his worth.

'Calm down, Emily,' he said softly, lowering his hands, palms down in a calming motion, 'What's wrong?'

'I can't take it!' she screamed, 'I can't take it any more!' Skinner was very impressed by her performance.

'Calm down. Please, calm down. There's no need for this. We'll have you back with your husband before you know it. It's just going to take time.'

'My husband? What do you know about my husband?'

'I've seen him. I saw him yesterday and I'm certain he's still out there, doing all he can to see you again. You just have to give it time.'

'It's so difficult. I feel like I can't go on.'

'You can make it through this, Emily. You have to.'

Emily sat down and cast Skinner a questioning look. He gave her the thumbs up.

'Can I get you anything? Maybe some water?' Skinner asked, nodding his head.

'Yes. I'd like some water. Thank you.'

Skinner turned and left the room, finding himself faced with Roxy and Jackson. He locked the door behind him and led them back up the corridor away from Emily's cell.

'Well done,' Roxy said.

'Thank you,' Skinner said, 'Sometimes you just get a feeling about someone, don't you?'

Roxy nodded her head but had a look on her face like she had something else on her mind. Skinner left Roxy and Jackson, his mind on getting a glass of water to Emily and setting up her chance of escape.

85
Snooping

Doctor Owen had spent the past few hours running more tests on the substance that was contained in the syringes Agent Clarkson had given him. The more he tested it, the more confident he became that his treatment and this mysterious yellow liquid were one and the same.

How is this possible?

Jane had used the hour or so of down time as an opportunity to do a bit of snooping. She wanted to find out what kind of woman Becky Clarkson was but there weren't too many clues dotted around the bare apartment. Jane wasn't surprised. If Becky had to move around a lot, or had to be able to bail at any time, it was hardly surprising there were no photos of friends and family to be found.

Doctor Owen barely acknowledged her presence as she returned to the kitchen table and began to examine the contents of the weapons case Becky had flashed before their eyes. There were a few blank spaces where Becky had tooled up before leaving them earlier, but there was still a veritable arsenal in front of them. Pistols, daggers, silver-plated throwing stars, grenades and all manner of weapons that Jane didn't recognise. All had their own slot carved into the foam inlay.

Looking inside the case, then outside and back inside again, Jane realised the base of the inlay didn't go all the way down to the bottom of the case. She found two small handles cut into the foam and wedged her fingers in to lift out the top layer. Underneath, she discovered pieces of a dismantled long-range rifle with a powerful telescope. In the bottom right corner of the second layer of the case was a tray full of the longest silver bullets Jane had ever seen.

Vampire sniper.

She returned the top layer to the case and drew her gun as she heard a noise at the front door.

'It's me,' Becky said as she entered the kitchen. She emptied the contents of her backpack onto the kitchen table. Jane moved the weapons case onto the floor to make room for the tumbling documents and flasks, which Jane immediately picked up and placed in the freezer.

'Is that everything?' Becky asked, and for the first time in a long time Doctor Owen looked up from his microscope.

'Yes, that looks like everything. Thank you,' he said, and returned his full attention to the samples of blood he was treating.

'Did you have any trouble?' Jane asked.

'None at all,' Becky said, 'The sites were abandoned. The doors were wide open and everything I was looking for was left out, as if they were expecting me.'

'Well, there's nothing we can do now until the morning. We've got everything Doctor Forrest needed and now we have to turn it over to the vampires.'

'Not if I can help it,' Becky said, 'I'm sure the vampires don't know about me. They'll only be expecting the doctor, maybe you as well. We've got that on our side. Anything on the news?'

'Nothing new. I'm worried that we haven't heard anything from Tom or Skinner either.'

'I'm sure your friends would let us know if they were in any trouble.' Becky patted Doctor Owen on the shoulder. 'Come on, guys,' she said, 'We've undoubtedly got another hard day tomorrow. The sun rises in a few hours. I think it would be a good idea if we all got some rest.'

86
A Long Long Time Ago

Doctor Edward Forrest had lost count of the number of times he had checked on the syringes he had prepared for the mission. With ten of his brothers and sisters preparing to board British Airways flight 159, he had packed ten cases each containing twenty-five syringes. The Boeing 737 would seat one hundred and eighty-nine passengers so he was confident there would be enough to go round.

With all ten cases stacked neatly on his workbench, his attention turned to another set of syringes. He was eternally grateful to Jackson for collecting his supply of Virex for him. He had expected the operation at Hartley House to be successful, they all had, so he was unable to stock up on the treatment he desperately needed. It was necessary for them to maintain a low profile, at least for another day or so.

He rolled up his left sleeve, reached for the small plastic box on his workbench and picked out a packaged syringe. He tore off the plastic wrapper and cast it aside, having lost track of the many thousands of times he had done that before. Without having to tap his arm with his right hand, the vein rose as he looked at it and stayed there as he took the cap off the syringe and tapped the bubbles out of the yellow liquid inside.

What a beautiful creation. What would I have become were it not for this concoction?

Edward Forrest cast his mind back to a special day in his life. His wife, who had come down with a terrible fever, turned to her husband, a pharmaceutical expert. He used her as a guinea pig to develop a makeshift treatment that kept her alive for three months. But on the day when he was preparing the largest batch of the treatment, with a view to seeing her through the coming winter, she was overcome with emotion and became someone that the doctor didn't recognise.

As he approached her with a dose of his creation, she sunk her teeth into his arm. He couldn't believe his eyes as she feasted on the blood that flowed from his veins. From that day forward, he had devoted every waking hour to developing his treatment.

Such a long long time ago, he thought.

His journey to the past was cut short as Roxy entered the room. She saw that he was about to take the treatment and started to excuse herself. The doctor didn't bat an eyelid.

'Don't worry,' he said to her, 'This won't take a second. It's been many years since this knocked me out.'

He pushed the needle into his vein and injected the yellow liquid into his bloodstream. The familiar pain spread around his body, the kind of pain that becomes more and more easy to handle with experience. He felt his mind drift away for a second then snapped back to reality.

'Now then, Roxy,' he said, 'I take it you've come for the syringes?'

Roxy nodded.

'They're all here. Ten packs of twenty-five. Has there been any indication of intervention?'

'None at all.'

'Excellent. It should be a walk in the park.'

87
Leaving The Lair

I spent the next hour doing what I had been learning to do for most of the day: soaring like an eagle from one side of the training hall to the other.

Well, probably more like a baby eagle. I was alone again but it gave me the chance to teach myself to change direction and move up and down in mid-air. Even though I was growing in confidence with my new skills, I hoped to God that I didn't have to use them as the night moved on.

The feelings of my brothers and sisters were becoming stronger and stronger. I didn't know if that was because I was venturing further down the path to the point of no return or if it was because everyone's feelings were so strong. I could tell they were all growing in confidence. The idea of leading the Rising against the humans was giving everyone an increased sense of optimism and self-importance.

'Over here everyone!' Peter shouted from far below, 'We're moving out!'

For the last hour I had been hoping Skinner would walk back through the door and tell Peter I was being excused from the night's operation. As the minutes ticked by, this pipe dream failed to become a reality and I realised that I would have to come to terms with the fact that I was going to be on that flight. I had no choice but to go through with their plan.

I weighed up the options in my head. If I made a break for freedom when we got outside, either I'd be caught or they'd turn on Skinner. Ditto if I made a run for it at the airport, which would be even more dangerous for me if there were indeed men on the inside looking out for us. If I tried to stop the operation while we were on the plane, I would almost certainly be overpowered and killed by everyone else on the team. If I tried to cause a scene on the plane, I would put the passengers in even more danger.

It didn't matter which way I looked at it, there was no way I could stop them infecting a large number of innocent people.

I resigned myself to the fact that I had no choice and dedicated my thoughts to keeping in mind the possibility of following the operation as far as I could. Roxy hadn't told us where the bodies were being taken following the crash. There was a plan for the bodies when we had finished with them and I had to find out what it was and where they were being taken.

I let go of the wall and glided down to the ground, touching down with a thump but still managing to stay on my feet. I joined my brothers and sisters and Peter led us out of the training hall.

I followed the single-file line as we marched up the corridor and turned down another corridor to the right before we reached the entrance hall. After another twenty or so paces we reached a tight spiral staircase carved into the rock. One by one we stomped up the stairs that seemed to go on forever and ever. Flaming torches were built into recesses in the walls but they were few and far between and light was low all the way to the top. Unable to see clearly, I stubbed my toe on the next step a few times.

I tapped my brother in front of me on the shoulder.

'Hey, why do we have to walk up these stairs? Why can't we just fly up to the top like normal?'

'They do this to get us used to walking around like humans,' he said, 'It's supposed to get us out of the habit of flying and start acting like normal people.'

With each step I remembered how far I had fallen into the chasm. My legs started to ache but before they started to burn with the build-up of lactic acid, I felt the warmth of my blood flow from my upper body down to my thighs and calves. I felt a little light-headed but from that moment on the pain in my legs disappeared. Suddenly I felt like I could have run up and down those steps all day long.

My blood spread out around the rest of my body when we reached the top. Another small corridor lay ahead with a wooden door at the end. Peter marched us through the door, round a patch of trees and bushes that concealed the entrance, and out onto a familiar clearing.

Even though I knew we had spent a long time in the vampires' lair, I was still surprised to see that darkness had fallen outside. Clouds above obscured our view of the stars and the only light came from the headlights of the vehicles in front of us, which cast long shadows of my new brothers and sisters across the grass. I spotted the car Jackson had picked us up in, along with two large coaches.

Roxy was waiting for us and walked up to Peter. 'Pick two of our brothers to join the recovery team.'

Peter turned round and pointed at me and the vampire I had followed up the stairs. 'Him and him.'

'Not him,' Roxy said, looking right at me. Peter picked out another member of our squad and the two chosen ones walked over to her.

Now I was really worried. It was clear that she wanted to keep me and Skinner apart.

Is it me or Skinner she doesn't trust? Or does she know exactly what's going on?

'Good luck to all of you,' she said to us and turned to the other two vampires, 'You two, come with me.'

'Right then,' said Peter, 'Let's do it.'

88
Losing The Edge

'Another beer?' Ali asked.

'No thanks,' Dave said, finally managing to put a stop to the long line of beers that had been bought for him all night long by his new friend and his silent partner.

'Come on, man. Just one more.'

'No, I've really got to hit the sack now. Thanks anyway.'

Dave got to his feet, realising the night had passed him by. Even though he had been keeping one eye on the road outside, he had lost track of time. One too many drinks had made him lose his edge. In an effort to maintain his watch on the window next to him, he had avoided visiting the men's room and his bladder now felt like it was bursting at the seams.

'Okay man, have a good night's sleep,' Ali said and shook hands with Dave.

'Well you guys better hit the sack as well if you're back at work tomorrow.'

'Don't worry about us, man. We'll be okay. Got a big day ahead of us tomorrow.'

'Oh yeah, what's that?'

'Big sale at the department store. Got a real early start. Doors open at five, but we're in at seven with the second group.'

Dave looked at his watch. It had just gone midnight. 'Clock's ticking, guys.'

'Nah, we don't need much sleep, man. Ain't that right, Bill?'

'Yaw.'

Dave left the bar and nearly fell as he slipped on the wet floor outside the door. It had stopped raining and the air was humid. He would have thought the rumbling noise that filled the air was thunder were it not for the two coaches that thundered past the hotel.

Do I get in the car and follow them? What if Tom isn't on one of those coaches?

Dave wasn't exactly light on his feet at the best of times, and after more than a couple of beers he decided to return to his room and continue his vigil by the window.

What the hell am I doing here? Dave thought to himself, *Stuck in the ass-end of nowhere waiting on a car going past that may or may not contain my friend. And what am I supposed to do when it does go past?*

After protecting his wife and children, who he hoped were tucked up in a motel somewhere up the coast where no one could find them, finding his friend and partner was his highest priority but Dave had a pressing concern growing in his stomach. More specifically just below his stomach.

Breaking into a jog, he made his way across the car park, up the front steps to the hotel and through the main entrance. None of the elevators were available so he ran up the stairs, praying his key card would work first time when he reached the door to his room. Thankfully it did and Dave made it to his bathroom just in time.

Back in the bar, Ali returned to his table and sat down next to Bill, handing his buddy one of the two beers he had in his hands.

'Feeling hungry, Bill?'

'Naw man, not yet.'

'Okay. We'll wait a while but I tell you, I gotta eat tonight, man.'

89
Dreams

Our coach was in the lead, charging round the tight bends in the road after we left the place I hoped I wouldn't have to call home ever again.

As we sped through Blackchapel, I looked out of the window and spotted Dave's car in the car park outside the hotel. I didn't know how or when I was going to see him again but it was comforting to know where an ally could be found.

I turned my attention to the pile of clothes I'd sat down next to. Upon boarding the coach, Peter had told everyone to find a change of clothes that looked good for them. Mine was a dark grey suit and blue shirt. Taking the hint from everyone else on board that privacy isn't a God-given right of vampires, I stripped down and slipped into my new attire.

As I removed my trousers I managed to transfer the syringes in my sock to the inside pocket of the suit jacket without being seen. The suit wasn't a perfect fit but was a little too big instead of a little too small, which is always the preferable option if you're not picking your own clothes.

At the front of the coach, Peter got to his feet and picked a handful of medical zip-up cases from the seat next to him.

'Listen up everyone!' he announced and started to walk down the coach, handing out a case to every one of the troops, 'I'm going to give each one of you one of these cases. Each case contains twenty-five syringes. There will be no more than two hundred targets on the plane, including the crew. You will each be responsible for treating twenty targets. Your reserved seats are arranged so that your targets will be seated in the rows across from you and behind you. Remember: work fast. You will only have five minutes from the moment the gas is released.'

Peter returned to the front of the coach and sat down. I inspected the case he'd dropped onto the empty seat next to me. I unzipped the case to reveal my ammunition and a plane ticket. The movement of the coach made the vampire blood shake around inside the syringes.

Certain death for twenty-five people. I hope you can live with yourself, Tom.

It had been a long day and I was sure I was going to have a long night so I decided to close my eyes for a few seconds. I wondered where Jane and Doctor Owen were and hoped they were safe.

Have they already met up with Doctor Forrest? Are they hard at work on the cure for me right now?

I doubted the answer to either of those questions was yes but I allowed myself a little hope. For the first time in twenty-four hours my thoughts turned to Sarah, my wife who had been killed five years ago. I pictured us sitting in the park, eating dinner in our favourite restaurant and doing all the things we loved to do together.

She was beautiful. I told myself then as I do now that I didn't deserve her. She was punching way below her weight when she settled for me and I wished she was still around today for me to tell her how much I loved her.

My thoughts then turned to someone else from my past. Michael Hudson. The man who had brutally beaten my beautiful Sarah to death with a baseball bat. I could see him standing in our kitchen, splattered with blood as Sarah lay on the floor, seconds from death. Michael knelt down beside her. He leaned over her and whispered something in her ear, then opened his mouth and sunk his teeth into her neck.

I lurched awake and heard Peter shout, 'We're here, people. Let's go.'

90
Boarding The Plane

I tried my best to cast my insane dreams from my mind and focus on the job in hand. The dream had been vivid, so realistic, but I knew it was just my exhausted mind playing tricks on me.

Everyone stood up but Peter had one more thing to say to us before we left the coach.

'We're going to go into the airport one at a time. We've got people on the inside but that doesn't mean we won't arouse suspicion if we all go in together. We won't need to go through luggage check-in so head directly for departures and follow the signs for flight BA159. See you on the plane.'

Peter stood at the end of the coach and waved us all off. One by one my brothers and sisters left the coach and made their way towards the main terminal building. The syringe packs had straps on them that we used to secure them round our waists. As I reached the front of the coach I asked Peter a question.

'What do we say if anyone asks to look inside these cases?'

'Just tell them you've got a medical condition and you might need to treat yourself on the plane. Trust me though, no one will ask to look inside them.'

As the last of my brothers and sisters made their way into the main terminal building, I left the coach and did my best to walk naturally across the road. My heart was pounding, which made me wonder whether this was just due to nerves and if my body actually still had a biological need for my heart to beat.

If my heart's still beating, do the rest of my internal organs still work? Is it still possible to save my body?

I reached the main entrance to the terminal and was faced with a sight I hadn't seen for a long time. It had been many years since I had flown and even longer since I took a holiday. Feelings of nostalgia and sadness gripped me as I took in the sight of countless families waiting in line to pack their luggage onto the planes that would take them to far away lands for a well-deserved break.

Some of you aren't going to get there. We're going to turn you all into vampires.

Massive flat screens hanging from the ceiling showed which gates everyone had to go to. I looked up BA flight 159 and headed for gate four. Without a second thought, I walked past all the retail outlets where I would normally have spent a small fortune on music and aftershave if I had been heading away with Sarah without a care in the world.

Instead I headed directly for the departure lounge, where a long queue for security checks was waiting. Standing at the back, I looked down the line. I couldn't see anyone from the coach.

Did they make it through already? Have they all been found out?

The line seemed to take an eternity to shuffle towards the security team. With each step forward I was getting more and more nervous. A member of the security team kept walking up and down the line looking at everyone. On one of his journeys past, he stopped right next to me and looked me in the eye.

'Sir, will you come with me?'

I didn't know what to do. 'Me? Why me?'

'Come with me please, sir.'

With no other alternative, I followed him past the line of passengers waiting to walk through the metal detectors and put their hand luggage through the X-ray machines. He unhooked a rope barrier and we walked round the security section towards a door in the corner of the room.

'Where are we going?' I asked, my voice breaking slightly with fear. I received no response.

He opened the door and asked me to walk through. Very reluctantly I did so, expecting to see a tiny room where I would be held and probably beaten, but instead I was faced with the departure lounge. People who had made it through the security checks were milling around the retail outlets and enjoying their last coffee or something stronger before they boarded their flights.

I turned round and quizzically stared at him.

'Good luck my brother,' was all he said and shut the door behind him.

Peter was right. They're everywhere in here.

I heard the call of the public address system announcing that my flight was now boarding and made my way towards gate four. As I arrived at the gate I recognised the faces of my fellow vampires. Some were drinking coffee, some were reading the early editions, but all of them were blending in with the crowds. No one knew what was about to happen.

The cabin crew were checking tickets and ushering people onto the plane. I showed my ticket and made my way down the tunnel and was greeted by more members of the cabin crew as I boarded the plane. I was shown to my seat by the window and removed my case of syringes, placing it in the pocket attached to the seat in front.

Peter was right again. No one asked me about the case.

The one thing I hoped above all was that no one would sit down in the two seats next to me. I needed some semblance of privacy to get my head round what I had no choice in doing.

My hope was not realised. Two people sat down next to me: a tall man who looked to be about thirty-five years old sat on the end and his daughter sat down between us. He was wearing jeans and a jumper and was well built. His daughter was wearing jeans and a pink jumper, with her long brown hair tied in a ponytail. She couldn't have been any older than eight and was quite possibly the cutest kid I'd ever seen.

'Hello mister,' she said, 'My name's Poppy. What's your name?'

91
Making New Friends

'Don't bother the nice man,' her father said.

'No, it's okay,' I said and did my best to smile naturally at the little girl, 'My name is Tom. Are you going on holiday?'

'I'm going to live with my mummy.'

I looked at her father, who was hiding the sadness in his mind beneath the obvious love for his child. Poppy opened the tiny pink bag she had carried onto the plane, took out a puzzle book and pen and turned her attention to a half-completed crossword.

'It didn't work out between her mother and me,' her father said, seemingly desperate for someone to talk to. Given the situation and my history with Sarah, I was hardly the best person to dish out family advice but thought I'd better try my best.

'I'm sorry to hear that,' I said, 'I know what it's like. I went through a similar thing a few years ago.'

'You have children?'

'No, but I split with my wife. We got back together for a while, but… I guess some things aren't meant to be.'

He nodded and shrugged, then held out his hand. 'My name's Jonathan. Friends call me Jonnie,' he said as we shook hands.

'Pleased to meet you,' I said, then struggled to think of anything else to say. The uncomfortable silence was interrupted by Poppy, who was struggling with one of her crossword clues.

'Eight across. Ship of the desert. Five letters.'

'Camel,' I said. She checked that it would fit, then turned and gave me a big smile. 'Thank you, Mister Tom.'

The sight of such a cute, innocent little girl cut me deeply. For the first time in hours I thought of another little girl. The one whose blood I drank that morning. The one who I couldn't resist feeding on, no matter how hard I had tried.

Is she still dead? Did she turn into a vampire? Have I turned someone into a vampire? Am I about to do the same to these good people?

The cloud that had been masking my thoughts of the girl and my feelings of guilt was blown away. The image of the dead girl's body, her blood soaking into her clothes, popped into my mind. I knew I had to do something, anything to salvage some semblance of humanity. Once more I thought of the syringes tucked in my sock and gave myself a call to action.

I did my best to look round the cabin and couldn't see any of my brothers and sisters. Not knowing whether I was within earshot of them, I decided to play it safe. 'Do you mind if I have a go at one of those puzzles?' I asked Poppy.

'Okay,' she said, and flicked to a new page for me. I took the book from her and started to write in an empty space on the page. When I was done, I handed the book to her father. 'Maybe your daddy can help you.'

He took the book from me and looked at me quizzically. I nodded towards the page and he looked down. My message read:

Please stay calm. There are people watching.
There are terrorists on board. After take-off you will all be gassed and infected with a virus. I have no choice. I am being forced to do this, which is why I want to help you.
I have the antidote.
If you want to help your daughter, you must give her the antidote now. There will be no time later.
I wish there was more I could do.

He looked at me again, wide-eyed with disbelief. 'You're serious aren't you?'

I nodded.

He thought to himself for a minute. The pilot announced that the plane would be ready for take-off in a few minutes, which prompted him to turn to me and hold out his hand.

'We haven't got much time. Give it to me.'

I took the syringes out of my pocket and handed them to him, trying to keep them out of Poppy's sight. He put them in the pocket of his jumper and stood up, taking Poppy in his hands.

'Come on, sweetheart. One last trip to the bathroom before we go up in the sky.'

92
Open Doors

Skinner had told Emily to wait a while, at least an hour after she heard everyone leave the lair. He said there would still be vampires there but there would only be a handful of them and she should be able to avoid them as they would most likely be hanging around the entrance hall.

She walked over to the door to her cell and listened for any kind of noise from outside.

Nothing.

She tried the door handle to make sure what Skinner had told her was true. He said he had left it unlocked when he had finished pretending to calm her down, which would get him in a lot of trouble if anyone else found out. The door opened slightly and she closed it again, listening for a reaction from anyone who might be waiting on the other side of the wall.

There was no noise again so Emily pulled the door open slightly, just enough to peer through the opening. The corridor seemed to go on forever, the light from the flickering torches hanging on the walls fading into darkness. She opened the door a little more, just enough to edge her upper body out. She turned to look down the corridor in the opposite direction. It looked exactly the same. No one to be seen. Not a sound to be heard.

Skinner had told her to turn right out of her door and head for the spiral staircase that would take her to the summit. He said the door at the summit was rarely locked so that would be her best chance of getting out. All she had to do then was find her way onto the main road and try to flag someone down who would take her back to the city.

That was the plan anyway. *One step at a time*, she told herself. Even though the stone walls were cold, the air was warm with the heat from the torches that lit the path ahead. The corridor curved to the left slightly so she couldn't gauge the distance she had to travel. She

242

didn't think it was too far but she had been almost catatonic when they had brought her down to her cell. Judging distances hadn't been on her mind at the time.

Wooden doors just like the one she closed behind her lined the corridor. Emily hoped the rooms behind them were all empty as she took her first steps. The silence of her footsteps made her thankful she had decided to put on her flats rather than heels the day before.

Step by step, she inched her way down the corridor, all the time looking out for the turning Skinner had told her to make and any hint of someone approaching her.

Then she saw something ahead. Not the turning she was looking for, but a shadow being projected onto the wall. Then she heard the heavy footsteps, getting louder and louder.

Shit! What am I going to do?

Emily was certain it was too late to turn round and run back to her cell. She'd already walked to far. She frantically looked around. There was a wooden door to her left and a heavy metal door on the opposite side of the corridor. Praying the wooden door wasn't locked, she took a quick light step towards it and tried the handle. It opened and she stepped inside, closing it behind her as quietly as she could.

She took a second to regain some calm, then turned round to survey the room where she had thankfully taken refuge. It looked like a lab but the details didn't sink in. Her full attention was taken by the familiar figure standing before her, who she hadn't seen in a long time.

'Emily?' said Doctor Forrest.

'Oh my God, what are you doing here?'

93
Take-off

Fortunately there were plenty of noisy children taking their seats on the flight so no one took any notice of Poppy's crying as her father brought her back to their seats.

'You'd better be right,' Jonnie said under his breath as he sat down with his daughter in his arms. I couldn't imagine how mad I'd be if a stranger had just talked me into injecting an unknown substance into the veins of my only child, but looking at the expression on his face, I had an idea.

'I wouldn't ask you to do it if I wasn't serious,' I said.

'So what happens?' he whispered.

'I know the man who's picking us up. I'll make sure you're looked after.'

'You'd better,' he said, still with anger in his voice. Even though he was undoubtedly under a lot of pressure, I didn't like his tone.

'Look man, it's not my fault you're in this situation. I'm trying to help you and your daughter. If my help isn't appreciated, you can f...'

Poppy turned to look at me.

'You can find your own way when we land,' I finished.

Jonnie took in what I said. 'You're right. I'm sorry, Tom. Are you sure there's nothing else you can do?'

'Positive,' I said as the plane started to move, 'Just sit back and try to act natural. I'll look after you the best I can.'

The plane turned to face the right direction on the runway. My heart was pumping hard in my chest. I knew there was no going back. Every scenario I ran through in my head would mean the death of me and probably everyone on the plane.

It's better to keep everyone alive as vampires than dead as humans. Isn't it?

I knew that if I could at least save Poppy and her father for now then it might be some kind of victory. Most of all, I hoped that saving Poppy would make the feelings of guilt that had resurfaced go away again. I hoped that Skinner would be able to get them back to Doctor Owen, or at least find them another supply of the syringes before the effects wore off.

We were thrown back in our seats as the plane accelerated from a standing start to take-off speed. Jonnie held Poppy's hand as we lifted off the ground. As the back of plane dipped I heard a few 'oohs' from fellow passengers as their stomachs jumped upwards.

I checked the time on my watch and made a mental note of the position of the second hand. As we climbed, I watched the time tick by. Four minutes were gone in no time and I leaned forward and fished around below my seat. Just as Roxy had told us, there was no life jacket, but I could feel something heavy. I lifted it out and placed it on my lap. With ten seconds to go, I unzipped the bag, took out the gas mask and placed it over my head.

Poppy looked at me and screamed. My heart broke as I saw the vision of pure innocent fear on her face. Jonnie put one arm round her shoulders and covered her face with his other hand. The seconds ticked by and one by one I saw the passengers drop off into a deep sleep. Poppy's body slumped forward and Jonnie fell to his side, his head lolling around in the aisle.

The plane levelled off. There was a low ping as the seatbelt lights went out on the panels above us.

94
Choking

I took the case of syringes out of the pocket in front of me and rose to my feet, placing a hand on the headrest in front to steady myself. Looking round the cabin I could see that all of my brothers and sisters had done the same. Some of them were already brandishing their blood-filled syringes.

We've got five minutes.

I unzipped the case and placed it on my empty seat. I took a syringe in my right hand. With the gas mask obstructing my vision I had to hold it up high to remove the cap. Having watched plenty of hospital TV dramas in the past, I held the syringe upside down, flicked the chamber to pop the air bubbles and pressed the plunger until a small drop of blood squirted out. If I was going to turn these people into vampires, I wanted to at least make sure they didn't have air bubbles flowing through their veins as well.

I didn't want to make Poppy my first target so I sidestepped past her and focused on Jonnie. I moved into the aisle and knelt down next to him. I straightened his head in his seat and rolled up his sleeve. Tapping the top of his forearm and trying not to think about the fact that I'd never given anyone an injection before, I tried to find a big fat vein on his muscular arm that would make it easy for me.

I looked at my watch and realised I had already wasted over a minute. *Damn it, I'm supposed to do at least five of these every minute.*

The cabin shook and Jonnie's head fell forward. I straightened him up again and looked into his lifeless eyes.

I can't do it, I thought, *I can't turn him and his daughter into vampires. I can't do this to anyone on this plane.*

I put the cap back on the syringe and placed it in the case, which I then zipped up and sat back down in my seat. Within seconds, the tall figure of Peter was standing in the aisle, the stare of his eyes burning into mine through our gas masks.

'What the hell are you doing, Tom?' he demanded in an eerie, muffled voice.

I didn't offer a response.

'Shit,' he exclaimed and shouted on another member of the team, 'Hey, are you done yet? Tom's choked! I need you to treat as many of this lot as you can. We've only got a couple of minutes!'

Peter leaned over and snatched the case of syringes out of my hands. I tried not to react, knowing that giving the impression that I'd bottled it would be my best chance of getting through the next few minutes and the best chance of survival for the passengers around me. He opened the case and took out a syringe. Without checking for air bubbles, he jabbed it into Jonnie's arm and pressed the plunger, sending a measure of vampire blood surging into his veins.

Another one of my brothers arrived and picked up a handful of syringes, immediately turning to the passengers seated across the aisle from me. Peter took the cap off a second syringe. He leaned over Jonnie and roughly grabbed one of Poppy's tiny arms.

I saw red.

In one move, I flicked his gas mask off his head with my left hand and buried my right fist into his jaw. Peter was sent sprawling backwards and fell on the vampire behind him. They both hit the ground. Peter quickly put his gas mask back on before he could breathe in any of the remnants of the gas that still hung in the air.

The vampires got to their feet and turned to look directly at me. I was convinced they were going to tear me limb from limb. But for a moment my life was spared. They had more important things on their minds. At that second, the plane started to dive.

95
Hiding In The Lab

Emily was in shock. When she opened the door and stepped inside, the last person in the world she had expected to meet was Doctor Forrest.

She cast her eyes around the room. The interior was a stark contrast to the décor of the corridor outside. A large workbench stood in the middle of the room with barely any space visible among the scientific paraphernalia. Emily recognised some of the equipment but she would have been lying if she said she knew what purpose any of it served. However, the burning question was: *what the hell is he doing here?*

She had met Doctor Forrest a few times in the past, mostly when he had a moment of inspiration in the middle of the night and called round to wake up her husband.

'Emily, I'm so happy to see you,' he began, 'When they told me about the explosion at our lab, I feared the worst. But then they said that Andrew was okay. Do you know where he is?'

'No, I don't know. I haven't spoken to Andrew since the explosion. I've just been dragged around the city by everyone looking for him.'

'How did you get here?'

'Someone took me away from the police station and I've been stuck in a room down the corridor ever since.'

'But you're in here now. How did you get out?'

Emily was about to tell him all about Skinner but then she realised something was amiss.

'What are you doing in here? The door wasn't locked,' she asked.

'I'm doing work for the vampires,' he said, 'I have no choice.'

Emily heard more footsteps outside the lab. She turned back to the door, opening it a fraction. It was Roxy. Emily watched as she opened the cell door without even attempting to unlock it and looked inside. Then she turned and headed directly for the lab.

Emily spun round, hoping Doctor Forrest may be able to offer her somewhere to hide but he had quietly moved closer and she bumped into him. When the door opened, she was trapped between the doctor and Roxy, who looked down at her with her dead brown eyes.

'You were right,' Doctor Forrest said.

'It means we've got an infiltrator,' Roxy said, 'I know who it is. I'll take care of him.'

Emily looked Doctor Forrest straight in the eye. 'You bastard! All this time you were one of them! But you were working on a cure with Andrew. Why?'

'The treatment has been ready for years. I was just making sure The Brotherhood didn't do anything they shouldn't. Your husband was part of that work.'

'Don't worry,' Roxy said, 'You'll be joining your husband very soon.'

96
Crash Landing

Peter and his henchman got to their feet and made a run for their seats. 'You're a fucking dead man!' I heard Peter mumble from beneath his gas mask.

I strapped myself in and held onto the armrests as tightly as I could. The pathetic little seatbelt was hardly designed to keep passengers in their seats as a vampire pilot made a nosedive towards the sea below. I resisted the usual instruction of assuming the brace position, knowing that it's only designed to break your neck and finish you off quickly. After all, if I could now call myself a vampire then a broken neck would only make my existence more painful in the short term, not end it.

The noise around us became excruciating as the cabin rattled furiously. Louder and louder it shook, with loose objects rolling down the aisle. The engines outside added to the cacophony by struggling with all their might to deal with the unnatural strain that was being put on them.

My insides were rising inside my body, a similar feeling to the drop from the top of a roller coaster, but this was going on and on, far longer than our bodies were designed to cope with. The force of our descent made it difficult for me to even attempt to adjust the seating positions of Poppy and her father, who were violently shaking and flailing in unison with each movement of the plane.

I knew the situation I was in was almost impossible. Even if I survived the impact, I would have to make my escape as soon as we hit the water if I was to stand a chance of surviving the night.

But I had to get in touch with Skinner to make sure Jonnie and Poppy weren't put in any danger. I hadn't managed to stop Jonnie being injected with vampire blood but I was relieved that his daughter had been spared. However, I knew her fortune may not last very long if I couldn't find a way to stop her being used as food for the batch of new vampires she would soon be packed in with and transported to God knows where.

When I thought I couldn't take any more of our descent, I felt the plane start to level off. The respite from our fall only lasted for a split second before my ears rang with an almighty bang. Everyone on board was thrown forward in their seats, some of which dislocated from the weak bolts that held them onto the floor, flying forward and crashing into the other passengers.

The doors to the overhead lockers flew open and a shower of bags and cases rained down into the aisles. Flying debris hit the unconscious passengers from all angles. I heard the crack of breaking bones all around me.

As soon as the dishevelled contents of the plane started to come to rest, blood rushed to my head and I knew exactly what I had to do. The warmth flowed back down my body, into my arms and legs and I tore myself free of my seatbelt. I pushed the seats in front forward just enough to make room for my escape and made a run for the emergency exit just across the aisle.

As I took three long steps to reach the door, I was already working out how to open it. In one move I smashed the glass panel and pulled on the handle inside, cutting my hand deeply on shards of broken glass.

I thought nothing of it. I heard the shouts of Peter and members of his team but before they could get to me, I threw the door out into the darkness ahead of me and leapt into the cool black night.

97
The View From The Pier

Skinner stood at the end of the pier and watched the coastguard boat heading out into the sea. It was his job to guard the docking point on the coastline.

When they had arrived, a large truck had been waiting for them. Its container was empty, ready and waiting to take their new brothers and sisters away. Where they were being taken, Skinner didn't know.

They have to survive the landing first, he thought and looked up at the sky to see a set of blinking lights appear overhead, then start to drop very quickly.

The coastguard boat changed direction to where the pilot thought the lights would hit the water ahead of them. Skinner could hear the faint sound of the plane's engines struggling overhead. In a matter of seconds, the plane splashed down into the sea and the flashing lights were extinguished.

'They're down. The plane's still in one piece. We've got to move fast,' a voice said over Skinner's crackling radio.

So far, everything's going according to plan. I hope Tom's okay.

Skinner's radio crackled into life again.

'The door's open. Hey, where the hell's he going?' then in a different, distant voice, someone shouted, 'Kill him!' The sound of a short loud burst of gunfire was transmitted over the airwaves and the volume shocked Skinner into almost dropping his radio.

'Skinner, this is Peter. Come in,' the radio crackled.

'This is Skinner.'

'Tom's coming towards you. You have to kill him.'

'What? Why?'

'He went crazy. He refused to treat any of the passengers and attacked me.'

'But how can I kill him? I haven't got any weapons.'

'There should be something you can use in the front cab of the truck. Something we'll need in case this lot get too rowdy.'

'Okay,' Skinner said, 'Leave it to me.'

Skinner ran for the truck and flung the driver's door open. He frantically searched around the seats and found nothing, but opening the glove box revealed a pistol and two silver-plated daggers. He took one of the daggers in his hand and went back onto the pier.

He didn't know what to think about what he'd heard over the radio. The idea that Tom had refused to inject any of the passengers with vampire blood was heartening. Skinner hoped that he had stood up for the humans and did what he could to stop the vampires, as futile a stand as that may have been.

On the other hand, Skinner had seen him flip out at the outpost that morning and wondered if he might actually have to use the dagger on his new friend.

98
Flying Again

I was happy. Not because I'd been on a plane that had crashed into the sea. Not because I had watched a perfectly good man get injected with something that was likely to cause him an eternity of pain, even if the treatment I had given him kept it at bay for a few hours.

I was happy because I was flying again.

Upon leaving the plane, I had heard Peter shout to the vampires that were on board the coastguard boat and they started to shoot at me. I was unsure whether their guns were loaded with regular or silver bullets but that didn't matter. I had taught myself enough basic manoeuvres in the training hall to avoid their shots.

Somehow I knew that Skinner wasn't among my brothers on the boat, so I headed in the direction of the wake it had left in the sea. I looked down at the water and saw that it was becoming choppy, with large swells spraying water into the air below me. I could taste the salt spray as I removed my gas mask and threw it into the water.

With my sixth sense I suspected there was only one person standing on the pier ahead of me. As I got closer, I could tell it was a vampire.

Skinner.

I told the blood in my body to flow towards my feet. With equal feelings of fear and awe, I felt the warmth in my arms and upper body that was carrying me through the air start to move down through my waist to my legs. I slowed down and started to drop towards the wooden pier that was getting closer and closer.

My body fell down and it was only as I was about to land that I realised I was falling too quickly. It was too late for me to slow myself down. My legs buckled under me as my feet hit the pier. I thumped into the ground and rolled over, clinging on to the wooden beams and almost fell over the side into the water.

'Tom, are you okay?' I heard Skinner ask. I got to my feet and dusted myself down.

'Just happy to be alive,' I said and clocked the weapon he was holding, 'What's with the knife?'

'One of the guys from the plane radioed over to me. He told me you'd gone crazy on the plane. He told me to kill you.'

'And you believed him?'

'I didn't know what to think. Especially after…'

'What? After this morning?'

Skinner nodded. I was going to protest my humanity but I knew he had a point. I was a monster. I was a vampire who drinks the blood of children. But now I was trying to redeem myself.

'Look, I need you to do something for me. There are two people on board the plane that I tried to help: a man and his daughter. Their names are Jonnie and Poppy. She's wearing jeans and a pink top. Probably seven or eight years old. You have to keep them apart from the rest.'

'I'll do whatever I can. I promise. Now you'd better get out of here. They're expecting me to kill you so you'd better not be here when they get back. I left Doctor Owen's wife with instructions of how to get out. Check the outskirts of the lair for her. If she managed to get out, she won't have gone too far.'

'She'll probably head back to Blackchapel. That's where I last saw Dave. I'll try and find both of them.'

Skinner handed me the silver-plated knife. 'Take this. You might need it.'

I thanked him and ran along the pier and jumped off the end, arcing backwards high in the sky and soaring over the trees. I forgot all about the virus coursing round my body. The troubles I'd had with alcohol hadn't crossed my mind all day long. I no longer wanted to forget where I was. I wanted to stay like this forever.

I was flying. And I loved it.

99
Room Service

The TV news had all but stopped reporting on the attack on the police station. Twenty-four hours was a long time in journalism. No new information had come to light about the attack or the missing individuals the police were supposedly looking for so the reporters had been fed various pieces of banal news to pass the time.

Just that second a bright red band flashed across the bottom of the TV screen, along with large white letters that read 'BREAKING NEWS'. The male reporter said that a plane had gone missing shortly after take-off and was thought to have crashed into the sea.

Dave didn't hear the report. He was asleep.

Slumped in his chair by the window where he had held his vigil for Tom, Dave had reached the point of no return and given in to the insistence of his eyelids. However, he did hear his phone ring and the piercing sound jerked him awake. Without thinking, he got to his feet and answered the call.

'Hello?' he croaked.

There was no answer. The caller hung up almost immediately.

Must be a wrong number. Dave thought nothing of it and hung up the phone. He rubbed his eyes and checked his watch.

What the hell am I doing here? he thought, not for the first time since checking in at the Cliffside Hotel. *Tom saw me in the car. He must know I'm here. I'll stay here as long as it takes to be sure he's okay.*

Dave considered calling his wife again to check how she was but then looked at his watch again and thought better of it. He decided to get his head down and have a few hours' sleep in his bed. He picked up his mobile and was about to program the alarm function with a time to wake him up when his thoughts were disturbed by another sound.

There was a knock at the door.

Very carefully and as quietly as he could, Dave edged towards the door and put his eye up to the spy hole.

Oh, for Christ's sake! Not him again.

It was the concierge.

'Hello?' Dave said.

'Hello sir, may I have a word?'

'It's past two in the morning. Is this absolutely necessary?'

'Yes sir, I'm afraid it is. I'm very sorry. I wouldn't wake you at this time if it wasn't important.'

'What is it?'

'Sir, may I ask you to open the door? I'd rather not wake the other guests by shouting through the door.'

Dave flipped the metal coil over the bolt on the door and opened it slightly. The concierge immediately pushed on the door and it banged against the bolt.

'Sir, will you please open the door? I'd prefer not to talk through a gap in the door.'

'Will you tell me what this is about first?'

'Room service, sir.'

'But I haven't ordered any room service.'

The door burst from its hinges and knocked Dave on the head, sending him sprawling backwards onto the floor. He looked up and saw the concierge standing before him, flanked by Ali and Bill from the bar. They all showed their extended canine teeth.

'No,' said Ali, 'But we have.'

100
Landing In Blackchapel

I reluctantly touched down on the empty road leading down into Blackchapel.

For the past thirty minutes I had been living a dream. The dream of flying was a dream that never lasted. For the moments I remembered after being jerked awake by the thought of falling out of the sky, I had been as happy as I had been at almost any point in my life. But that feeling was fleeting and impossible to recreate. Only the happiness I felt when Sarah took me back could compare.

Now I could get the feeling whenever I wanted, at any time. The excitement was intoxicating. The fact that I was turning into a vampire and had to feed on human blood to sustain my existence didn't even cross my mind.

I can fly. I can take to the fucking skies any time I want.

I had circled the mountains and clearings around the vampire lair. I saw no one that looked like they had just escaped. My sixth sense wasn't strong but I knew there were no humans around. I couldn't sense any vampires either.

At least until I walked past the sign at the side of the road that read 'Welcome to Blackchapel'.

I was suddenly hit by the terrible sense of belonging that had been present in my mind all day in the lair, only this time it was stronger. Much stronger.

Other than the kid working in the petrol station, I couldn't see anyone around. I looked closer at the kid and felt certain he was a vampire. On the opposite side of the road there was a gap in the barrier that was supposed to protect wayward drivers from a sheer drop. I wondered how many drivers had had their veins sucked dry by the kid or his friends and then been dumped over the edge of the cliff into the mists below, never to be found again.

As I kept walking towards a small row of shops, I became aware of the noise coming from a bar at the end. I could hear people shouting and laughing. It was after two in the morning and by the sound of it the party would be going on until sunrise. My gut feelings became stronger as I walked past the bar.

Wall to wall vampires.

I checked my hand where I had cut it during my escape from the plane. It had already healed. Just thirty minutes earlier the glass panel on the emergency door had sliced a deep gash in my hand. I still had blood all over my jacket and shirt to prove it, but now the wound had disappeared, leaving not even the tiniest of scars.

I stopped and looked up at the Cliffside Hotel, a structure so massively out of place that it towered over the rest of Blackchapel. I knew Dave had to be here; his car was still parked outside. The lights were turned off and the curtains closed in every room apart from one.

Something's wrong.

With the luxury of not having to go through the reception area to see what was going on in the room above me, my feet left the floor and I started my ascent.

101
Vampire Hotel

Dave shuddered as terrible feelings of panic and realisation washed over him.

I've checked into a vampire hotel.

He lifted a hand to feel his nose. He was sure it wasn't broken but that didn't stop the stream of blood trickling from his nostrils. He ignored it and tried to get to his feet, but a kick to the kidneys sent him tumbling back onto the floor. Another hard boot in the back kept him down.

Dave tried to put the growing pain in his body out of his mind, just for a few seconds while he inched his way over to the bedside table where he had left his gun. He lifted his hand to reach for it but a falling boot stamped his hand into the ground and made it stay there. The concierge picked up the gun and removed the clip, examining the regular bullets inside.

'I'm not sure what you were expecting to do with this, sir.'

'Fuck you.'

'Well, that's not a very nice way to treat a member of staff.'

'Come on,' Ali shouted, 'The hunger's killing me.'

The concierge kicked Dave in the back to stop him trying to get up again. 'You'll have to wait,' he said, 'I've told you before. We can't feed in the bedrooms. Do you know how much work it causes the cleaning staff?'

The concierge picked Dave up by his collar and held his head in front of Ali, who took a swing at him with one quick, hard punch to the jaw. The last thing Dave felt was his eyes rolling back in their sockets. He blacked out and his body slumped in the concierge's arms.

'Take him down to the kitchen,' the concierge said, 'And try not to get his blood on everything.'

Ali and Bill grabbed an arm each and dragged Dave's heavy body out of the room and down the corridor towards the elevator.

The concierge remained in the room and started to gather together Dave's personal items. All he had with him were his gun and his jacket. The concierge wondered why someone would check into a hotel first thing in the morning without any luggage and spend all day just hanging around.

He said he was waiting for a friend, but no one else has shown up.

The concierge tucked the gun in his belt and threw Dave's jacket over his arm. He cast his eyes around the room. Something caught his eye in the mirror by the desk. The mirror was pointing at the window. It looked like a man was outside and he was coming closer.

102

Gatecrasher

I didn't know how Dave had got himself into this situation but one thing was clear as I saw what was happening to him through the window.

They're going to kill him.

The concierge spun round with a startled look on his face. I smashed through the window and flew across the room towards him, grabbing his neck and pinning him against the wall.

'Where are you taking him?' I growled.

'Who are you?' the concierge whimpered.

'Dave's my friend. Where is he?'

The concierge instinctively glanced towards the door. A vision of a hotel kitchen flashed into my mind.

'Thanks. That's all I need.'

I drew the silver-plated dagger from my belt and jabbed it into the concierge's neck. He tried to scream but the unstoppable reaction now taking over his body had already eaten away his voice box. The ash was still falling from his wound as I left the bedroom with murder on my mind.

I looked up and down the corridor and saw two vampires struggling to drag Dave's limp body into the elevator. I started to run. The sound of my feet stomping along the corridor alerted them and one of them hit the button to close the doors. I took longer and longer steps until I was almost flying again, but I just failed to reach the elevator before the doors closed in front of me.

With no door leading to a staircase to the left or right, I decided to test my abilities again. I told myself I needed more strength in my arms. In less than a second, warm blood had flowed into my biceps and triceps. I squeezed the tips of my fingers into the gaps between the elevator doors and tried to pull them apart. It was no problem. I was prepared for a struggle but I flung the heavy metal doors apart with ease.

I leaned forward and gazed into the black chasm below. The elevator had just stopped at the ground floor and I heard the doors open. Without a second to spare, I jumped forward and fell down onto the elevator. With power still in my arms, I punched a hole through the roof like it was made from tin foil and tore a strip away, just big enough for me to fit through. I jumped down.

Dave was at my feet. He lay between me and his captors, who were trying to drag him away by his collar. With hatred in their eyes, they stared me down like they were going to jump on me and tear me apart. Then in unison, their gazes clocked the silver dagger in my hand.

They know I've killed their friend. They know I want to do the same to them.

The two vampires let go of Dave and his head thumped to the ground, but the impact failed to wake him up. They both took a step back and held their hands in front of them. I leaned over and picked Dave up by his collar. Even though my left arm was full of blood, pumping my muscles larger than they had ever been before, I knew I wouldn't be able to carry Dave for long.

I've got to get the hell out of here.

I held the dagger out and edged out of the elevator, forcing the vampires in front of me to take further steps back into the reception area. Just over their shoulders, I saw something that made my heart sink, something that would make getting out of the hotel very difficult. A mob of at least twenty people walked through the front door to the hotel.

Correction: a mob of at least twenty vampires.

103

'You Are Now Leaving Blackchapel'

By the glazed happiness on their faces, I assumed they were the cause of the noise in the bar outside. One by one the vampires moved into the reception area and their expressions changed. Smiles turned to shock, which in turn quickly morphed into anger.

Still brandishing the dagger to keep the two closest vampires at bay, I dragged Dave towards the mob. They all kept their distance but looked at me like they were trying to burn a hole in my head with their stare. With their legs bent and arms out to their sides, any one of them was ready to jump me if they thought they had an opportunity.

I could kill any of them with a single jab from the dagger, but can I take them all on?

My heart was pounding again. Adrenaline was flowing through my body to my brain but I did all I could to maintain a calm front as I edged us closer to the front door. The vampires circled us at just over arm's length and kept their distance. Thoughts and voices flashed into my mind.

We're going to kill you.
We're going to feast on your friend.
You killed our brother. You must die.
He's one of us.
He killed one of our brothers. He's one of them.
He's an infiltrator.
Kill him!

With the last voice, I heard a scream behind me. Keeping hold of Dave's collar, I spun round and was faced with a vampire leaping towards me. I swung my right arm out, the silver blade pointing at him.

He flew right into me. I stumbled backwards but kept my footing. I heard a familiar noise. It was the faint fizz of a vampire's body turning to ash. I looked down and saw that the blade had stabbed him square in the chest.

There were more screams around me. I pulled the dagger from his still-dissolving body and my victim fell to the floor screaming. I held out the dagger, swinging for arms that were reaching for me.

'Come on then!' I shouted, 'Who's having it next? I've killed two of you bastards already. It's too easy!'

Still threatening them with the dagger, I took larger steps towards the door. They all wanted to attack me but none of them wanted to meet with the same fate as their brother, who was now nothing more than a pile of ash and clothes on the floor. The circle broke and I kicked the front door open.

Dragging Dave's heavy body out of the hotel and down the steps, I kept looking at the vampires that were staring me down from inside. We reached Dave's car. I stuck my hand in his pocket and breathed a sigh of relief when I found his car key. I opened the back door and threw Dave onto the back seat, then got into the driver's seat and hit the gas.

As we passed the sign thanking us for passing through Blackchapel, I made a mental note never to return. Or if I did, to bring plenty of silver with me.

Warmth spread all over me as my vampire blood regulated my bodily functions. The fight was over. Keeping my eyes on the road, with one hand I reached back and felt for Dave's wrist. I found his pulse, just wanting to double check that I hadn't wasted my time rescuing a dead body.

Every few seconds I shot a glance in the rear view mirror, half expecting to see the sky filled with vampires on our tail, but saw nothing out of the ordinary. They had decided not to give chase and I wasn't that interested in knowing why. All that mattered was getting back to the city in one piece and finding our old friends.

The road was empty, which I hoped would allow us to make good time. The only traffic I saw was two coaches going in the opposite direction.

Skinner.

104
Triumphant Return

Skinner could sense something was amiss. The crew had successfully unloaded the bodies from the plane onto the boat, then from the boat into the truck, which was now travelling towards an unknown destination.

But now that the mission was over and everyone was on board the coaches heading back to the lair, Skinner was getting a feeling in the back of his mind. He was an infiltrator, alone in the group, but the thoughts going round in his head were more than just a fear of being discovered.

They know I'm not one of them.

When the boat docked at the pier, he'd told them all that he'd killed Tom. He said that Tom had gone crazy after being a vampire for only a few hours so he had no choice. At the time he wasn't sure how convincing his story of stabbing him with a silver dagger then dropping the dagger in the water had been. Now he was certain they were all ready to turn on him. Skinner looked round the coach. Even though no one looked at him, he could feel their minds trying to delve into his.

As the coaches passed a sign that told them Blackchapel was just five miles ahead, Skinner saw a car go past at speed in the opposite direction. Tom's face flashed into his mind. The other passengers on the coach looked at each other and started to whisper between themselves.

Do they know? Did they see the same thing?

Skinner was relieved that Tom was alive. He felt confident that Tom had found his friend Dave and the two of them were driving away to safety. He hoped they had found Emily but couldn't feel her presence in their car.

As the coaches passed through Blackchapel, the empty lead coach stopped outside the hotel where a crowd had gathered. Skinner sensed the presence of vampires. Dozens of them.

The remaining coach passed through Blackchapel and made its way through the metal gates that secured the entrance to the lair. It stopped in the grassy clearing and the crew disembarked. Finally free of the normal human front they had to put up in the airport and on the plane before take-off, they all ran to the end of the cliff and jumped down into the chasm.

Peter remained in the clearing for a few seconds, just long enough to stare at Skinner, to look deep into his mind. He then held out an arm in the direction of the chasm and said 'You first.'

Skinner flew down into the chasm and landed on the wooden platform. The main doors to the lair were open and the vampires were all filing into the entrance hall. Roxy had been waiting for them and was congratulating them all one by one.

Peter landed next to Skinner and closed the doors behind him as they walked into the hall. Roxy shook Skinner's hand and patted him on the shoulder. 'Good job,' she said, but her gaze was drawn by Peter behind him. Her eyes narrowed.

Roxy turned to Skinner. The tone of her voice changed. 'Come with me, Skinner. We need to talk.'

105
Ashes To Ashes

Now Skinner was really worried. Bad feelings hung in the air and as he followed Roxy down the corridor, he weighed up the possible outcomes.

He hoped Emily had successfully escaped from the lair but suspected she hadn't. After all, it was a difficult climb all the way up the stairs and she had to get out without being seen. If she had been seen or caught while trying to escape, it seemed likely that she would give away the name of the person who had helped her, either consciously or subconsciously.

Someone could have tipped Roxy off to the fact that he and Tom were more than just brief acquaintances. Now that Tom was on the loose, they might suspect him of being an infiltrator from The Brotherhood. Of course there was a slim chance that Roxy wanted to congratulate Skinner for a job well done and show him the plans for the next attack.

So there were two possible outcomes: Skinner would either live or die. Skinner was no pessimist but it didn't feel like the odds were in his favour. Either way, he was sure he was in trouble.

They reached the door to Doctor Forrest's lab, but Roxy pointed to the metal door on the other side of the corridor.

'In there please,' she said.

Skinner apprehensively turned the handle and edged the door open. The room inside was dark, almost pitch black save for the torch light that spilled through the crack in the door.

There was the faint sound of whimpering from inside. Skinner opened the door to reveal Emily, gagged and tied to a wooden chair. She was terrified. Tears streamed down her face over the industrial tape that stopped her screaming at the top of her lungs.

Skinner turned to look at Roxy. He was ready to make all kinds of excuses for her attempted escape but didn't get the chance to say a word. Roxy punched him square on the nose. He lost his footing as he stumbled backwards into the room and sank to his knees. Roxy grabbed the handle and pulled the door shut.

Skinner jumped to his feet and tried the handle but the door was locked from the outside. The faint sound of him banging on the inside of the door was barely audible from the corridor. The darkness of the room meant he was only just visible through the small window in the door, but he could clearly see Roxy staring at him with the cold, lifeless eyes of a murderer.

The door behind Roxy opened and Doctor Forrest appeared behind her. He walked across the corridor and hit a button on the intercom panel next to the door. The fuzzy sound of Skinner shouting filled the air.

'You don't know what you're doing! This is a mistake! Please, let me out!'

'I know exactly what I'm doing, Skinner,' Roxy began, 'You tried to help Emily escape. Your friend is missing and we believe you have something to do with the problem on the plane.'

'You're wrong! I don't know what happened on the plane!'

'I can't believe anything you say any more, Skinner. Not even that bullshit you gave us about what happened at the base. I know you won't tell me where we can find Doctor Owen and it's not really that important. We're close to finding him ourselves, which makes you useless to us.'

'No, wait! What are you doing?'

'I'll make it as quick as I can,' Roxy said and hit another button on the wall.

The faces looking through the window in the door glowed purple as ultraviolet light illuminated the room. Skinner punched the door in vain. As the first specks of dust fell from his face, the tape over Emily's mouth broke free and her screams pierced the air. Roxy turned off the intercom.

She watched in silence as Skinner ran aimlessly around the room, searching for shade that he would never find. Exposed areas on his hands and face were slowly dissolving into ash, leaving a dusty trail behind him. Smoke rose from his open wounds and filled the air. Emily struggled to breathe and coughed furiously as she took lungfuls of black dust.

The chemical reactions took hold and Skinner's body started to burn faster. Ash poured from all over his face until his head had completely disappeared. He sank to his knees and tumbled onto the floor. The pile of clothes lost their shape as the remnants of his body dissolved. Roxy turned off the ultraviolet light and left Emily alone in the darkness, coughing and screaming.

'Shouldn't we get her out of there?' Doctor Forrest asked.

'No,' Roxy said without a hint of mercy in her voice, 'She'll be leaving here for good very soon so leave her where she is. We haven't got time to baby-sit her. I've got a call to make.'

106
This Is How It Begins

Doctor Owen had tossed and turned all night.

Okay, so Becky Clarkson had been trying to lie low for the past two years and soft furnishings hadn't been top of her priority list, but God damn it, this sofa's lumpy.

He'd managed a few hours of sleep but never more than thirty minutes at a time. As he struggled to find a comfortable sleeping position for what felt like the millionth time, he decided that his chances of getting any more sleep had passed. Not only was the sofa restricting his slumber but more importantly he couldn't get thoughts of Emily out of his mind.

Where is my wife?

What are they doing to her?

Will I ever see her again?

He knew these thoughts were unhelpful but he couldn't shake them. Trying to turn his mind to something else, he sat up on the sofa and rubbed his eyes. He saw Jane sitting close to the TV, watching the news with the volume turned down.

'Hey,' he said, 'What's going on?'

'I couldn't sleep,' Jane said, 'so I turned on the TV to see if there was anything more on the news about us.'

'Was there anything?'

'No, nothing about us any more. There's been a plane crash and that's all that's been on the news since I woke up.'

'Really? Where?'

'Here. Just off the coast a couple of hours ago.'

Jane turned up the volume and they listened to the reporter's voice from the helicopter circling the wreckage of the plane that was floating in a choppy sea.

'The wreckage is being searched by the coastguard who arrived on site first. From up here I can't see any signs of survivors but it's very difficult to see anything with the weather as bad as this. The pilot has just told me we have to land the helicopter now before the storm gets any worse.'

The reporter continued her conversation with the news anchor in the studio but it just became background noise as Becky entered the room.

'I just heard on the radio. There's been a plane crash, hasn't there?' she asked.

'Yes,' said Jane, 'You don't sound too surprised.'

'I knew something like this was coming. I just hoped it wouldn't happen so soon.'

Doctor Owen frowned in disbelief. 'You mean this is related to us?'

'That's right. It's one of the stages.'

'Stages of what?'

'The Rising. The wheels are already in motion. We need to get ready.'

'Ready for what?' Jane asked.

'War.'

Doctor Owen spluttered a nervous laugh. 'War? Come on, that'll never happen. What about the treaty, the Costas report?'

'Haven't you learned anything today? That's just a smokescreen. It's all bullshit to make you think we were going to be okay. Only a few key people know what is really going to happen.'

'And you're one of them?'

'No, but I do know that it will all begin with a strike on the general public. A huge event made to look like an accident or a natural disaster.'

They all focused on the TV screen again. The picture from the helicopter was becoming shakier as the weather outside got worse. With no new information, the reporter continued to do her best to string out what little she did know.

Doctor Owen's phone rang. 'Hello?' he said as he answered the call from a withheld number.

'Doctor Owen. This is Roxy. Pay attention. You will meet us at the main south entrance to the Morningside Mall at five o'clock. Bring all the samples and documents and you will get your wife back.'

'Is she okay?'

'She is fine. She will be with us.'

'Let me speak to her again. Please.'

'No. I don't have time for all that again.'

'Look, if you don't let me speak to her then…'

'Then what?' she barked, 'Who the fuck do you think you're talking to? We're not negotiating. It's simple: do as I say or she dies. End of story. Goodbye.'

107
Disciple

Steve Ellis sunk the last mouthful of his cup of coffee. It had been a very long day and he'd lost count of the number of coffees he'd consumed since sunrise.

Ever since he had received the call from Marcus, he knew he couldn't go home. This was one day he'd prepared for but sometimes doubted whether he'd ever see. He was one of the few people who knew the real details of the treaty. Since assuming the role of Operations Director, he had worked every hour he could to enable the true intentions of the humans and the vampires.

He wasn't a vampire but he did everything he could to make sure they received the place in society they believed they deserved. The vampires called him a disciple, one of their followers who would benefit from their eventual power and wealth.

It was the wealth that Steve was most interested in. Vampires did not believe in money as a societal driving force but since the humans did, the disciples would automatically receive a share of all monies generated from the Rising. This was on the condition that the humans forfeit any political power over the size of the vampire community. The population levels had been agreed fifty years earlier but the humans had decided to trade certain rights, effectively selling out their species.

This didn't bother Steve. He knew that now the Rising had begun, there was nothing anyone could do to stop it. Within days every government around the world would be crying out for the one thing that would slow down the spread of the virus.

Stockpiles of Virex were positioned all over the world in anticipation of this day. Controlling the flow of Virex to the infected would determine which territories were most heavily affected, but most importantly it would control what each territory paid for their supplies. It was a perfect plan and he would soon be reaping the benefits.

The phone on his desk rang. He answered it and was greeted by Roxy. She spoke quickly and hung up as soon as he acknowledged her orders.

'Morningside Mall. Five o'clock. Seal all windows and cover all exits. This is a population expansion exercise. Use deadly force for containment only. We suspect your missing agent will be joining our targets on site. Extract her and leave the other members of her team behind. Understood?'

'Yes.'

With that, she was gone. Steve kept the phone in his hand and dialled the number to reach General Graham. It was time to call in the troops.

108

Back To Civilisation

We made our way out of the mountains and back towards civilisation without incident. As we neared the freeway, I stopped the car at the side of the road and got out to check Dave for injuries.

I opened the door and found him still unconscious on the back seat. I checked his pulse again then ran my hand round his neck. I was confident he hadn't been bitten at the hotel but I needed to check. No blood on my hands confirmed my suspicions. I searched in his pockets and found his mobile phone.

Full signal, full battery.

Thank God.

I called Doctor Owen's number. 'Yes?' was his curt answer.

'Hey Doc, it's me, Tom. Are you okay?'

'Oh my God, Tom, I wasn't expecting you. Where are you?'

'I've been all over. I'm just coming back to the city now. Are you watching the news?'

'Yes. The plane crash is all they've been talking about.'

'It was them. I was on the plane. Have they recovered any bodies?'

'No, they haven't mentioned anything about any survivors.'

'Shit. I don't think they'll find any. Where are you? I'll come and pick you up.'

'No, there's no point. We're about to leave to get Emily and Doctor Forrest. Meet us at the Morningside Mall, in the car park by the north entrance in an hour's time.'

'Will do. I tried to find your wife but searching the mountains is like looking for a needle in a haystack.'

'Don't worry. They have her but we should have her back soon.'

'Is Jane okay?'

'Yes, she's fine. Is Skinner there with you?'

'No, but Dave is. Skinner can't get away from the vampires. I'm not sure when we'll see him again, they're keeping him on a short leash. I'll tell you all about it when I see you.'

We exchanged farewells and I pocketed the mobile as I sat back down in the driver's seat. I hit the accelerator and took us onto the freeway but had to slam on the brakes as soon as we reached the top of the ramp. Ahead of me a queue of bright red brake lights stretched out into the orange glow bathing down from the streetlights hanging overhead.

A few spots of rain hit the windscreen. It was only a brief warning before the heavens opened and the downpour started again. I turned on the radio and heard the travel reporter saying that all flights had been cancelled. Everyone who had been waiting on a flight was now trying to get out of the airport and go home.

'Stay off the freeway,' was his advice. I could have done with that just minutes earlier.

I sat with my hands on the steering wheel and allowed myself to calm down a little. I felt like I had been running all day.

Syringes, little girls, a plane crash and a hotel full of vampires had made this the craziest day of my life. And I could fly. I expected to wake up at any moment. Ever since I had woken up on the bed at Hartley House I had wished the whole thing was a terrible nightmare that would soon be over, but now I felt different. I hoped it wasn't a dream. I hoped I wouldn't wake up in my own bed and have to go back to being a detective.

I'm on the inside of the biggest conspiracy the world has ever known.

I've seen things almost no one else in the world has ever seen.

I can fly.

I'm a vampire.

And it feels amazing.

A loud whirring noise invaded my moment of peace. I turned round and saw a helicopter in the background edging its way along the growing queue of traffic, not twenty metres above the vehicles.

I recognised the helicopter. It belonged to The Brotherhood.

109
Stein

Captain Stein was ravenous. Twenty-four hours as a vampire hadn't been kind to him.

Whether it was the burning in his stomach that went away then came back twice as bad an hour later or his so-called brothers taunting him, he had no one who knew what he was going through and no one on his side. Everyone he knew was trained to kill him.

They had held him in a bare hall, chained to the thick heating pipes. When the sun rose, the soldiers entered the room and opened the blinds and windows. All day long he had to watch the sunlight edge its way across the laminated floor towards him. It was mid-afternoon when one of the more sympathetic members of the squad entered the room to bring him a bottle of water and shut the curtains just before the deadly sunlight reached his body.

The same soldiers that taunted him were sitting across from him in the helicopter as it floated over the trees and fields of the countryside towards the freeway intersection. They all stared at him with fear and hatred all over their faces, their hands gripping their automatic rifles, ready to take him out with a single shot should he make a move they didn't like. Most of them had known members of the crew on board Alpha One and Alpha Two and now that Alpha Three was airborne, they swore they wouldn't let another vampire take down one of their gunships.

Stein was certain they would kill him as soon as they discovered him at the mountain base after the detective and his friends escaped. It was only after they realised they could use him as a sniffer dog that his life was spared. For what it was worth.

The detective.

The motherfucker who turned me into an animal.

Stein knew that where they were going he would be dumped with the rest of the rebirths, the people who would think themselves lucky when they realised they hadn't perished in the plane crash but would soon wish they were dead. He looked down at his boots. His new feet had finished growing back just after they arrived at Hartley House. It amazed him how similar they were to his old feet that Detective Ryder sliced off in the base the night before.

He thought of the mission ahead for everyone else aboard the helicopter. It was a joke. He couldn't believe how far The Brotherhood had strayed from their true intentions. The intentions of the founding members hundreds of years ago had been to protect the human race from the vampires at any cost. Now that had been lost in five hundred years of bureaucracy. The treaty. The Costas report. Nothing but bullshit that got in the way of ridding the world of pure evil.

All this talk of coexistence was crap. The Brotherhood had not put enough effort into the treatment that would kill every vampire. They had become almost subservient to the vampires and now, there they were, on their way to perform their role in the next phase of the treaty.

Baby-sitting.

As the gunship glided over the crowded road below, Captain Stein was hit with a familiar feeling in his mind. It was something that he hadn't felt since the night before, when the detective had bitten him and turned him into a vampire.

The detective.

Stein felt a warmth flow into his arms. He yanked his arms up and tore them free from the handcuffs that were holding him in his seat. Before the soldiers could fire off a shot, Stein had thrown himself free of his captors and was falling towards the ground below.

110
Emergency Lane

I turned round in my seat and looked out of the back window. The helicopter didn't look like it was heading towards us, but the shock came when I saw a body fall from the main cabin. It fell towards the ground but stopped before it hit the grassy field next to the road. I knew who it was, the only person it could be.

Stein. He knows I'm here.

Not wanting to stick around and wait for him to find us, I hit the accelerator and swerved over to the emergency lane. I knew my actions would alert him to our presence but I saw no other option.

Get the hell out of here.

I saw a flash of white in the rear view mirror, followed by another, and another. A second later, more vehicles were following me down the emergency lane. I drove as fast as I could, knowing that some of the commuters behind me would get caught in the hail of bullets raining down from the helicopter.

I was certain that Captain Stein had escaped from the clutches of The Brotherhood. Were they taking him to be killed? Whatever their reason for transporting him in the gunship, they were surely regretting it now. He was free, and the more they tried to neutralise him, the more attention they were drawing to themselves and the fact that there was a vampire flying around a freeway intersection filled with normal people who had no concept of what was going on around them.

The windscreen wipers were going as fast as they could but it was still difficult to see through the torrent of rain ahead at eighty miles an hour. I took a deep intake of breath as a car in front of me pulled out into the emergency lane. I jammed on the horn and narrowly avoided smashing into the back of it as it pulled back into its place in the traffic jam.

One look in the rear view mirror told me that Stein was getting closer. The gunship was larger and flashes of gunfire were still falling down towards the road. I heard a screech and looked again. The car that was following me skidded and flipped over onto its roof, smashing into several cars in the process. I was certain I could see bullet holes in its bodywork.

'What the hell's going on?' asked a voice from the back seat.

'Dave!' I exclaimed, 'Are you okay?'

'I think so,' he said and surveyed his surroundings, 'Where am I? Why are we going so fast?'

'We've got a vampire on our tail. The Brotherhood are trying to kill it, and probably us as well. Can't explain any more right now.'

There was a loud thump from the back of the car. Dave looked out of the back windscreen. 'Holy shit! I guess this is the vampire.'

Almost crashing into another car, I turned round. Captain Stein was lying along the back of our car. He looked frantic. I heard a voice echo deep within my mind.

Ryder. I'm going to kill you.

Pieces of the road ahead flew into the air and landed on the bonnet. The gunship was directly above us and they were taking pot shots at the vampire that was clinging on. I knew I had to get Dave away from this situation. He would be the one that Stein attacked first and I couldn't let that happen.

'Dave, climb over here and take the wheel!' I shouted.

He squeezed his ample frame between the seats into the passenger side. I hit the horn again to stop another car pulling out in front of us then turned to Dave.

'Take the wheel,' I said, and let go of the steering wheel when he gripped it with both hands.

'Where are you going?' he asked.

I checked that I still had the silver-plated dagger tucked in my belt. 'To get that bug off our car,' I said and jumped out of the driver's door.

111
'I'm Going To Tear You Apart'

Suspended in the air, I slid down the side of the car and grabbed onto the pair of legs that were hanging over the end of the rear wing. Stein's hands gave way and the weight of his body pulled me down.

We hit the road with a thump. I gritted my teeth and grunted with pain as the left side of my face scraped along the rough surface of the road. A car that had pulled into the emergency lane stopped right in front of us and the driver sounded the horn.

We were bathed in the white light of the headlights. Stein sat up and looked right at me. For a second he looked deep into my eyes, penetrating my mind with his thoughts.

You did this to me, you bastard. I'm going to kill you. I'm going to tear you apart.

The tarmac exploded next to us. We both looked up to see the gunship hovering over us. Small white hot bullets were almost masked in the rain as they shot down out of the sky towards us. I quickly got to my feet and made a leap for the field next to the road. I wanted to get the attack as far away from the traffic as possible. But no sooner had my feet left the ground than I felt Stein's hands grab my ankle and pull me back down.

'Come here, you motherfucker!'

His hands made their way up my legs and grabbed onto my waist. Stein lifted us off the ground. I looked up and saw the gunship getting closer and closer. We were rising into the air, flying towards the deadly rotating blades above. Stein chose the opposite side of the gunship to where The Brotherhood had planted their heavy machine gun.

We rose faster and faster. Stein held me out in front of him, trying to throw my body into the deadly blades. As we reached the gunship, I threw out a hand and gripped the edge of the opening to the main cabin. I held on tight and we stopped. Stein lost his grip and the downdraft from the blades blew him away from me. Before the soldiers on board could lift their weapons to shoot at me, I let go and the downdraft pushed me back towards the ground.

Blood flowed up through my body into my arms and shoulders. I stopped falling and hung in the air ten feet above the ground. The gunship started to turn to allow the gunner a clear shot at me, but a second later Stein flew into me from behind and pushed my body down. He let go and threw me towards the traffic.

My heart skipped a beat as I crashed through a car windscreen. I heard the screams of the passengers but got to my feet and stood on the bonnet. I looked down and saw blood all over the dashboard, which was quickly being diluted by the falling rain. I thought nothing of it, knowing that my body would repair itself before long.

I felt pain all over, but it wasn't the type of pain that made me want to rest. It charged me like adrenaline, driving me on to push me harder than ever before. Looking down the emergency lane to see that Dave was disappearing into the distance, I turned all of my attention to the one thing that my life depended on.

Kill Captain Stein.

112
Kill Captain Stein

I spotted Stein standing on the roof of a car two lanes across from me. I didn't have time to make a jump for him before I heard the rattle of bullets tearing through the bodywork of the car I was standing on.

I rolled over the side and crouched down, out of the line of sight of the gunner on board the helicopter above. As I hoped he would, the gunner turned his attention to Stein and started to fire at will in his direction. As far as The Brotherhood were concerned, we were just two vampires and we had to be killed at all costs, no matter how many humans were injured or killed in the process.

When the shooting stopped for a few seconds, I heard the screams of the people stuck in their cars. Glass and bullet casings peppered the road's surface. I could feel the pain of everyone around me. Too scared to leave their cars, too panicked to stay still, they didn't know what to do.

The passenger door of a car in the next lane flew open and a young woman in jeans and a white t-shirt made a run for the emergency lane, hoping to find some protective shelter among the trees that lined the edged of the road. Her companions in the car were shouting at her to come back but she didn't listen to them. She made it to the barrier and jumped over, but she never landed on the other side.

In a flash, Stein flew from his hiding place and plucked her out of the air as she jumped. Her screams became lost in the sound of car horns and the pouring rain as Stein carried her high into the air, tracked by a line of gunfire from the helicopter.

I lost track of them. So did The Brotherhood. The gunship had changed positions and I was now a sitting duck. I made another leap for cover, this time behind a large van that I hoped was empty as its rear compartment was torn apart by a hail of bullets, narrowly missing me as I darted behind.

I knew the van would only offer cover for a matter of seconds before the gunship moved again. Looking around for suitable cover, I spotted a tanker a few vehicles ahead with a badge on the back that signified a non-hazardous load. I took a step forward but I was stopped in my tracks.

A body hit the ground at my feet with an almighty thump. It was the body of the young girl, only her jeans and white t-shirt were soaked through with rain water and her own blood, which was pouring from a gaping wound in her neck. Her eyelids flickered and with her last breath she gargled blood in her throat.

I looked up and had no time to move out of the way. Stein's hands caught me firmly on the shoulders and the force of his falling body hammered me into the ground. I would have cried out in agony as my left arm popped out of its socket but the force of Stein's knee crushing my chest forced the wind out of me. He began pounding my face with his fists.

'Fuck you! Fuck you! Fuck you!' he chanted maniacally as he unloaded his rage on me.

My thoughts went to the silver dagger tucked into the back of my belt but I couldn't reach it with my right hand and my left arm was limp and useless. I felt and heard the horrible crunch in the middle of my face as his last punch broke my nose.

Over Stein's shoulder I saw an arc of yellowy-white bullets cut through the air and rattle through the van next to us. Stein sensed the danger immediately and let go of me, flying away into the traffic behind. With the pressure on my chest now gone, I had just enough time to take a deep, wheezy breath and roll to my side before the tarmac where I had been lying was shredded to pieces. The pain in my shoulder was magnified a hundred times as I rolled onto my left side. I shrieked in pain and tears welled in my eyes.

With no agility or poise whatsoever I threw myself over the bonnet of the car next to me and crouched down. My eyes were fixed on the tanker once more, but my plans had changed. I no longer wanted to use it as cover. Getting to my feet and ignoring the unbelievable pain in my shoulder and face, I took two powerful steps, feeling my blood flow from my legs into my torso.

Narrowly avoiding another barrage of bullets, I threw myself forward with all of my might. I was airborne, no more than four feet off the ground, heading directly towards the tanker. I looked ahead, making sure I was on my intended course then closed my eyes. I told all the blood in my body to head for my left shoulder and winced in anticipation of the pain that was to come.

My shoulder hit the tanker square on the edge. I heard the pop as my arm reconnected to its socket and screamed in agony as a bolt of electricity shot through my spine to my brain. I blacked out for a second but the impact of crashing headfirst onto the surface of the road brought me back to consciousness.

The warmth of my blood spread all over my body as I wobbled to my feet, using my hands to steady myself against the side of the tanker. I rolled my arm around to confirm it was functional again.

Burning with unbelievable pain but functional.

I took a few seconds to compose myself and heard the thunder of gunfire once more. I looked at the gunship and saw the line of bullets raining down in the direction of Stein, one lane across and two or three cars down.

I took a step sideways and looked round the side of the tanker. I could see Stein darting from one car to another, dancing around the certain death of the trail of silver bullets that was following his every move. The shooting stopped and I began to run. I was almost on top of him when he turned round, but there was nothing he could do to stop me.

I grabbed him by his shirt and head butted him on the nose. When he instinctively lifted his hands to his bleeding nose, I reached for the dagger with my left hand and quickly drew it forward, slicing through his right hand and severing his little finger.

He screamed and looked at his hand. His little finger had almost completely dissolved into ash before it hit the ground. Frozen with the terror of knowing he had only a few seconds left to live, Stein was mine to do with as I pleased. Still gripping him by his shirt, I jumped high into the air, taking his shaking, decomposing body with me. Moving faster than the gunship could rotate, I flew round to the opposite side to where the gunner was stationed and threw what was left of his screaming carcass into the cabin.

I made my escape and searched the traffic ahead for Dave's car. I looked back only once, to see the gunship flailing in the air, attempting to land in a field. I spotted our car less than a mile down the road. With the adrenaline subsiding and the reality of what had just happened to me setting in, I started to feel faint as I fell towards the rear windscreen.

113
Mid-Season Sale

Sunrise was still an hour or so away but the staff at the Morningside Mall were already arriving for work. In less than an hour, the biggest department store in the mall was going to open for its mid-season sale. Every sale began in the early hours of the morning and the car park closest to the north entrance was already starting to fill up.

The workers all ran from the coach that dropped them off and made their way inside, past the queue of eager shoppers that was building on the concourse.

On the roof of the mall, several groups of men were working hard, unaware of the reason for the tasks they were performing. All they knew was that someone had called their boss in the middle of the night and offered to pay them all a ridiculous amount of money to get on the roof and nail thick sheets of metal over the skylights that dotted the ceilings inside. No one had told them why they were doing it, but they didn't care as long as they got paid.

As the shop workers arrived at the store, their supervisors thrust racks of clothes in their direction and barked orders at them to make sure the shoppers were faced with the sale stock as soon as they walked through the door.

The store manager clicked her fingers as she realised she had left her handbag in her car. Following a spate of break-ins in the car park recently, she decided it was best to fetch it as soon as possible. She surveyed the surroundings and saw that all of her staff were busy re-arranging the store layout. Everything was going according to plan so she told herself she had a few minutes to nip down to her car.

She walked back through the store and cut through the fitting rooms. She opened a door marked 'Employees Only' and walked down the undecorated stone walled corridor, down the stairs at the end and into the cold darkness of the employees' car park.

That's weird, she thought as she looked around and sensed that something was amiss.

In the middle of the car park, a truck sat across several parking spaces, with the driver's door wide open. She walked up to the truck and looked inside the cabin. As she suspected, there was no one there.

'Hey, is there anyone here?' she shouted. Her voice echoed off the cold stone walls but no one answered her call.

She walked round to the back of the truck. One of the doors was ajar and the realisation of what was going on hit her as she opened it. She was faced with a truck full of unconscious bodies.

Everything fell into place.

Of course. The sale. All the people.

She knew that today was the day. And she would be part of it.

114
Not A Scratch

'Why the hell is it so busy?' Becky asked as she took her helmet off. She walked towards the car where Jane and Doctor Owen were taking their bags and cases out of the boot.

'It's sale day,' Jane said, 'The department store opens early today.'

'It doesn't happen very often, does it?' Becky asked.

'No, why?'

'Just seems too much like a coincidence, that's all.'

Jane stifled a laugh. 'You think everything's a conspiracy, don't you?'

Becky didn't share her light-hearted mood.

'Yes I do, Jane. So would you if you'd seen the things I've seen over the last two years.'

Doctor Owen piped up as he threw a bag full of documents over his shoulder. 'Let's just get in there, dump all this crap, get my wife and get the hell out of here.'

'Can't argue with that,' Becky said then returned her tone to serious. 'Okay, here's the plan. They don't know about me so you two go in there and meet with Roxy. I'm going to find a lookout point and watch over you. You can't take any weapons but remember that I'll be watching you through the viewfinder of my rifle. I can take a vampire's nose clean off from a thousand metres away.'

Jane believed her and suspected that she had done just that on more than one occasion.

'Then what?' Jane asked.

'I know someone who can help us,' Becky said, 'Someone who owes me a favour. He's a scientist as well. He should be able to keep us safe and allow you to continue your work.'

'Finish my work?' Doctor Owen said, 'Is there any point now that we're handing all of this over?'

'Look, Doc, we have to go into hiding once this is over. We have to lie low and stay away from the vampires, The Brotherhood, everyone. But if there's anything you can do to help us stop them, you owe it to everyone out there, especially your friend Tom. We're running out of time. Where the hell is he?'

Jane was ready to say she didn't know when they heard a car screech into the car park and skid to a halt next to them. The rear windscreen was smashed and the countless bullet holes made the car's bodywork look like a cheese grater on wheels. Dave jumped out of the driver's seat and shouted 'Help me with him!'

They all ran to the back of the car and opened the doors. Lying among shattered glass on a seat soaked with his blood, Tom was unconscious.

'I don't know what happened to him. I was driving and he fell through the back window. He just told me to head for the north car park at the mall then passed out. He looked like hell when he got in the car. I'm worried he might need medical attention.'

Jane leaned into the car to examine the body, but couldn't find an injury among the shredded clothes.

'I don't believe it,' she said, 'There's not a scratch on him.'

115
'Give Me A Minute'

My body jerked and I was awake. I looked up and saw everyone standing around me. Everyone.

'Jane!' I said with surprise and relief in my voice. I got up and jumped out of the car. I tried to embrace her but she reeled backwards, like she didn't want to touch me.

'What's up?' I asked.

'Look at the back seat,' she said with a look of horror on her face.

I looked at the spot where I had been lying. It looked like someone had been killed. Glass was strewn all over the seat, which was soaked through with blood. My blood. I bent down and checked my face in the car's wing mirror. Not a scratch.

I felt the spot on my back where I had crashed through some poor commuter's windscreen. Nothing.

'What happened to you?' Jane asked.

'I got in a fight. A few fights, actually. Captain Stein is dead.'

Becky walked over to me and introduced herself without any prompt.

'Hello, Tom. My name is Becky Clarkson. I used to work for the World Health Organisation. I've been working with your friends today.'

We shook hands. 'Pleased to meet you, Becky. So what are we doing here?'

'We're going to exchange all the papers and samples we have on the primary treatment for the doctor's wife.'

'But doesn't that mean that the vampires will have all the research, all the work you've done for The Brotherhood?'

'That's right,' said Doctor Owen, who looked very tired, 'But there's nothing else we can do.'

'Hey Doc, did you know someone else is using your treatment?'

'Did you come across the Virex syringes as well?' Becky asked.

'Yes. I took two and gave them to a guy and his kid on the plane.'

'Did they use them?'

'I think so, yes.'

'Before or after they were infected?'

'Before, but only he was infected.'

'What happened on the plane?' Jane asked.

'They gassed everyone and injected them with vampire blood. The crash was supposed to look like an accident but the bodies were taken off the plane almost as soon as it went down.'

'Where were they taking the bodies?'

'I don't know. Skinner was staying with them. Have you heard from him?'

'No. I assumed he was with you.'

The whole situation was disorganised and confusing. After a day of running around, it didn't feel like we were any closer to finding out what was going on in this city or how we could stop it.

Doctor Owen picked up a medical case and started to walk towards the mall. 'Can we go?' he asked.

'Wait,' Becky said, 'Let me go on ahead. Give me a minute to get through the mall, find a spot and get set up. Jane, put this in your car.'

Becky threw an earpiece at Jane then ran to the back of the car, picked up a black holdall. She threw it over her shoulder then ran towards the entrance when she saw the coast was clear.

'How are you doing, Dave?' Jane asked.

'A hell of a lot better than I would have been if it wasn't for this guy,' he said and pointed to me, 'Last thing I remember was getting punched out by a couple of bloodsuckers, then I woke up in the back seat of the car with this son of a bitch behind the wheel. I've got a bad feeling about this place, though.'

'Why's that?' I asked.

'Some of the guys who attacked me work here. In fact, everyone who was staying at that hotel works here and they were all vampires.'

'Try not to worry,' Doctor Owen said, 'We'll be in and out of there. Has she been gone a minute yet? Let's go.'

We all picked up bags and cases and made our way into the mall.

116
Loud And Clear

Becky ran up the stairs to a small area on the first floor of the mall that was cordoned off for a selection of coffee and cake stands. She thought the plants, potted trees and statues dotted around the empty tables and chairs would offer adequate cover, at least for the duration of the hopefully short meeting. A single door marked 'Employees Only' stood in the corner. Becky tried the handle. It was locked.

As quietly as she could, she dragged a table and chair over to the largest statue and sat down, establishing line of sight to the south entrance and the fountain just inside the doors. In under thirty seconds she had unzipped the holdall, placed all the pieces of her rifle on the table and pieced it together. She surveyed her surroundings.

No one here.

With the rifle no doubt visible to anyone who made their way up the motionless escalator, she would have no choice but to silence them. She knew the rifle would be no good for close combat but she felt confident that one of the many weapons held in her combat suit would do the trick.

'Jane, are you there?' she said into the tiny microphone on her collar.

'Yes, I'm here. Can you hear me?'

'Loud and clear. Where are you?'

'We're just making our way down the mall towards the south entrance now.'

'Good. Try to stay between the doors and the fountain. That's where I've got the best shot.'

'Understood.'

Jane peered through the high-powered scope mounted on her rifle and saw Jane walk past the fountain with Doctor Owen. 'Where are the other two?'

'They won't be expecting Dave and Tom so they decided to try and blend in with the crowd of shoppers and hang around as lookouts.'

'Good idea.'

Jane and Doctor Owen placed their bags and cases on the floor then perched on the edge of the fountain. Becky was focused solely on the job at hand.

Guard these people with your life. You need their help. You haven't got a hope of stopping the Rising on your own.

The silence was broken by the click of a door unlocking. She looked up from the rifle and saw the handle of the door in the corner move. Sunrise was only minutes away. The vampires would be here any second. She didn't have time for a fight.

Neutralise the threat.

She got to her feet and took three steps forward and one to the left, moving her out of the immediate field of vision of whoever was behind the door. Without looking down, her right hand went to a pocket on her jacket and drew a small throwing knife.

The door opened.

As soon as the man behind the door showed himself, Becky threw the knife as hard as she could. Silently, it flew through the air and embedded itself deeply in his temple. He was dead before he hit the ground.

Becky looked down at the fountain. *They're still safe. I've got a few seconds.* She ran over to the door and couldn't believe what she saw.

'Becky, they're here,' Jane said.

Becky stood over the dead body of a man in camouflage gear. He had an automatic rifle in his hands.

'Becky, are you there?' Jane asked again.

'Yes, I'm here.'

'Becky?' asked another voice, one she hadn't expected to hear.

'Will, is that you?' Becky asked, aware that Jane would be listening to this conversation.

'Yes. I haven't got long. I'm sorry I haven't been in touch sooner but I haven't been able to get away. I don't know what will happen to me if they find me but I have to tell you.'

'What?'

'Get out of the mall. Get the fuck out of there right now.'

Becky stared at the body at her feet. A small trickle of blood ran down his lifeless face. 'No shit.'

'They know where you are. You, Agent Simpson and the doctor. They know everything. Oh shit.'

'What?' Jane asked with desperation in her voice. There was no answer from Will but she heard another voice in her ear, a voice she didn't recognise.

'Agent Clarkson. My name is Captain Sayers. Put your hands on your head and walk through the door.'

Before she could challenge the order, a gloved hand reached round the door and opened it fully. Behind the door stood two soldiers in camouflage suits. The red spots from the infrared sights on their rifles painted targets on her body.

Becky put her hands on her head. 'Jane, if you can hear me, get out of here now. This is a setup.'

117
'Wake Up, Daddy!'

'Daddy! Wake up, Daddy!'

Jonnie woke up to find his daughter Poppy shaking his body as hard as she could with her tiny hands. He immediately sat up and grabbed her, hugging her, holding her tightly.

'I'm here now, sweetheart. Everything's going to be okay.'

Where the hell are we?

Jonnie looked around him. They were in a metal container. The doors were ajar, allowing faint artificial light from outside to spill inside. Everywhere he looked, he saw bodies lying on the metal floor.

The plane.

His last memory was injecting himself and his daughter with a mysterious yellow liquid. A yellow liquid given to him by that man on the plane.

Tom.

At least he knew he was right to trust the stranger. Both he and his daughter were alive. Jonnie didn't feel any different. He rolled up his sleeves and checked his arms. Sure enough, there was a bruise on his left arm.

Shit. What the hell did they inject me with?

He didn't want to hang around and find out what all the other bodies were infected with, especially if he and Poppy were temporarily immune. Jonnie got to his feet and took his daughter in his arms.

'Come on, sweetheart, we're getting out of here.'

He opened the door and jumped down from the edge of the container. They were in an almost-empty car park. Jonnie looked at his watch.

Just after five. Jesus, we've been out all night.

The thought of the plane crash hit him again. *It must be all over the news. Poppy's mother must be going mad with worry.*

Jonnie headed for the door, hoping their surroundings would soon become familiar to him. He also knew that he somehow had to find Tom again. He had to know what happened on the plane. Why did those people do this to him?

Holding Poppy in one arm, he jogged up the stairs behind the door. As he reached the top, he spotted a single door at the end of the corridor ahead of him but the sight before him was the last thing he had expected as he opened it.

They found themselves standing at the back of a bustling department store. Jonnie instantly knew he was in the mall but he had no idea why. He blended into the crowd who were more bothered about searching for bargains in the early hours than a man and his daughter sneaking past them and out into the mall.

Jonnie's feeling of complete helplessness turned to hope when he saw a face he recognised across the mall. Deep inside he knew that his presence couldn't be a good thing. It was too much of a coincidence, but he didn't want to think about that for now. All he cared about was getting help from someone who might know what they were doing there.

'Tom!' he shouted as he ran across the marble floor.

118
'The Rising Has Already Begun'

Jane's heart sank when she heard the last broadcast from Agent Clarkson.

This is going to end badly. It's too late to try to run away.

'Emily!' Doctor Owen shouted and ran to embrace his wife as she walked through the south entrance of the mall.

Roxy was standing next to them but they ignored her. They hugged so tightly that they almost crushed each other's bodies. Doctor Owen couldn't even comprehend what his wife must have been through.

'Are you okay?' he asked.

'I am now,' she spluttered, fighting back the tears, 'But there's something you don't know…'

'If you've hurt her…' Doctor Owen started to threaten Roxy.

'She's fine,' Roxy said, 'Can we get on with this? We haven't got much time.'

Doctor Owen pointed at the pile of bags and cases on the floor by the fountain. 'Take it, it's all yours. Where's Doctor Forrest?'

Roxy smiled and waved to a van that was parked just outside the entrance. Two vampires in black suits escorted a man in dark trousers and a white shirt into the mall. It was Doctor Forrest.

'You're okay!' Doctor Owen exclaimed as he walked through the doors.

'Have you got everything there?' Doctor Forrest asked, ignoring any concern Andrew had for his well-being.

'Er… yes. It's all there.'

'Including the backup tapes?'

'Yes, everything.'

'Excellent,' he said and turned to his vampire escorts, 'Take these back to the van.'

The vampires walked over to the fountain and picked up the bags and cases. As they left the mall, Doctor Owen realised the terrible truth.

'You're one of them!'

'What?' Jane exclaimed from behind him.

'He's right,' Doctor Forrest said, 'I'm one of them. I'm a vampire. I always have been, Andrew. I'm sorry I had to deceive you all these years.'

'But it was you that kept us working on the cure when The Brotherhood were forcing us to work on the primary treatment.'

'That's right. You see, Andrew, the work on the secondary treatment is already complete. It has been for four years. It was my job to make sure you didn't make any new developments in that time.'

'In what time?'

'In the time it took The Brotherhood to build up stockpiles of the secondary treatment all over the world.'

'But why would they do that? Why would you want them to do that?'

'To maintain a balance of the species.'

'You mean you're going to go public? There will be anarchy. It goes against the terms of the treaty.'

'Controlled anarchy, Andrew. That's the whole point: control. I know you haven't seen the treaty so let me spell it out for you. This whole chain of events was agreed fifty years ago. The mass-production of the treatment. The building of stockpiles. Even the plane crash earlier today, while not spelled out in such detail, is implied by the need to greatly increase our numbers in a short time frame.'

'To what end?'

'Co-existence. The Rising has already begun.'

'But the Rising would result in total extermination of the human race. You've read the Costas report. Vampires wouldn't be able to stop themselves from drinking the blood of every human. Once that happens, the vampires would die out from hunger.'

'That report was only released to make people think it could never happen. The key ingredient left out was political control. This plan is backed by the highest positions in world governments. Once we take our rightful place alongside the humans, a treatment program will begin to maintain certain layers of human society in the event of them turning into vampires. This will ensure peaceful co-existence.'

'But the treatment isn't complete. Once you've been bitten, you need to keep taking the treatment every day.'

'I know. That's the beauty of it. Regular treatment means regular payments to Mantek from every national health organisation around the world. Fifty years ago, we stood on the edge of our rise to power. A treaty was signed that agreed a fair share of the future of our planet. That includes its wealth. Mantek is part-owned by us, part-owned by the World Health Organisation.'

'I don't believe you!' Jane shouted, 'This could never happen!'

'It could happen and it did. Fifty years ago, you were almost beaten. You would have agreed to anything. Now you get to be part of the Rising today.'

'What do you mean?'

'Some of our brothers and sisters are here, waiting for you. Farewell, my friend.' Doctor Forrest turned and walked out of the mall. The sun was just starting to rise outside so he ran for the van.

Roxy addressed Jane and the doctor one more time before leaving. 'Your friend Skinner is dead. And don't even think of trying to leave. Your friends, our babysitters The Brotherhood, are waiting outside for you with orders to shoot on sight.'

As she left the mall, the doors automatically closed and metal shutters started to drop behind the doors.

'Andrew, what's going on?' Emily asked.

Screams echoed from the other side of the mall.

119
Bad Feeling

Everything had moved so fast in the past few hours that I had almost lost track of what was going on. Jane and the doc were handing over all they had on the primary treatment in exchange for Emily and Doctor Forrest. Once we were done here I hoped to God we could go back to wherever they had been hiding out all night so Doctor Owen could continue his tests and work out what the hell was happening to me.

I hadn't been hit by the hunger for almost twenty-four hours. Not since I'd lost control at the outpost. I wondered how long it would take to come back, and what had happened to my body in the time since my last dose of the doc's treatment.

How long does it take for my body to become beyond repair?

Will I ever be human again?

I thought of the joy of flying I had experienced and questioned whether I could ever go back to being fully human.

'It doesn't feel right in here,' Dave said.

'I know what you mean,' I said. Ever since we had walked through the entrance, I'd had a strange feeling nagging in my mind. It was a feeling of belonging but also danger at the same time. I'd felt the same way at the hotel in Blackchapel. I knew vampires were nearby, but we couldn't know whether they were just part of the crowd or had other intentions.

'Tom!' I heard the shout from behind us.

I looked round and saw the two people I didn't expect to see in the mall at five in the morning. Jonnie was running towards us, carrying his daughter in his arms.

'Tom, I'm so glad we found you.' He sounded exhausted.

'Jonnie, what are you doing here? What happened after the crash?'

'I don't know. We just woke up now.'

'What, here?'

'In the back of a truck in the car park downstairs.'

A terrible thought entered my mind.

'Were all the other passengers with you?'

Before he said 'Yes', I had already worked out what was going on. There were hundreds of shoppers in the department store. They were so focused on grabbing the latest bargains that most of them didn't notice the metal shutters start to drop on the entrance to the store. A handful of them noticed and got out before it closed.

'Oh shit. Why the hell didn't we work it out? The best way for them to rapidly increase their numbers is to lock the infected bodies in with a large number of people and let nature take its course.'

'What do you mean?' Jonnie asked. I realised I hadn't given him the whole story on the plane.

'You know the infection they injected into everyone on the plane?'

'Yes, what was it?'

'It was vampire blood.'

Jonnie stared at me blankly. 'Vampire blood? You mean I'm going to turn into a vampire? I don't believe you!'

'Well you should believe me. I know it's hard to take in but it's true. You're not going to turn right away. The treatment I gave you should hold it off for the rest of the day. We'll get you more. You'll be okay. I'm sorry I couldn't stop them from injecting you, but I made sure they didn't touch your daughter.'

As he thanked me, we heard screams from behind the metal shutters.

'Come on,' I said and led the way towards the south entrance to the mall, where I hoped everything was fine and we could get out of here before the vampires that were about to enjoy their first feed worked out how to get through the metal shutters.

We ran down the mall as fast as we could and met Jane and Doctor Owen running towards us.

'What happened?' Jane asked.

'The department store has been locked down. There must be two or three hundred people trapped in there with about a hundred and fifty vampires.'

We all looked around us. All the entrances were reinforced with metal shutters. All windows were covered. Not one speck of sunlight was allowed in the mall.

'Where's Becky?' I asked.

'She's been captured. The Brotherhood found her and forced her to go with them. I overheard them on the earpiece.'

'Well, can you still hear them?'

'No.'

'Maybe they can hear you.'

'Good point,' she said and started to address whoever may be listening to her voice, 'Hey, if anyone is out there, you have to come in here. There are hundreds of people trapped in the department store. They're in danger.'

'Agent Simpson. This is Captain Sayers of The Brotherhood. I have been ordered not to let anyone in or out of the mall until further notice. You may like to know that Agent Clarkson and the member of our team that was helping her out have been apprehended. It's doubtful you'll see them again.'

'What are you going to do with them?'

'It's not what's going to happen to them that you should be worried about.'

Jane hung her head in despair.

'We're fucked, aren't we?' I asked.

Jane nodded.

The people who had ducked under the shutters before they sealed the entrance of the department store were frantic. They didn't know what to do. They were watching their friends inside getting ripped apart by creatures of the night they never thought existed in the real world. Blood sprayed on the inside of the tall, thin windows next to the shutters, which rattled as the bodies of the victims were slammed against them.

With The Brotherhood outside and their rifles trained on every possible exit, and a population of vampires inside that was set to double, or even treble as soon as they'd finished carving through the shoppers in the department store, we all knew there was only one outcome of this situation.

We're fucked.

Tom Ryder will return

Thank you for reading *The Rising*, I hope you enjoyed it. Tom, Jane, Doctor Owen and the gang will return soon...

Contact the author:
Scott McKenzie
s.a.mckenzie@gmail.com
www.stardotfiction.com

Rebirth and *The Rising* were both published online in blog format. This practice, called blooking, is increasing in popularity. There are hundreds of blooks out there. If you enjoyed reading my work, you may like to consider the following…

blook
http://en.wikipedia.org/wiki/Blook

Blogs as books
With the advent of the blog people started to publish books serialized on their blogs. Chapters are published one by one as blog posts, and readers can then subscribe to the blook via an RSS feed, tag it and comment on it. This type of blook was popularized by Tom Evslin in September 2005, with the launch of hackoff.com, a murder mystery set in the dot-com bubble.

Useful links
Novelr
News, reviews and commentary of blooking
www.novelr.com

Pages Unbound
Library of blooks, with user reviews
www.pagesunbound.com

Printed in the United Kingdom by
Lightning Source UK Ltd., Milton Keynes
136592UK00001B/126/P